Strange Camp Fellows

Joshua Calkins-Treworgy

BooksForABuck.com
2017

For Dennis Habulinec. Ever a colleague, always a gentleman.

Chapter One

Digby Narick slipped silently through the shadows abutting the wall of the manor on its north side, grateful for the eight foot stone wall blocking the broad rear lawn from street view. It wouldn't do, after all, to have one of the city's well-armed guards spot him at his work: no, no. Generally speaking, they tended to frown upon cutpurses like himself skulking around wealthy estates in the dead of night, looking for all the world like they might be up to something along the lines of breaking and entering, at the very least.

Peering up the outer wall of the manor, taking a moment to admire the polished brick and evenness of the mortar between each layer, Digby narrowed his eyes and watched the window just five feet or so over his head, waiting for any subtle sign of light. After more than a minute, he unslung his bag from his shoulders, reaching inside and pulling out a collapsible tube with an angled head, a lone slash of glass fixed inside a curved bulkhead. He pulled it quietly open, looked up again, and held the bottom, narrower and also hosting a thin membrane of glass, to his eye. Using this tool, he peered with one eye up into the room beyond the window.

The window itself, blissfully, was constructed of the sort of expensive glass that left the casual observer with the impression that there was no glass present at all, so clear it was. Digby had a perfect view into the room beyond, and what he found encouraged him more than he could have hoped for at the start of the evening.

The room was dark, with no candles lit, nor any oil lamps or any of those new sorts of lights that had become so popular in the last thirty years, the electrical overhead fixtures that mimicked the street lights cities like Desanadron and Ja-Wen had been installing everywhere throughout their boroughs. Yet with a cloudless sky overhead, a full moon, and his own naturally enhanced night vision, the veteran thief could see perfectly well into the room.

To anyone not in the know, the chamber would appear to be a music room and nothing more, with sheet music stands lining one wall to the left, several instruments in their cases against the opposite wall to the right, and a gorgeous walnut piano dominating a corner farthest from the window. But a lone item held Digby's eye fast, a simple green violin case sitting on a small circular table beside the piano.

"Joy of joys," he muttered to himself. Pulling the tool away from his eye and setting it gently on the ground, he then pulled out another extendable tool, a thin black metal bar like an 'L' with a little wheel on one flat surface near a taped handle. *Now to test my luck,* he thought, carefully wedging the razor-thin edge on the lip of the top end just under the window jam. He shook out his left hand and smoothed the fine red fur on the back and white on the underside and palm, grabbing the nub attached to the wheel between thumb and forefinger.

Slowly he turned the wheel, feeling for resistance through his fingertips but detecting none right away. Being a vulpesin, one of the fox-men native to Tallowmere's central and southern forests, Digby benefited greatly from an enhanced sensitivity in his hands and feet when it came to delicate operations such as this.

After a full three rotations of the crank wheel with no discernable problems, he sped up the process for another four rotations; the window overhead now opened enough for him to easily fit his arm through once he managed to scale the wall up far enough to reach in. He withdrew the pry tool, slid it shut, and put it back in his bag. Next, he took the scope up once more and extended it, creeping to the stone wall abutting the street. A quick check up and down the road showed him no patrolmen in the vicinity and he swiftly tucked the scope away, strapped the bag on his back once more, and made a short sprint to the manor outer wall, kicking up the wall far enough to shoot his arms through the opening and grab onto the inner window sill.

Adjusting his arms, he pushed the window the rest of the way up, then hauled himself inside, sliding the window most of the way shut behind him. Not a sound did he make, as practiced as ever. Crouched low, he surveyed the room once more, sniffing the air with his sensitive nostrils to try and detect anything out of the ordinary. The only aromas were those he might have normally expected from wood and pine resin and a few containers filled with cork grease somewhere on the shelf unit situated to his left. Absent were the familiar, tell-tale scents of ash or ozone that would indicate typical security spells locked onto objects to alert owners to potential theft or cause severe damage to the would-be thief.

Digby shook himself softly, settling his dark brown tunic and drab green trousers, visually inspecting himself for anything that might trip him up in the event he needed to make sudden movements. Satisfied that he could securely cross to the table and his target, he took several steps forward, knees bent, crossing his legs in a side-step shuffle that offered no audible clue to his passage. His whiskers twitched as a brief breeze played through the crack in the window he'd left behind him, but he kept himself in check with a force of will and continued on, finally arriving at the table. Then, he carefully reached down to a gray pouch on his left hip. From within he took a thin glass dropper, pulling out the plug and hovering it over the green case before squeezing a single clear droplet on the case.

The moment the liquid landed, the case wavered, then shrank with a soft suctioning sound to the size of his palm. He set the dropper back in its vial, the vial back in his pouch, and eased his pack onto the table. Proceeding with every ounce of caution, he set the case in his pack, put it back on, and crept back toward the window.

He was three cross-steps away when he saw the lip of another pry tool slide into the crack. Baffled, he nearly stumbled mid-step, correcting himself with the eerie grace of long practice, and completed his return to balance. He looked down out the window, and found himself locking eyes with a pinch-faced young human all in black. He quietly opened the window as the other burglar removed his tool and backed away from the manor door, then hopped outside, landing in a ready crouch next to the other man.

"Hey Digby," the other thief whispered. "Um, this is awkward," he added, scratching the back of his head.

"Just a tad," Digby replied, slowly rising to his feet and keeping his hands loose at his sides, keeping a close eye on the human. "Care to shut the window, Randall?"

The human reached up with a separate tool from his belt, a thin rod with a suction cup on it, sticking it to the exterior of the window and pulling it shut.

"That's handy. I usually use my pry tool and have to leave a gap."

"Nero made it for me," said Randall with a touch of pride, tucking it away.

Digby had taken the opportunity while the human was closing the window to slide toward the stone perimeter wall and use his scope to check the street. A pair of city guardsmen approached from the west, and he suspected they'd be in visual range in about half a minute. Randall turned toward Digby then, eyes narrowing on the vulpesin. "Come on, man, I really need this. I've been hanging around the bottom rung so long. Just let me have the violin, I'll give you partial credit."

"We can talk about it when we get out of here," Digby rasped, crouching on one knee and putting his hands together in a scoop. "Come on, I'll help you over," he added, tilting his head toward the wall. Randall's expression went from suspicious to relieved instantly, and he approached quickly.

"Thanks, man. I always thought people had you figured wrong." He stepped up onto Digby's hands and grunted as Digby lifted. Randall pushed off, jumping over the wall.

Immediately the air filled with twin shouts, followed by grumbled curses and the clamour of feet.

The vulpesin ambled around to the west side of the manor property, hopped over the wall himself, and whistled as he traveled along at a light jog toward the guild hall.

Scoundrel though he was, he managed to locate one of his friends in the night watch along the way and asked her to arrange for Randall's release, slipping the heavily armored human woman four gold coins to guarantee it was done before dawn.

"Well aren't you a fucking saint," she groused from behind the nose guard of her gray iron helm.

Digby shrugged, a coy grin on his foxy face.

"It could be worse," he professed as he walked away. "I could have left him to rot." He sauntered away then, onward through the benighted streets of the city of Breck. 'City' was perhaps a loose term at best for what Breck was; compared to the other metropolitan centers in the Freehold Territories in Tamalaria's north-central plains, it might be best to call it a collection of three towns. Square mileage defined it as a city, but only barely.

The Manor District, through which Digby skulked, flitting from shadow to shadow with the casual ease of a career sneak, was easily the most tightly packed in layout. The wealthy people living there thought this would ensure greater security, but he rejoiced in proving that theory untrue wherever possible. The job he had taken did just that.

But all was not to be songs and wine, as a fellow says. Nearing the northern border of the Manor District, Digby settled in to be at his best as he moved along. As they had been designed more to keep the common riffraff from being too close to the well-to-do of the city, the roads separating the Manor District from Prima District were a solid twenty feet across to the nearest buildings. Between street torch lamps, the newer electrical lamps, and paranoid business owners setting out magical devices that flooded the area in front of their stores with light when someone got close, that was a large area to cross with nowhere to hide.

For a thief, it was a hellscape of 'Don't Get Caught'.

There were only really three ways of approaching this problem in a non-magical way and his options cycled through the vulpesin's head as he came to a halt near the end of the alley from which he would begin his crossing. *Option one, run like all the demons of the Hells are in pursuit. Sure, that might draw notice, but if you're quick enough, nobody's going to be able to remember with any accuracy what you look like,* he thought to himself, now standing stock still as he stared at the open stretch of street that began only about six feet away now. *Option two, walk across nice and casual, as if you belong here, nothing is wrong, nothing to see here people. It may give people a good look, but if you don't show panic, they might just dismiss you.* Digby rolled his head on his neck, several soft 'pops' echoing in his ears. *And lastly, option three, creep all the way back to that other alley intersection, head east all the way out of town, then approach Prima District from the outside as if I was just coming into town. That way, if anybody does happen to notice, they'll remember someone coming into town itself in the dead of night.*

Despite going through all of his options in his head, the crimson-and-white-furred sneak had known all along what he was going to do. Head down, he leaned forward slightly as he sprinted across the empty stretch. When he drew within a few feet of the alley opposite the one he'd left the Manor District by, a powerful beam of light flooded the area in front of the store ahead and to his right, but by the time he registered how bright it was, he was several yards into the alley, tripping over something solid and tumble-rolling forward, going from his shoulder to his hip as he'd learned many years before. He came up in a daze, leaning against an alley wall, and looked back over his shoulder when he heard a rumbling curse behind him.

"Sorry, friend," he said to the homeless man who'd been sleeping in the alley before he ran into him.

The shambling, gruff-looking figure, its head and face obscured by a cloak hood, grunted wordlessly at the vulpesin and flapped a filth-covered hand at him in dismissal.

Digby snickered, the nerves of having passed through the open street now straying out.

Ten minutes later, striding through the batting doors into the entry room of the guild hall, he offered the burly jaft at the duty desk to his left a grin. "Evening, Gallit," he said, walking over.

The blue-skinned, bald humanoid grunted non-committal acknowledgment in reply.

"Quiet night?"

"Steward Heflin was asking about you," Gallit replied, leaning forward in his chair, the springs protesting loudly. "Seemed a might bit peeved at you. What'd you do to the old man?"

Digby feigned an offended scoff with hand pressed to chest.

"Why my good man, whatever do you mean? I am the walking image of delight and charity!" He pulled at his chin, eyes upward in faux contemplation. "Though, he may have taken offense to me putting peppers in his sandwich."

Gallit harumphed and shook his head, leaning back with his arms over his chest.

"You're a right prick, fox. Go on with ya. I'll tell him I ain't seen you if he asks."

"There's a good lad." Digby headed through the double doors opposite the entrance. These opened upon a large, circular chamber that stretched about twenty yards in diameter, with broad archways leading off in three different directions, each narrowing down into hallways that led off to various wings within the guildhall. Another doorway, only wide enough for one large person, had a solid green door which would open upon a staircase that led down to a kind of barracks the guild members could use as temporary housing. A few members had set up semi-permanent occupancy, but not many had overall, leaving plenty of available space at most times for new members.

The sound of a couple of muffled conversations barely filled the air, several of the guild's regulars sharing shop talk in the quieter hours. Digby recognized Tofar Nelson, a snub-faced human brawler who took mostly escort and bodyguard contracts from the mission rolls. Nelson sat with a half-elf the vulpesin didn't yet know well, a transfer from one of the other branches of the guild. *Ja-Wen branch if I remember correctly,* he thought as he passed them by on his way to the north wing of the hall.

"Narick," Nelson said, calling Digby by his surname.

Digby paused, back sliding on the balls of his feet to stand beside the human.

Nelson dipped his head toward the half-elf and said, "Jeremy here needs to drop off some gear to the quartermasters. Any chance you could show him down there?"

"It's on my way, sure. Come along, rookie," Digby said amiably, patting the half-elf man on the shoulder, realizing now how young the fellow looked. Jeremy had the doe-eyed look of a man who is not sure he's made a wise decision, and as he awkwardly grabbed up his travel bag from the floor, Digby assessed that the answer was a solid 'no'. "So, how long have you been in our fair city," Digby asked as he led the lamb along through the entry arch to the north wing.

"About ten days," Jeremy replied. "I'm from Sorepha, one of the villages east of Ja-Wen. I had a few missions for the guild branch in the metro before headmaster Quillian suggested I transfer out here to gain experience."

Digby cringed inside; such transfer cases usually ended up taking on jobs well beyond their skill level in a misguided effort to prove themselves. Most of these ended up being brought back by veterans in pieces.

At the first junction of hallways, he turned left, pointing at a crimson scrawl of paint on the beige wall that read 'Quatermastr'. Jeremy raised an eyebrow at the vulpesin rogue.

"We're all painfully aware that our less literate members should not be in charge of signage, young Jeremy," Digby responded to the unasked question. Down the hall and around another bend, they came to a solid oak door painted blue with white trim, and Digby knocked on it.

A window panel slid open around his head height, a mesh grill obscuring the guild member behind the door. Digby produced a winning smile and said, "So which of our lovely hoarders of all things gear do we have on duty right now? This young man has gear to hand over," he added, draping an arm companionably around Jeremy's shoulders.

The grill window slid shut, several locks snapped open, and a whirl of blue-and-white light simmered on the door. With a creak the door opened, revealing a gnome woman hovering in mid-air, her magic giving off a subtle shimmer as she lowered herself to the floor. She was unlike most gnome women, who kept their sideburns and neck hair, opting instead to be completely clean-shaven. She smiled up at the vulpesin, who beamed down at her.

"Nancy," Digby exclaimed, swooping forward to snatch the laughing gnome mage up in a twirling embrace. They chuckled together a moment before he set her down and stepped back, hands on his hips. "By the gods, when did you get back?"

"Yesterday," she replied, flicking a hand idly at the door, shutting it with a minor magical trick. "The boys in charge were all too happy to have me back." She gave Jeremy a brief up-and-down, nodded, and made a few quick gestures with her hands. From elsewhere in the wide, sprawling chamber, outfitted with dozens of trunks and equipment racks, a low wheeled cart rumbled up, the wheels glowing the same blue and white as the seal spell she'd had on the door.

"Jeremy, this is Nancy Prennit. The greatest quartermaster a guild could ask for," Digby said.

Jeremy undid the ties on his travel bag and put several items on the cart, starting with a length of rope that had seen better days.

"She'd been on loan to our head office out of Desanadron for a while, and I wasn't sure we'd get her back!"

"Pleased to meet you, mum," Jeremy said softly with a nod, setting a pair of empty vials on the cart, then a grappling hook that was bent out of true. Lastly, he added a small pouch that rattled and clanked, and had the word 'farsight' scribbled on it. "Erm, had a bit of an accident with the scope, mum," he said as Nancy pulled open the drawstring and poured out several broken bits of metal and glass.

"Gods, what happened here?" she asked, shaking her head, upper lip pooched out.

"Goblin got the drop on me, tackled me off my cart," Jeremy said. He shrugged his shoulders and added, "Was the only weapon I had on hand."

Digby grimaced, noticing the spots of blood on the bent metal.

"Did you kill the little guy," he asked with a half-chuckle.

Jeremy's blank look served as an answer, and Nancy whistled appreciatively before sending the cart away with a wave of her hand.

The vulpesin clapped his hands together and hitched a sigh. "Well, Nancy here's your go-to gal for gear, and she's also quite square for appraisals, if you should need it. Nancy?"

"We'll catch up later, Digs," she replied. "As for you, young man, allow me to run you through the paperwork for damaged equipment." She guided Jeremy toward a desk, and Digby took his leave, heading for taskmaster Coby Jerrick's office.

After navigating a few more turns in the north wing main corridor, he came to an open door which led into a darkened chamber. On the right hand wall was a simple military cot, a lumpy form bundled in blankets upon it. In the center of the room sat a table with a thick leatherbound tome, a gaggle of pens and pencils around it, and a single coffee mug. Next to the tome also sat a turned down oil lantern.

Digby crept into the room, as ever looking around the walls. Newspaper clippings covered them, all stories associated with the guild and its most notable members' reported deeds. In the grand scheme of things, it wasn't much, really. The Freelance Adventurers Guild of Tamalaria took on and completed an estimated three thousand contracts per year, and they had been in operation across the continent for nearly a century. But they often got confused with and overshadowed by the organization they'd branched off from, The Unified Adventurers' Guild. Even in some of the clippings, most of which Digby had read over his years in the guild, reporters confused and misnamed the collective, using their better-known competitors' name in the stories.

The vulpesin used the wheel on the side of the lantern to increase the light in the room, then gently padded over to the huddled form on the cot, easing his hand down on the figure's arm. He shook the fellow gently and whispered, "Coby, hey. Come on, old timer, it's Digby."

The figure groaned and rolled onto his back on the cot, revealing a thickly bearded, older human man in a dark blue hooded robe. His long, horsey face crumpled in a wrinkle-heavy smacking of lips, followed by a yawn that saw his spindly arms stretch wide up over his head. Rheumy faded blue eyes blinked open and peeked up at the vulpesin, and a soft smile graced his lips.

"Ah, Digby," said Coby in his raspy tone. "Good to see you, young man. Help me up?" Coby tossed the blanket aside to reveal his long white cotton trousers and bare feet, covered in coarse gray hairs, a simple black tunic shirt on under the robe. The robe itself was covered here and there in strange, arcane sigils, several of which shimmered with a faint golden light as Digby helped him up to his feet from the cot. Something cracked loudly, and Coby winced, one hand reaching around to his back. "Sweet Lenos, that hurts," he grumbled. "So, what brings you to see an old codger like me?"

"I've got a top-end job to report completed," Digby said, helping Coby over to the chair at the table and easing him down into it with his hands on the old man's elbow and small of his back. Coby laboriously opened the tome and flipped through to the most recent entries, then took up a pen and set to paper. "Mark down, 'Wayne Leffert's violin recovered from Netche Estate by Digby Narick. Nobody alerted, nobody harmed in expertly executed infiltration.'"

"Got it," Coby said, scribbling with penmanship speed and elegance that might belong to a much younger man. His handwriting was looping and artistic, legible but flowing, and he did it with such careless grace that an uneducated man might find himself quite jealous. Yet when Digby saw written on the page was quite different than what he'd dictated; it read, 'Thief Digby managed to not bungle a B&E to nab up Wayne Leffert's violin, which we were contracted to steal back from the Netche family, who stole it first'. "Anything else, youngster?"

"Yeah, you might want to add in a bit about how brave and handsome I was while doing it," the vulpesin muttered. "No, just what's there should do fine. I'm going to drop off the violin to the folks over in Outbound. Master Jerrick?"

The old man looked up as he gently closed the tome, setting the pen aside. The look Digby wore made the taskmaster blink in confusion, and he eased back into his chair.

"What is it, my boy," he asked, the wrinkles on his face smoothing, the sigils and glyphs on his robes continuing to shimmer, now producing a low hum. "You look concerned."

"I am, sir." Digby took a step back as Coby Jerrick's peculiar enchantments carried on, making him appear younger by the moment. The beard had shrunk to hang down now just over his neck, and color crept through his hair, turning it steadily from silver-gray to light brown. The horse-like face was beginning to tighten, taking decades off of his outward appearance. "It's just, well, how long do you suppose you have, now? I don't mean to seem insensitive, but you may be forced out soon enough."

"This curse can be broken, Digby," the now-middle-aged Coby replied, his voice sounding stronger, firmer, his arms thickened to fill out the sleeves of his robes, legs filling what had been loose trousers. The sigils ceased glowing, and the hum vanished. "Father Regilin has already made progress in his research, and he is hopeful that he won't even need to find and interrogate the warlock. This magic is something very similar to things he has seen before, out in the wilds."

Coby stood and sauntered easily on his own over to a narrow bookcase at the rear of the room, passing an index finger over the spines of several books before plucking one out. He brought it over toward Digby, using a ribbon bookmark to open it to a point a quarter way in. He handed the book to Digby, and pointed to the illustration of a strange-looking, roach-like beast with seven legs covered in luxurious golden fur. "You are familiar with these creatures?"

"Chulcas, yeah, I've heard of them." Digby scanned the carefully written text. One of the underlined sections caught his interest in particular. "Wow. I didn't know that was how they killed their prey."

"A fascinating process," Coby remarked, folding his hands behind his back. "Nomo posits that the whole mechanism is something scientific, not magical, though I would counter that magic and science are cousins in the same clan. Of course, as an academic without any ounce of magical talent, one might understandably be skeptical about some of his findings."

"Well, he *did* write an entire series of observations in the wilds." Digby snapped the book shut and handed it back to Coby.

The mage taskmaster set the book on the table behind him and draped an arm over Digby's shoulders, guiding him toward the hallway, walking slowly with him toward Outbound's office.

"That he did, and we all owe him a debt for them. But this is one area where he and Father Regilin very much disagree. The priest believes the chulcas carry a curse in their very spirits, where Nomo suspects the secret is something called an 'enzyme' in their saliva, a clear venom that looks like drool but is, in fact, a kind of toxin. In either event, the padre has convinced a few of his braver congregants to try tracking down a few of the beasts to subdue and bring in for study. It's a better chance than trying to find members of the Cult of Sidius."

The two men finally came to another office, this one well-lit but unmanned. The chamber looked more like a storage room than an office, stretching a good twenty yards forward from the door and with iron shelves securely anchored in the walls. The entryway held no door, but neither man dared try stepping directly into the room. Instead, Digby pressed his left hand to a faded place on the wall to his left, just outside of the entrance, and said aloud, "*Vessa antis.*"

An audible click echoed up and down the hall, and the two men then proceeded into the room a few paces. Digby then turned around, put his right hand on the wall opposite where he'd put his left out in the hallway, and said, "*Vessa costis.*"

Another loud click snapped the air, and he sighed. "We really should try to work out a different way of securing this room."

"Why? That spell has worked just fine the whole time I've been here."

"Right, but what happens if someone figures out where to aim a disenchantment?" the vulpesin asked. "Or worse, when the headmaster passes away? All of his protections are contingent on his being alive."

"We'll cross that bridge if and when we come to it," Coby said. "Come now, let's get the violin squared away."

Digby rooted around in his bag and pulled out the shrunken instrument case, setting it on the floor.

"Dinky drops?"

"Cheap and effective, though it'd probably wear off soon on its own." Digby pulled out a dropper with a light red fluid. He released a single drop of the substance on the case, which stretched back out to its original size in moments. He picked up the case, and together, he and Coby walked to the back of the room and started opening drawers until they found the most recent emptied one. From atop the cabinet, Coby took down a blank parchment, filling out the form for the Outbound missions officer to record and set up, sliding the sheet into a holder slot on the front of the drawer. Digby dropped the case into the drawer, slid it shut, and the two men then headed back out, the vulpesin repeating the entry and securing sequence once more.

"You sleeping here tonight, then," Coby asked as they stopped at his office once more, Digby remaining in the doorway.

"Yeah, it's been a long night," Digby replied with a yawn and stretch. "You have the latest contracts up in the Roll Call room for tomorrow?"

"I do."

"All right, I might check them out in the morning. Otherwise, I think I'll just grab my payment, then take a few days off. Have a good night, Coby."

Alone once more, the vulpesin headed down to the guildhall's lower level, selected an available bed, and crawled into it for a much-deserved rest after putting his gear in the trunk at the foot of the bed. *And they say there's no rest for the wicked,* he thought as he drifted off to sleep. *Little do they know.*

Chapter Two

Whenever he entered a new place, Biff Mclargehuge had been taught growing up, the first thing he must do is look around and find somebody who looked like they knew the place pretty well. The thing to do was ask as many questions as he could about said new place to this person, and hope that he could remember as much as possible of what they told him. "You may have to ask several times, lad. You're none too bright, but that's a tradition among the men of our blood," his father had told him many and many-a. "It comes with being a Mclargehuge."

The massive human held the straps of his pack with hands too big for the average male his age, the knuckles scarred many times over from countless brawls and combats engaged in the wilds with the various brigands and rashum, monsters, of the lands between Naletech and this township. He had been wandering for weeks, trying to find a new place to call 'home' per his father's wishes, and that time had seen him into more battles than most militiamen or adventurers would see in a full five years of service. He never meant any harm, or to get into fights: people and critters just seemed to get angry at him. Even the ones that started out being nice to him got angry and turned on him, though he could not understand why.

Understanding was not Biff Mclargehuge's forte.

As he entered the outskirts of the town, the first thing Biff observed was the strange way people here walked around. They mostly wore no armor, and only a few folks seemed to carry any kind of weapons. *How do they protect themselves?* he wondered. *They all must be very nice people to not want to have something to cut or bash with on hand.* This warmed his simple heart: how wonderful it must be to live in a town where he could not see a single fight taking place in the streets!

The hulking human found himself the subject of some few stares, however, mostly from young human women as he plodded toward the front porch of a creaking wooden establishment that smelled, even from a distance of about thirty yards, of graf and beer. An older man sat with a pipe on the porch, and he looked like the sort of man who, to Biff's understanding, would probably be a 'local', as his father called learned men who never went anywhere. The glances and stares from the young women made him feel funny, and color flushed his cheeks as he smiled at them and waved, and they invariably waved back.

At six and a half feet in height, with the body frame of a gladiatorial champion, blond hair and blue eyes, he fairly exuded 'alpha male' to them. He'd been complimented on his physical appearance many times over the course of his short life, despite having the intellectual capacity of a rock.

Biff climbed the steps up onto the pub's front porch and beamed at the old man, who just stared wonderingly up at him. "Hello, sir," Biff said. "What's the name of this town?"

"This is Breck, young man," the gentleman replied. "Sweet gods, they make 'em big where you come from, don't they?"

"Um, yes?" Biff did not quite understand the question. "Papa says I was made from my mom's crotch. I didn't know more could be made from there," he said.

The older man burst into a gale of laughter, which confused Biff even further. He didn't realize he had made a joke. The older man shook his head, trying to calm down, which was good. That meant Biff could ask more questions. "What can you tell me about Breck?"

"Plenty, youngster, plenty. I've lived here my whole life. But I suspect you're just passing through, aren't you?"

"Where would I go if not here?" Biff asked. "Papa told me to find a new place to call home, on account of I was always breaking something in the house. So he packed me some things and told me to get walking, so I did, and now I'm here." There was a pause, and Biff asked, "Are you okay, mister? You look confused and sad, which is bad, I know because sometimes I feel that way too."

The older man just subtly shook his head and took a drag on his pipe.

"Your father just packed your things and sent you out into the world with no direction? You do realize that's not normal, right, lad?"

Biff shrugged his shoulders and smiled again.

"Well, doesn't seem to have dimmed your spirit any, at least. How old are you, son?"

"I'll be twenty in a couple of months," Biff replied. "Can I sit down in that chair? Mom says you always have to ask permission, it isn't polite to just assume."

"Well, your mum sounds like a wise woman, son. Sure, have a seat." The older man waved a hand to the chair next to his, his simple brown tunics rustling as he rummaged in his pockets, pulling out a pouch of tobacco to tamp into his pipe.

Biff took off his pack and dropped it next to the chair with a resounding 'thud' that shook the porch, then sat.

"What's your name, son?"

"I'm Biff. What's your name, sir?"

"I'm Randall. So, you're not just passing through to the militia training grounds?"

"No sir, Mister Randall. I'm no soldier, though my papa did say I'd make a good one. He says I'm a barbarian, though, and apparently barbarians don't make very good soldiers. So, where should I stay in Breck?"

"Depends, lad. You have any money?"

"I've got a little, though I ain't got much. Papa said it's enough to get me a few days at an inn. He said I'll have to find a job."

"You ever had a job, lad?"

"Once, kind of. About four years ago, Mr. Burich had me chop wood during the summer. Then he had me do the same thing for some other folks around town. They all said I was really good, that I was made for splitting logs on account of I had a mind like the stump I chopped them on. That was nice of them," Biff said.

"You think that was nice of them? How, lad?"

"Well, a stump's part of a tree, and trees are nice. I like trees," Biff said casually, as if this point should be obvious.

Randall just shook his head and scoffed, then patted Biff on the leg, his hand rattling the chainmaille leggings Biff wore under his loose brown trousers. Sitting there in his boiled leather armor with a broadsword on his back, the young man looked like nothing less than a hero walking out of a tale of yore. *Yet he's got the mind of a simpleton,* Randall mused.

"Is there somewhere around here I could get a new job, Mr. Randall?"

"Fellow your size, I should imagine so, yes," Randall said. "Biff, I had planned to get my first wet of the day soon's this place opened business, but I think perhaps I'll delay that for now. Let's you and I take a walk, lad." He stood with a grunt and tucking away his pipe after one last draw and tapping out the remains. "I think we can get you situated quickly."

***

"That there's O'Grady's," Randall said ten minutes later, pointing to an open-fronted smithy's forge as he guided Biff through the heart of downtown. Breck wasn't a bustling metropolis like Desanadron, Ja-Wen or Palen, but its downtown was as busy as any of those cities of an afternoon. "Finest dwarven crafts and weaponry you could ask for, and O'Grady himself can do custom armors with a flair few others can claim."

Scritch, scratch, scritch, scratch. Randall had already gotten used to this sound; Biff had a small notebook in his huge hands, and a pen, and the big oaf was keeping notes in handwriting that looked no more skilled than that of an elementary schooler. *Still, at least he's trying,* Randall thought.

"Is Mr. O'Grady a dwarf himself," asked Biff, eyes wandering as he turned about in a slow circle to take in their surroundings.

"He is, Biff, though you would do well not to make too big a point of that. He was raised by Jafts in the Drelling mountains range, and thinks of himself as one of their kind. He even once tried to breathe underwater, like the big blue folks, but nearly drowned for his efforts."

Biff scribbled another note in his book, then folded it shut over one thick finger, the pen in his other hand like a toothpick.

Randall walked on a few dozen paces, then stopped, a ribald smile crossing his features. He pointed to a finely appointed three-story building with red lace curtains drawn over all of the windows and a fierce-looking wererat in half-plate armor standing in front of the door at the top of the steps leading inside.

"What's that place," Biff asked, notebook open once more.

"That, my lad, is Madame Prahl's Pleasure House, the only standing brothel in Breck," said Randall. He planted his hands on his hips and lowered his head for a moment, rubbing his mouth. "I imagine it's a place you'll eventually get round to visiting."

"Why," Biff asked, scribbling.

Randall just blinked at him, nonplussed.

"You do know what a brothel is, don't you, lad?"

Biff just shook his head, and Randall ripped into a fit of laughter that made the massive warrior worry that perhaps the older man had lost his mind for a moment. It came complete with slapping of the thighs, wheezing, and shaking of the head. "Oh, by the gods, the job can bloody well wait, lad! 'Ave you never had sex, boy?"

Biff once more shook his head, and Randall just sniffed, patting him on the shoulder. "Well, per'aps Jocko will let me teach you something of the world then, oh traveling youth. Follow me."

Biff tucked his notebook away now in a pouch on his hip, as well as the pen, and followed Randall across the dusty square of public space between them and the brothel. As they approached, the heavily armored wererat's flat look turned into an outright scowl, and his left hand moved deftly to the handle of a heavy steel truncheon on his hip. When Randall got to the bottom of the steps, the lycanthrope took a heavy step forward and put his right hand out in a halting gesture.

"Hold on there, Turp, you ain't gettin' in until you've paid off your last visit," the wererat snarled. "Madame Prahl's not extending any more credit to people until business picks up in the coming season."

"Jocko, normally I'd stand here and argue with you until you had to pound me stupid and send me away, but you have got to hear this," Randall said with barely restrained laughter. "Biff? Wait here, lad," the older man said, pouncing up the steps and pulling the bewildered rat aside to whisper quietly.

Biff just stood there with the straps of his pack held in his palms, idly running his hands up and down their length. *Left strap needs replacement,* he thought, his palm sensitive to every groove of fabric that felt out of place or damaged. He may not have understood things like sarcasm, or subtlety, or whispers and gossip, but Biff had always possessed a strange affinity for assessing things like damage to fabrics, how animals were feeling, or how to build something if he were just given the parts and shown what the finished product should look like.

A couple of minutes later, the wererat came down the steps with a broad, shit-eating smile plastered to his face, eyes dancing with impish glee. "Hello there, young Biff," he exclaimed. "I'm Jocko, the doorman to this fine establishment!" Biff did as he was always taught then, extending one of his huge, scar-riddled hands to shake.

The wererat seemed surprised by this gesture, but he accepted it and shook. "Randall is a many-time customer of ours, and despite his tab, I've agreed to take you inside on a little tour of our operation!"

"Oh, nifty," Biff replied enthusiastically. "So, what do you folks make here?"

Jocko and Randall both snickered, and the lycanthrope slung an arm round Biff's broad shoulders, guiding the larger lad up the steps companionably.

"We make smiles, lad, we make smiles," said Jocko.

"Don't forget babies and diseases here and there," Randall muttered as he took up Jocko's spot on the porch and Jocko and Biff headed inside.

The first thing Biff noticed was a combination of how dimly lit the entry room was, and the combination aroma of lilacs and honey. The entrance was a narrow passage with a couple of slatted benches against each wall, and coats hung off of iron hooks on either side. A long shelf also protruded from the left wall at about Biff's eye level, with various bags and pails settled atop. It reminded Biff of the break room at papa's workplace, the old saw mill on the edge of Naltech.

When Jocko slipped ahead of him, Biff followed dutifully, notebook and pen in hand. As the pair stepped into a lavish common room furnished with several plush chairs, three broad couches and a long trestle table with bowls of various fruits and cheeses, the lumbering young barbarian heard muffled noises coming from all directions. A curious turning brought his eyes upon several closed doors leading off of the commons room, then up a stairway against the far wall to a balconied second level, the ceiling of the commons room far overhead. Another set of stairs on the second balcony level led up to a third floor, a sight which boggled Biff's mind.

Not that such was a difficult thing to do.

"It sounds like someone's in trouble," Biff remarked as his eyes darted around at various doors around them. A high-pitched shriek split the air, and without a thought in his head, Biff stuffed the notebook and pen away as he darted for one of the nearby doors,

Jocko too stunned by the swiftness with which the giant brute moved to get a hand on him and stop his forward motion.

The enormous broadsword was in his hands as the barbarian kicked in a rickety wooden door, halting in his tracks as his eyes fell upon the room beyond. Laid on a plush four-poster bed was a middle-aged human fellow, his long brown hair matted to his sweaty head, naked as the day he was born. Seated atop him was a half-elven woman, also nude, her arms crossed over her tiny breasts as she stared at the intruding Biff, eyes wide, body clenched in alarm. The smell in the room was a bittersweet blend of salty sweat and jasmine perfume, coming mostly from the couple on the bed. A long, low dresser stood to Biff's right, covered with what looked like various torture devices and capsules full of makeup, the top dominated by a vanity mirror which stretched across most of its length. "Oh, um, sorry about that," Biff said awkwardly, letting his sword tip scrape the floor as he pulled the door shut, stepping back out into the commons room.

Jocko was bent over in a fit of gale laughter behind him, and as Biff turned around and sheathed his sword, he found himself grinning a little too. "By the gods, lad, you're a thick one aren't you," Jocko asked, straightening up.

"I guess, yeah," Biff replied. "You know, I've heard of places like this. But back where I'm from, I think they call it a gym." Jocko raised an eyebrow at him, waiting on the follow-up explanation. "You know, a place where people go to exercise."

"Exercise? Lad, what makes you think those two were exercising," Jocko asked.

"Well, once, a couple of years ago, when I was really worried about one of my teeth falling out in the middle of the night, I went to tell my papa and mom, and when I walked in, they were doing that," Biff replied evenly, pointing back at the door, behind which from no noise was presently coming (and beyond which a highly irritated customer was whisper-haggling with a distressed prostitute over payment, since they'd been so fantastically disrupted). "I asked my papa what they were doing, and he said, 'Exercising'."

"So what is it people are doing when they lift weights or go jogging," Jocko asked.

"Working out, or training," said Biff matter-of-factly, sending the wererat into another fit of laughter.

***

"I wouldn't have expected less, given our conversation a bit ago," Randall said to Jocko as Biff waited at the bottom of the steps leading from the street to the brothel entrance. "Still, he doesn't seem to mean any harm."

"Gods be thankful for that," Jocko replied, looking down at the huge young barbarian. "Where are you going to take him, by the way? For a job, I mean, because I've got a few ideas, lad that size."

"I was thinking I'd take him to the Freelancers hall over there on Pearl Street," said Randall. "They could use someone like our young Biff here. Strong, clearly has a working knowledge of that sword of his."

"And not much else."

"They'll be able to get him squared away. Otherwise, he's apt to wander around and get taken advantage of by some unscrupulous bloke or other, maybe one of Branson's Boys over on 7th or 8th. He'd be a nightmare for the constabulary to try to deal with if he became a street tough."

"I don't think they'd take him in any case," Jocko replied. "Them boys have to have a measure of wits about them, and he doesn't quite qualify for that, now does he? Best of luck with him, then, Randall. Oh, and you still owe a tab, friend," the wererat chided, wagging a finger at the scrawny human.

"I haven't forgotten." Randall nodded and headed down the steps, patting Biff on the arm.

"Ready to be off, then?"

"Yup." Biff followed Randall once more, the older gent occasionally stopping to point out places of importance along the way. He made sure to stay on West Main until they'd passed the rougher patches of 7th and 8th street before turning north and heading past their respective intersections, finally aiming himself and the lad toward a wide, squat building with an old-fashioned sandwich board on a stand to the right of the batwing entrance doors. "'Freelance Adventurers Guild of Tamalaria'", Biff read aloud, giving Randall a fresh surprise.

"You can read fairly well, then," he said, having worried when he'd seen the child-like handwriting in Biff's notebook. "Good. I'm thinking signing up with this bunch is going to be your best chance to get situated here in Breck, at least, until you get your legs under you proper." He planted his hands on his hips, elbows angled out, and beamed up at the barbarian. "Well, this is where we part ways, Biff. It's been a pleasure meeting you, I must say."

"Thanks, Mr. Randall. You've been awfully nice to show me around," Biff said. What happened next took Randall rather by surprise; the big man reached out and took him in a firm hug, but he didn't squeeze hard enough to hurt. He patted Randall on the back, then turned and headed into the guildhall, leaving a mystified Randall to watch him disappear.

Chapter Three

The conjurer loosed another phantasmal bird from his outstretched hand, and ducked with a yelp as a coruscating green comet of fire blasted it apart mere yards away from him, his dark purple robes flapping loosely about him, hands up to shield his face. Smoke drifting in front of him, the elven mage grumbled, "Gods, Memnock, you could wait a little longer before your release! Or at least slow that thing down a touch."

"That would rather defeat the entire exercise, Nigel," replied a mid-range female voice through the cloud between him and the opposite end of the Combat Magic Practice Chamber. Enchanted decades earlier, the room stretched nearly the length of a traditional cuyotai longhouse beyond its door, though the exterior dimensions of the guildhall would never have allowed such a construction within its visible confines. A tall, broad-shouldered woman in a white hooded cloak with orange, looping trim along the cuffs and edges stepped out of the smoke. Her long, crimson curls bounced as she hopped toward him playfully, a husky and exuberant woman with the brightest smile one could hope for.

Of course, most men were put off by both her stature and frame, along with her deadliness with offensive magic and knack for short sword work and grappling. Memnock Halcesh wore many descriptors, but 'dainty' had never entered into the equation. She bounded to Nigel's side and looped his head around into her armpit in a playful headlock, rubbing his thin, soft brown hair like a teasing sibling. "I'm trying to work on my speed and accuracy, after all. And besides, you've been trying to get your conjurations to maneuver on their own for months now. This ought to help us both, if we're trying to best one another."

"I wouldn't have any problem with that," Nigel replied, slipping free of her grasp finally and running a pale hand through his hair. "But we've only got so much energy to expend before the safety cube snaps. If that happens, one of us could end up killing the other with an errant blow." The magical devices had been made popular among guilds and military institutions throughout the realms since their creation nearly a century earlier, and even the Freelance Adventurers Guild had managed to make a bulk purchase of safety cubes. Activated by a small feed of magical energy, the cream-orange blocks would flash brightly and cover an area roughly the size of a chamber such as the training room with a faint glimmer. Anything that happened within the cube's domain would be undone the moment the cube ran out of energy, or burst from an overload of kinetic force within its boundaries. Yet all of the memories and experiences learned and lived through would remain in the mind, thus allowing for tremendous extended training.

"There's a hefty supply in the cabinets if we need more," Memnock said, strolling over to a wooden locker and pulling it open. Yet it seemed the heavens wanted her to look the fool; only a paltry dozen or so of the small blocks remained in the supply cabinet, and the other three such doors opened upon little more than dust and some worn bits of gear. "Well, shit," she muttered, shaking her head.

"It's just as well, Mem." Nigel snapped his fingers. The chamber flashed with an orange light, and the faint glimmer that had lain upon every solid surface, the guild members themselves included, vanished without a trace save for the telltale aroma of black licorice that the cubes smelled so heavily of. "I've taken an Outbound job. Digby brought us in a very lucrative retrieval last night, and I'm off to take care of the second leg of the journey."

"I'm guessing it was something that skirts the line of legality," Memnock commented, eyes half-lidded, shaking her head. "Where is the fox today, by the way?"

"Last time I saw him was in the grand commons about an hour and a half ago." Nigel hooked one arm around hers, striding easily toward the door with his head leaned to the side against her biceps. "You ever think they'll rank me up past journeyer, Mem?"

"Of course they will, Nigel," she said, patting him on the head with her free hand. "Of course, I might be an old crone by the time it happens, but I'm sure you can do it."

He snickered and squeezed her arm as hard as he could, a feeble overall effort, all things given.

"Well, that's only a year or so off, so I'm in luck," he retorted, slipping free of her before Memnock could give him a headlock or any other roughhousing attack. Off he went down the hall toward the Outbounds office while Memnock turned left out of the room, heading for the grand commons. Digby often spent entire days hanging out there, alternating between chatting up his fellow guild members, chasing down leads, and napping while laid out atop one of the long trestle tables that sat against the outer walls of the chamber. Once in a while she would find him half-asleep in one of the cozy wingback chairs by the fireplace in the northwest or southeast corners of the room, a book in hand, paying little actual attention to whatever he was reading. Invariably the book in question would be some romance novel or other, a curiosity she didn't find herself willing or able to ask about just yet. She'd known him for two years now, and though she might ask at some point, Memnock suspected it wouldn't be any time soon.

As she entered the grand common room, she spotted the vulpesin seated across from the ever-armored Sirock Delpa, a pok-chi board and cards set between them on one of the round tables that dotted the interior of the chamber. Sirock was the tallest dwarf Memnock had ever met, and possibly the tallest in all of Tamalaria, standing a massive four and a half feet high with a frame like a moving cliff face. Decked out in the traditional full plate armor of his deity, the goddess Reyko, the dwarf oft found himself having to choose his seats with care, as he had here. While Digby, with his back to her, had procured one of the wingback chairs for his play session, Sirock had dragged over one of the stone chairs from where it usually stood forgotten near the north entrance of the room.

The heavily-bearded battle priest darted a look up and spotted her, nodding without a word as greeting. Memnock strode up alongside Digby's chair, propping her elbow along the back corner of it over his shoulder and leaned down, stage whispering, "So, who's winning?"

"Thanks to a piss-poor draw of the cards, the preacher here," the vulpesin groused as he considered the three cards in his hand before moving one of his red infantry tokens into Sirock's foremost territory for contest. "Infantry two against infantry one." Digby plucked one of his cards out of his hand and slapping it down on the table next to the right side of the board. "Ranged advantage plus one," he said, reading the card. He then scooped up two of the dice on the left side of the table, blew on them, and rolled them farther right of his downturned draw deck. He snarled as a one and a two came up.

"Well, it's a four at least," Mem said. "It's only two out of six he bests that." The battle priest of Reyko plucked up a single six-sided die, cast it to his left, and smiled silently as it came up six. Digby slapped his own knee and grunted a curse, shaking his head. Mem patted him on the shoulder and said, "Well, I suppose I'll know better than to open my mouth in the future."

"Blessed be they who take heart in the order of training and diligence," said Sirock, quoting from the scriptures of Reyko. The dwarf didn't speak often, a taciturn man even by the standards of the dwarves of the Northwestron Mountains from whence he hailed. Yet when he did speak, it was usually in carefully selected passages from the holy book of his religion, a faith to which fewer than a hundred adherents still belonged across the known realms. He'd been a true priest once, Mem had learned, but when all of the members of his congregation in Traithrock finally abandoned the faith, he simply packed up some meager belongings and left, without a word to anyone.

How he had settled on working with the Freelance Adventurers Guild, she didn't know, though she'd heard a few wild tales conjured up among the guild's other members. None of these seemed to fit the stoic battle priest's demeanor or nature, so she dismissed most of them out of hand. One story seemed like it might be somewhere in the region of possible, though, and she considered it as Sirock moved one of his cavalry units into a flanking position alongside one of the vulpesin's combat mage battalions.

From one of the senior members she had once heard that Sirock had been merely passing through Breck some years back when he came upon a group of shameless thugs laying waste to an entire squad of constables. It was said that the battle priest dropped his gear bag, took up arms, and without a sound uttered launched himself into their midst, swiftly killing half of the criminals and felling another quarter more before the remainder ran off out of the city for dear life. One of the constables who survived the battle resigned his post afterwards, and before Sirock could press on out of town, the former officer invited him to join ranks with him with the Freelancers.

"So, anything new and exciting going on today?" Mem asked, having spent most of her morning in the training room.

"Nothing much, near as I can tell," replied Digby. "Heard some murmurs about half an hour ago about a potential new recruit taking the grand tour. Big as an ox, Rinata says, and she's a pretty keen eye."

"She learn anything else about him?"

"No, not as yet, but senior hand Palmer is showing him around," Digby replied. "Doubtless he'll be coming through here soon enough. Sit a spell, we might get a chance to eyeball the fresh meat when they pass."

Mem did just that, bringing a simple folding chair over from another table and seating herself to Digby's left and Sirock's right.

The battle priest indicated his attack phase with wordless jabs of his finger, indicating a strike from his cavalry against the mage battalion. With a flip of a card, he gave himself three extra dice to roll for 'Plus 3 Vs Mages', and soundly trounced Digby's defenders, clearing the way for direct path to the vulpesin's capital base.

Three rounds later, Digby resigned, clearly beaten, and shook hands with the dwarf. Digby and Mem swapped positions seamlessly, and reset the board for a fresh start, with the mage shuffling the cards as Sirock surveyed his options for force allocation. Once Mem split the cards and handed him his half, the dwarf waved one hand to invite her to select her forces first. As she eyeballed her arrangements, she caught a look from the dwarf, and she turned to follow his gaze over her shoulder.

The man padding along beside senior hand Palmer looked like nothing so much as a demi-god carved out of pure muscle and boiled leather armor, an enormous broadsword strapped to his back. Tall, blond haired and handsome in the way of rugged country folk, he would have looked right at home in a gladiatorial arena. Yet he carried a notebook in one hand and a pen in the other, and his expression gave off an impression of studiousness she had seen before.

On the faces of children, she thought with a sigh. *Just what we need in this guild, another brainless brute.*

Dylan Palmer, a svelt lizardman scholar and second in line behind the chapter's headmaster, Vikas Tsur, was moseying along with his hands clasped behind his back, speaking softly to the huge human.

With an amused grin he led the big man over toward the trio around the table and cleared his throat. "Mister Narick, Miss Halcesh, Mister Delpa, how are the three of you doing today?"

"Just fine, senior hand," Digby said. "And who's this young fellow?"

"This is Biff," Palmer said, leaning his head toward the young barbarian. "He's looking for a job, and someone recommended he join our ranks."

"Well, welcome, Biff," Digby said with a playful smile. "I've lived in this city for some time now, would've thought I'd seen someone your overall size and look before, but I can't say as I recognize you."

"I'm not from Breck." Biff nodded. "I'm from Naletch, born and raised," he added with a measure of pride. Digby raised one eyebrow at the big fellow, and quirked his canine lips.

"Wait, I've been there once, about three, four years back," the vulpesin said, casting back in his mind for the memory. "As I recall, there's a few human families that seem to make them big like you there. It's got the lumber mill, right? Up on that peat moss hill, just north of town?"

Biff nodded happily, mouth half-open like a dog that has been shown approval by its master.

"What's your family name, Biff?"

"McLargehuge," the barbarian replied, the result of which was unkind snickering from some of the other scattered guild members nearby. Digby had it, now; he'd met a man in the town by the name of Sten McLarguje, most likely this young brute's father. The man had bought him drinks in the town's lone pub to help the whole of the town thank him and Nigel for locating a den of bosakin that had been snatching up the livestock in the surrounding farms the town relied upon for food. The queer, giant-eyed reptilian monsters had been holed up in a burrow not more than a mile out of town, just past the lumber mill that employed most of the menfolk of Naletch. Between Digby's traps and Nigel's spellwork, they had eradicated the entire lot in a couple of nights' time. The guild had been paid rather handsomely for the work.

And here is that man's son, and he can't even pronounce his own name correctly, Digby thought. *What a dunce.* Despite this inner dialogue, he rose from his seat and offered the big boy a hand, which

Biff took with surprising (and appreciated) gentleness. Biff then reached his hand down to Memnock, who shook as she tried not to stare, and finally the barbarian shuffled around her and offered his hand to the dwarf, who just looked up at him in stony silence. Biff kept his hand held out, his dullard smile showing no ounce of give, no single inch of surrender. After nearly a minute of this, feeling horrendously awkward, Digby cleared his throat theatrically.

"Take no offense, young Biff," said the vulpesin. "Sirock here's not what those in the entertainment business would call a crowd-pleaser. It's nothing personal, you understand?" But his words washed like so much air over Biff, who remained as still and unflinching as the battle priest.

When another full minute passed, with an expectant hush laying thick as everyone in the room looked on to see what would happen, Digby witnessed a miracle; Sirock's cheeks creased up in a genuine smile, and he took the boy's hand.

"If thy enemy be true to his heart and to his duty, hate him not," said Sirock, once more quoting as he pumped Biff's hand up and down. "For he is no enemy true, but instead a warrior whose orders are not thy own." Finally the two men let go of one another, to scattered applause and several sighs of relief from the various men and women in the chamber, all of whom returned to their previous positions and pursuits. Senior hand Palmer bade the trio farewell, and guided Biff away, speaking softly to him once again.

"By the gods, I hope he signs up," said Digby, shaking his head and resuming his seat. "We could use someone that determined."

"Agreed," said Memnock, making her first move and drawing her starting hand of three cards. "And we could use a fourth at some point. I'm tired of being the biggest one of us out there."

***

"Sign here," said Vikas, pointing at the contract scroll laid out on his desk before the massive human, Biff. When Palmer had informed him that young Mr. McLargehuge somehow bested Sirock Delpa in a staredown, causing the dwarven battle priest to actually break into a smile and quote his scripture in a complimentary fashion, the aged elven soldier knew he *had* to convince the big man to sign up. Thankfully, it hadn't taken much of an effort. Massive and undoubtedly dangerous as Biff was, chatting him up into doing something proved almost unnecessary. With pen in hand, the barbarian signed his name in a barely legible scrawl near the bottom of the scroll.

"Excellent." Vikas rolled the contract up and rose from his seat to face the wall of scroll cubbies behind his desk. He slid Biff's into the most recently opened cubby, then faced his new grunt. "You are familiar with what my title means, yes?"

"Yup," said Biff. "It means you're the big boss here."

"That is correct," said the elven man, his twig-like frame slipping back to his seat like an insect. "As headmaster, I am in charge of this branch of the Freelance Adventurers Guild of Tamalaria. The contract you just signed commits you to one year of service to our ranks, and gives you access to all of the perks and privileges being a member affords. Your current rank is junior wanderer, a rank you shall hold for no less than three months. Your percentage earnings shall be three percent of all jobs completed for less than fifty gold, and six percent for anything over and above. Any and all extraneous gatherings collected while on a job, as a result *of* that job, should be turned in and appraised in the quartermaster's department. The taskmaster is in charge of doling out and offering open contracts, as well as receiving reports and recording the results of jobs taken whence they are completed. Do you understand thus far?"

"Uh-huh," said Biff, scribbling madly in his little notebook.

"There are four primary ranks in this guild, and each rank has a junior and senior level. There are also the specialists, who focus solely on one department or area of our needs as an overall operation," said Vikas, folding his fingers together atop his desk. "The ranks are wanderer, journeyer, foot, and hand. Above the hands are vice headmasters, of which most branches only have one. Finally, above them are the headmasters themselves, such as me. Among the specialists," the elf soldier said, slowing down his speech to allow Biff to catch up, "there are the quartermasters, in charge of our gear. There are the taskmasters, in charge of records and assignments. Then there are the grooms, who care for the various beasts of burden and labor that each branch owns and uses for official business. We also employ three full-time barristers, who represent guild members and the guild itself when there are," he said, taking a deep breath, thinking of that damned wizenheimer, the vulpesin, "Legal issues," he finished in one long breath.

"Okay," said Biff. "Um, do I have to remember all their names just yet? Only, I'm not very good with names if there's a lot of them." Vikas pulled his folded hands to his narrow belly and eased back in his plush leather chair, which creaked faintly as he shifted back into it.

"No need to try memorizing them all right now, Biff. Now, ours is a guild that is, in many respects, very much like the United Adventurers Guild of Tamalaria. We take outside contracts from various peoples of the realm, and perform the tasks and services requested so long as they fall within our abilities and are profitable. However, unlike they, we do not mandate any member take any job they don't like, so long as they meet a certain minimum quota."

"A what," Biff asked, pen paused, face scrunched up in confusion.

"A quota, dear lad. It means a required number or quantity of a thing," the elf said, providing Biff a pause to scribble some more. "This quota differs from most people's expectations. Ours is not based on the income of the contracts you take or the number of jobs overall. Taskmaster Jerrick, vice-headmaster Rollins and myself determine the importance of the contracts that come in, and we give each a rating out of ten. For each earnings quarter as a junior wanderer, we require a minimum quote of six points. The greater your rank with us, of course, the greater the quota."

"What if I don't make the quota some time," Biff asked, his tone that of a child who has been threatened with no more Gift Day presents.

"Well, we then assess a payment penalty for the jobs completed in the next quarter. Not much, so no worries, but after enough shortages, it can lead to quite the crimp. In any event, we don't expel members for not meeting it," he said, and felt a strange twinge of sympathy for Biff as the young barbarian visibly relaxed. "We also occasionally classify certain contracts or tasks around the guildhall as 'clearance posts', meaning that they can be completed to automatically put members in good standing for their quota, even if they're currently under penalty."

"Kind of like how some folks do a penance, depending on their religion," Biff observed.

Vikas, impressed with this bit of proven knowledge, nodded.

"Precisely like that, young Biff. Now look, we won't likely see much of each other for a while after this," the headmaster said, rising from his seat and coming around the desk. Biff stood up as well as the elven man took him gently by the arm and guided him toward the office door. "But we will have a meeting tomorrow morning. Every new member gets paired up with a more experienced one for their first couple of jobs, sort of a 'learn the ropes' apprenticeship. Be here in my office at eight o'clock in the morning, and we'll have you paired up. For now, you have the freedom to come and go as you like, and of course to use the barracks in the basement."

Biff thanked him for his kindness, pulling the door shut behind him as he left.

Vikas sauntered back to his chair, propped his feet up on the desk, and grabbed the little blue box from the corner which gave him a direct communication line to senior hand Palmer's matching device. "Palmer?"

"Yes, sir," the lizardman replied over the device.

"I need you to send someone to my office," Vikas said with a wolfish grin.

Chapter Four

Digby stared, dumbfounded, at the knife-eared cretin seated at his desk, a veritable cat-that-got-the-canary smile dancing like firelight in his almond-shaped eyes. "You're kidding me," he breathed, his palms suddenly clammy, feet twitching. "This is outrageous," he continued, unable to look at the headmaster, eyes lowering to the floor.

"Whatever you may wish to call it, it's perfect for our purposes," said Vikas. "He gets his training job in, we get the requested number of people on the job, and the contract stays under our control. You've rejected every other candidate who *wanted* to join you, Delpa and Halcesh, since at least one of the three of you had bad blood with them, so this presents itself as the perfect opportunity."

"But sir, he's only just come to Breck, from his hometown," Digby protested. He's never been outside of a fifty mile radius from the place he was born, I'll wager! We can't expect this to work." He slid one hand back through the hair atop his canine head.

Vikas's aggressively joyful expression vanished, replaced by a tight-mouthed glare, holding one finger up to still the vulpesin.

"We need to keep that contract, Digby," the headmaster said curtly. "We've two more weeks left on it before it lapses, and if we don't show some kind of progress by then, we'll have to forfeit the establishment bonus. That money's already spent. We could cover it, but it would hurt all of us."

"I know," Digby said, one hand in the crook of his other arm, fist perched under his long chin as his fingers pulled idly on the whiskers draped over the sides of his snout.

"And you *did* say that you'd gotten the other two to agree to go with you on the job, that you'd take a fourth if they suited you all."

"I know," Digby replied, a little more forcefully, his nods more exaggerated.

"And everybody needs to expose themselves to more outbound travel to grow the guild."

"I know," Digby fairly shouted, banging his fist on the arm of the visitor's chair, crossing his legs and half-turning aside, letting out a 'harumph' of disapproval. "This isn't exactly what I had in mind, sir. I'll gladly do a few short run jobs with just the boy, get him used to the flow of things, but this is too much."

A silence hung then over the room, one wherein Vikas simply leaned back in his chair, hands folded in his lap, thumbs twiddling over one another. After what felt like an eternity, the headmaster pulled open a drawer on the right side of his desk, took out a tightly wound scroll with beautifully polished wooden rollers, and set it on his desktop. No word was spoken as yet; he merely tapped the scroll once, then leaned back again. Digby finally broke the quiet. "Is that…" he began.

"It is," said Vikas. "I told you I would be keeping it on hand."

"It wouldn't hold up, you know," the vulpesin said, his voice wavering just a hint, eyes betraying him by darting to the insignia carved on each end of the roller handles. "No government in all of these realms would send me back based on that piece of parchment."

"It's not just governments you need to worry about, and you know that as well as I, Mister Narick," Vikas replied softly, barely moving his mouth to speak. "There's more than one copy of this scroll out there. Perhaps only half a dozen, but not many men in these realms know your whereabouts personally. And if some unscrupulous far-wanderer should realize how much profit there would be in taking you back, it wouldn't take long for you to be in serious trouble."

Digby wanted to scream, choke the elf, and run like a maniac all at once. He couldn't help but admire Vikas for his grit in this situation. Elves generally weren't known for their ability to be manipulative or underhanded: such traits typified illeck, known by most as *dark elves*. But Vikas had been a soldier for a long time, hundreds of years, and soldiers were nothing if not practical. The best way to ensure Digby's cooperation was to rely on tactics such as this. *Well played, you old war horse,* he thought.

"I wouldn't be dead, though," the vulpesin finally said. "And I don't care how many copies of that scroll are floating around out there, or who else knows where to find me, I'd have to be brought back very much *alive* in order for anybody to collect."

"True, but it doesn't say anything about comfortable or unharmed," Vikas countered. "Look, you know the contract will pay handsomely, and Biff strikes me as more than capable of handling the dangers of the wilds. It may be that having him along will result in a team that is somewhat imbalanced, but there are no other good options remaining to you. So, what will it be, Digby?"

Rather than verbally respond, the nimble vulpesin rogue roll-flipped himself back over his chair from a seated position, demonstrating nigh-impossible agility, and landed in a rigid stance back by the office door. He merely nodded, then wheeled about and kicked the door open, leaving the headmaster behind.

"Good choice," the old elven soldier muttered to himself, feeling wretched for resorting to such bullying.

***

Memnock and Sirock sat on one side of the table, slid together on a red cushioned bench by the cafe window, and Biff sat across from them with a broad, simpleton smile, fingers laced together around a coffee mug. He'd never had coffee before, and with a dollop of cream and some sugar, he'd discovered it was possibly among the most delightful things he'd ever had in this life. He had come to the cafe/diner per Mr. Digby's instructions, and located the tall lady and armored dwarf as recommended, then sat across from them.

For Memnock and Sirock's part, the vulpesin had located them the evening before and asked them to meet him at Dan's Diner, just a couple of streets over from the guildhall, to discuss the 'Last Shield' contract they'd signed on for months earlier. He had informed them both that headmaster Vikas wanted them to take Biff so that the four of them could finally take up the task and get the job done. His reasoning was fairly straight-forward: headmaster Vikas didn't want the contract to lapse, and since it paid so well, they needed to get the revenue in. Both mage and battle priest agreed, and set about making preparations the night before to ready themselves for the journey.

Dan's wasn't precisely packed, but the trio often sat in the same booth, and Digby himself felt quite glad to see them in the normal place when he strode into the diner and nodded his usual 'hello' to Megan, the hostess behind the counter. He leaned in close to a stout fellow in blue trousers and faded robin's egg vest with gray hair spilling down over his shoulders seated at the counter and said, "Morning, Harold. How goes the fishing?"

"Same as it ever did, fox." The older man turned a face toward him that had no features on the left side, a solid, smooth mass of flesh with no blemishes. His lone eye swirled with various colors, and his mouth, which dominated his left cheek, crooked down in a vague frown. "I manage to make a living, little more."

"Catch anything interesting lately?"

"Just some crawlies," Harold replied, turning back to his plate of bacon strips nearly burnt black. "Sold the lot to Becker's for a pretty penny."

Digby clapped him on the back companionably, then sauntered over toward his comrades, drawing out a copy of the contract scroll from his belt as he seated himself beside Biff. Megan came over with a fresh mug and poured refills for the other three, then got Digby squared up. "The usual, fellows," the vulpesin asked, to silent nods from Mem and Sir. "Biff, what'll you have? It's on me."

The barbarian looked over his menu, narrowed his eyes, and looked over at the waitress. "I'll have three pancakes, an omelet with cheddar cheese, and a rasher of bacon," he said, handing the menu across to her.

Megan took it, scribbled the order on her notepad, then shuffled away quickly. Digby took a sip of the coffee, grimaced, then added a heavy dose of sugar.

"Have to hand it to her, she's consistent with how much she burns the cuppa. So, my friends..." Digby unrolled the scroll between himself and Sirock, seated across from him. The dwarf shifted his utensils to hold down the top, Digby doing the same for the bottom. "We come to the heart of the matter, why I've gathered us here this morning. We are finally going to tackle this contract, 'The Last Shield'. Biff, I'm going to go over this mostly for your benefit, since you're new to the guild and haven't been read in for the job."

"Okay."

"One Toro the Bold is our client on this, a fairly well-known blacksmith out of Trec. He has requested that we locate and retrieve the last shield crafted by master blacksmith Jayen the Hammer. Jayen was quite possibly the finest dwarven smithy to ever grace the Freehold States, and his works have become ever-more valuable since his passing two years ago."

"How'd he die?" Biff asked, sipping down the last of his current cup of coffee.

"Well, Jayen was quite old, even for a dwarf, young Biff," Digby said. "He was nearly five hundred years old. Most dwarves only make it about four hundred before they pass of natural causes. He was discovered in his bed one day by his son Parthal, who had come for a visit. He suspects the old smithy just passed in his sleep. Ah, thank you, Megan," Digby said as the waitress topped him and Biff up. "Now, the very last shield Jayen made was said to have been the most beautiful piece he ever made, crafted from half a dozen different materials, striped like a rainbow. Toro would like to have the shield brought to him, as he had originally intended to have the piece placed in a tradesmen's museum in Ja-Wen, in honor of Jayen's accomplishments in the craft." He took another sip of his coffee and continued. "He'd contracted a caravan that was already *en route* to the city to add this piece to their cargo, with instructions on where to take it when they reached Ja-Wen."

"Weren't they rivals in the field?" Memnock asked, stirring her coffee lazily as she stared at the contract scroll. "I mean, how would Toro have come into possession of the shield to begin with?"

"Parthal gave the shield to Toro, actually, as a grieving gift. The two did indeed have a rivalry, but theirs was a respectful one. Often, Toro would refer clients looking for specialized armors to Jayen, and Jayen would refer clients looking for specialized weapons to Toro. They worked together upon a time some forty years ago, when Toro was a younger man. He 'prenticed with The Hammer, and developed a deep respect for the dwarf's technique. Now," Digby tapped the bottom of the contract with one clawed finger, "this right here is why I initially signed us up, folks."

"Why am I not surprised?" Memnock commented dryly. "That's quite a purse."

"Eight-thousand gold coin," Biff said, then whistled appreciatively. "That's a lot of money." He tapped his empty cup on the table rapidly, until Memnock finally reached out her hand and softly put it over his, ceasing the rattle.

"Sorry," Biff muttered, pulling his hand away off of the handle.

"The reward of coin is as nothing compared to the glory of victory over one's enemies," said Sirock, eyes locked on the mug clasped in his thick fingers. "The spoils of war may be reveled in upon the end of battle, and ne'er before."

Biff cocked an eyebrow at the battle priest, then turned his look upon the mage woman across from him.

"It's a quote from the holy book of Reyko, a dwarven goddess of battle," Memnock explained. "Most of the time, when Sirock says something, it's a quote from his scripture. He's a priest of Reyko, you see."

"Oh," said Biff, turning his attention to the heavily armored dwarf. "Forgive me for saying so, padre, but you don't look much like a preacher."

Sirock responded with a silent smile, followed by a sip of his coffee and nothing more. He looked to his left, then removed his utensils from the scroll and rolled it up, dutifully handing it back across to Digby just in time for Megan to start laying their plates down before them all.

"Have you two started packing for the trip?" Digby asked before tucking into his sausage patties.

"I've squared away everything for supplies for my part," Memnock replied. "Sirock?"

"As the sun doth rise in the skies above to make ready the day ahead, so too do we as warriors set aside what we shall need for the confrontations ahead," said Sirock.

"I'll take that as a 'yes'," said Digby between bites. "I've only got to fill out the paperwork to get us a wagon and some horses. Trouble is, I have no idea where we should get started."

Memnock raised a finger as she chewed, then pawed through the shoulder bag on the bench beside her, pulling out a red covered journal and pulling it open with the cloth bookmark sewn into the binding.

"You already have something to that effect, Mem?"

"Rumors I tracked down a couple of months back, when you first signed us up," she answered upon swallowing. She scanned her handwriting, then pointed to the page. "'Some rumors persist that the shield is being held by a clutch of rendermen in the wilds in the Ja-Wen city-state territory. The nature of these particular rendermen states that it is an amalgamated clutch, which is exceedingly rare in and of itself, which should make them easy to find. What's more, we know from the surviving caravan guard's testimony that the rendermen that attacked his group and stole the shield in the first place was also an amalgamated grouping. I was able to follow this up with four more people saying much the same thing, though the specifics vary a little from person to person."

"Who's your primary source on this," Digby asked.

"A Wayfarer veteran whose troupe passed through a few days after we took the job. His family troupe had been passing through Breck from Palen, but their course took them through Ja-Wen, then north of the Allenian Hills on their way to Desanadron. They came to the Freeholds for a bit of extra coin along the way."

Digby nodded, and a clatter of utensils on plates and bowls filled the air around them for a few minutes as they all concentrated on eating. When they were all finished, Megan came by and cleared the table of all but their mugs, scuttling away for only a minute before returning with a carafe with a green rim.

"Good call," Digby said as she poured for Biff, then the others.

Sirock grimaced at the sight of the green rim, and Megan brought around the red-rimmed pot from her other hand for him. Digby chuckled and said, "Never developed a taste for the decaff, eh, preacher?"

"And behold, the deceiver Sonamo came before blessed Reyko, offering her sweetness. Yet with the power of truth, which comes of seeing pure battle, she did know that he held before her offal, concealed with a glam. Then did she didst strike swiftly the Great God of Chaos and Darkness in the groin with a swing of her mighty foot," replied the battle priest. This bit of doggerel sent both Mem and Digby into chortles, leaning back on their benches, and Biff snickered along with, though he did not understand entirely the meaning of what had just passed between the two companions. As he sipped his coffee, he noticed it had a slightly different taste, but it was no worse the wear for the cream and sugar he added.

"I'll get the paperwork filled out when we leave here for the wagon and horses," Dibgy said. "I'd like for us to leave by tomorrow morning, so make every preparation you can soonest. Biff, when we leave, I'd like you to accompany me. You need to see how things are done properly as regards all the paperwork and filings for a job."

Memnock snorted, and Biff drained off the last of his coffee as Digby shot her a dirty look.

"What?" she asked, beaming up at the vulpesin as he slid out of the booth. "I'm just saying, the last four times we've worked together, you've fouled up the paperwork at some point or other, always in a rush to get things moving. Why don't you leave the paperwork to me?"

"Well enough. Biff? You'll go with Ms. Halcesh, she'll show you how to do it *properly*," he said with a sneer.

Sirock patted Digby on the back and ambled past him, leaving the diner before Digby could even attempt to stiff him with the bill again. He had learned from experience that the rogue couldn't be trusted to pick up a tab.

Memnock brushed past him next, followed closely by Biff. Digby caught the young barbarian by the wrist and turned him about momentarily, standing on tip-toe to whisper in his ear. "Now you be careful about what you say to Mem, Biff. She's a little sensitive about her size and a lot of people comment on it. Understood?"

"Okay," said Biff. "But why would she be sensitive about it? She's big like me, that's not a bad thing, is it?"

Digby just smiled and shook his head.

"No, Biff, it absolutely is not. Run along, now, so she doesn't leave you behind." Digby watched them exit, then retrieved a crinkled slip of parchment from one of his pockets and approached Megan at the till, handing her the slip.

"Gotta say, I'm a little surprised this Heflin of yours keeps giving you vouchers to pay for your meals," the human woman said, opening the drawer after scribbling the total on the slip. "He must really like you, fox."

"Oh, 'like' might not quite be the right word for it, dear," the rogue said as he waved a farewell to her, exiting the diner. When he got outside, he looked back at the front of the diner, and wondered for a moment what it might be like to have kitchen of his own again. He'd lived at the guildhall for a few years now, and before that, he'd been on the road for longer than he could immediately place. *When was the last time I had a home,* he wondered. *When did any of us, other than Biff?*

***

Memnock took the blank form from the duty desk and grabbed a seat at one of the two tables near the door that led off of the grand common room into this particular dreary little office. Run by an officious little goblin named Wennick, the Office of Requisitions was the most unpopular room in the entire of the guildhall. Wennick had no good reason to be liked by most of the members at the Breck branch of the guild: most saw him as High Headmaster Tennison's creature and viewed him with equal measures disdain and distrust.

Mem had been cordial enough asking for the forms for transport request, and the hook-nosed little man with his pale green skin and ragged woolen tunic had mumbled under his breath in his native tongue as he withdrew the form from one of the many boxes he kept on his side of the counter. The duty desk ran the entire width of the room, and an enchanted glass partition kept him safely out of reach of the guild's members. Ensorcelled too was his little access door, which would only allow him and the senior-most members of the guild as a whole to pass through from one side to the other.

Yet as he'd slipped the form through the little open chute to her, Mem had remained neutral of expression, keeping her eyes from wandering. She had, months earlier, spotted a critical flaw in the enchantment that kept the whole of the area beyond the counter safe from assault. It seemed an incredibly simple thing to her mind once she'd spotted it, but the mage figured that the defenses' simplicity was something most magic practitioners would overlook out of mere habit, always looking for expertise and convoluted explanations.

The glass and the desk are enchanted, but not the floor, she thought as she eyeballed the long line where the desk met the concrete. *A touch of gaiamancy, and the whole thing'd collapse.* She grinned briefly, then turned her attention to the form and the pen in her hand. "All right, Biff. The first thing we do here is look at the box in the upper left corner. See the little check boxes?"

"Uh-huh."

"There's 'horses', 'oxen', 'wagons', 'auto-carts', and 'artifacts'. Now, we're going to be requesting horses and a wagon, so we check off those boxes. Gear and equipment are allocated by the quartermaster, but for any of these five things, we need to inform the head office in Desanadron that we're taking from the overall inventory for a job." She ticked off the required boxes. "Now, here, in this box with the blank lines, we write the names of everyone in the group taking the job." She quickly jotted down her own name, then Digby's, then Sirock, and finally Biff. "Now in this box, we write down the contract title." She wrote out, 'The Last Shield'. "If we have a reference number from the contract, we write that too, since lots of jobs have similar titles." She pulled out her little notebook, then copied down the number she'd recorded back when Digby first brought the job to them.

"Okay. Um, what if there's other members on the same job, but not working together," Biff asked.

"Well, then if the other agent or agents wanted one of these five things, they'd have to fill out their own form," Memnock replied. "Now, the next thing we need to do is fill this out here." She pointed with her pen to the large space on the form with numerous blank lines. "We describe, concisely, what the goal of the job is, and justify why we'll need the supplies we're requesting. We could go out and secure any of this stuff for ourselves, really, but this way, the guild can cover some of our start-up expense. Give me a minute and we'll continue."

Memnock quickly wrote out a summary of the job, explained in ink why they would need four horses and a wagon, and then set her pen in one of the pockets of her robe.

"Is that all?"

"No. Now, we hand it back to Wennick." She rose from the chair and returned to the counter where she patted the little bell. The goblin, who'd laid back on a cot against the far wall, looked over with a laziness to his expression that had all the power of a man who might otherwise have been content to sleep for the next hundred days without qualm. With a grunt he swung himself over the side of the cot, ambled slowly back to the counter, and accepted the form through the chute. The wide, flap-like ears on the sides of the goblin's head twitched as he looked it over, nostrils flaring and shriveling as he padded over to what looked like a restroom booth, disappearing inside and drawing a curtain shut behind himself. Out of eyesight, the goblin could be doing anything and nobody would be any the wiser, though Mem had once convinced Wennick to tell her what he kept in the booth.

Situated on a narrow countertop beyond the curtain, the goblin had installed an enchanted mirror. The spell attached would allow him to contact either Nancy in the quartermaster's office, or High Headmaster Tennison, depending upon which hand the goblin touched the mirror's flat surface with. His left hand would send a signal to Nancy, his right to Tennison, and in either event, he would then pass along the information written down. With a slight adjustment of the magical energies flowing through the glass, he could pass the paper directly through the other side, whereupon a stamp of approval or denial would be affixed to the form and then passed back through to him.

As Mem thought on this, the goblin twitched the curtain back and returned, handing the form through the chute with a green 'APPROVED' stamped on the upper-right corner of the parchment.

"So, now that we have approval, we put one signature from a member on the job in the bottom left, then hand it back, and Wennick will then file the form away after making a copy for us to keep on our person when we go out to the stables for the horses." She handed it back, and the goblin slipped the form into a strange mechanical contraption with a large metal crank on the left side. He turned the crank a few times, then reached down to a tray on the device's underside, returning with a warm sheet that looked much like the original form, passing it to Memnock. "See?"

"Neat," said Biff with a glare of wonder in his eyes. "Um, what's this mean, right here?"

Mem angled her head around and looked at where his thick finger pointed, aimed at a small note in the 'Approval Notes' box. There, in High Headmaster Tennison's neat, curlicue handwriting, were the words 'Top Breed'.

"It means we've been approved to take the best horses the stables currently has, if we so choose." Mem narrowed her eyes at the handwriting, vexed for reasons she could not quite put her finger on. "Tennison doesn't usually make such approvals willy-nilly, and none of us are very high-ranking members." She took the form and tucked it into one of the many pockets on the inside of her cloak. "Would you mind terribly seeing yourself around a little bit, Biff? I'd like to get clarification on this from headmaster Vikas."

"Okay," said the large young brute, ambling out of the Requisitions Office with the tall mage woman right behind him. "Um, any suggestions what I should do?"

Mem paused a moment, then snapped her fingers and waggled one at him.

"I think I know what might be right up your alley." She wrapped her arm around his biceps and led him toward the main entrance of the guildhall building. "You might even earn a little coin, too, which is always helpful," she added as they stepped outside.

***

Biff waved farewell to Memnock as she headed back toward the guildhall, which was only a couple of blocks away, and as such, would be easy enough for him to find his way back to. That was good, because Breck already seemed much too easy to get lost in for a lad who had never been beyond the town he was born and raised in. When she was out of sight, the barbarian turned his attention to the mound of coal rocks and the shovel planted in the side of their little hill. An open furnace grate stood before him, with a faint scarlet glow coming from within. Seated a few yards away from Biff was a brawny jaft of middling height, the blue-fleshed, bald headed humanoid slumped back on a lawn chair with a filthy leather apron covering his bare upper torso.

"You'll want to shovel on a rhythm once things get going in there," the jaft said to Biff, who just nodded, gripping the handle of the shovel in his massive hands. "The next time you hear the whistle, you're going to want to pitch in at least three big loads, then settle into a steady feed, half a scoop every ten count or so. You ready, big man?"

"Yes sir," Biff replied, and the jaft got up from his lawn chair and moved around toward the back side of the squat, dome-like brick structure. Words were exchanged in a language Biff didn't speak, and as the jaft returned, an ear-scraping whistle sounded, and Biff quickly shoved three heavy scoops of coat into the furnace, slowing down and pushing the shovel into the pile about halfway before bringing the tool back up. He waited, counting to ten before pushing the next scoop in. In less than a minute, he had a perfect working pattern established.

He knew full well this was nothing more than busywork, a simple task foisted off on him to keep him out of the way so that Memnock could take care of a complicated task without him bumbling along and slowing her down. Thick though he was, Biff had been handled and managed by his papa all his young life and he'd come to recognize when he was being shunted aside to avoid making himself a burden. This was one such time.

Not that this man seems to mind, he thought, taking a quick peek out of the corner of his eye at the jaft relaxing. Though he suspected that this was the sort of task that was more rewarding if one understood how it benefited some other process taking place *inside* the dome-like building, Biff carried out his task, begging no questions, making no complaints. An expression his father had been keen on played through Biff's mind like a mantra as he shoveled- 'Work until the job is done, or until you're dead'.

And so he shoveled more coal, waiting for Mem to return to either tell him he was done, or until he was out of coal.

***

Vice-headmaster Rollins didn't even peer up from the heavy book she was scanning with her half-lidded, gold-ringed eyes. A rakah of the rare wizus tribe, she appeared physically like a tall, wiry barn owl/human hybrid. While most rakah, avian lycanthropes, could shape-change into either a fully humanoid or fully animal form for brief periods, like the other lycanthrope breeds, the 'owlies' as many called them could not. Yet the gods themselves seemed to have made up for this shortcoming by making the wizus tribe the most intelligent and magically gifted of all of the lycanthrope races as a whole.

Rollins had three of the four walls of her office lined with bookcases, each one containing six shelves. In all of them, with no exceptions, the top three shelves were crammed full of books of all sorts, arranged alphabetically first by author, then by title. On most, the lower three shelves housed various magical artifacts and relics of all sorts, each one accompanied by a small hand-scroll bearing information regarding the item in question.

Memnock spent the first minute in Rollins's office as she did every time she came here, staring with her lips slightly apart, surveying the cases with something approaching envy on steroids. After a moment, she gathered her senses, approached the desk, and withdrew the copied request form from her sleeve. "Master Rollins, a moment of your time, if I may?"

Rollins gave no response for a moment, finally taking a solid white bookmark from beside her elbow, and setting it in place. A single black horizontal line had been marked about halfway down the marker, and she set this line very deliberately at the start of a paragraph about three-quarters of the way down the page before looking up with half-lidded eyes.

"You are always welcome to interrupt me, lovely Memnock," she trilled, her voice low and melodious. "How go your studies?"

"Splendidly, and thank you, my lady," the tall, broad sorcerous replied with a shallow curtsy. "May I be seated?"

"Yes, you may," said Rollins.

Memnock had memorized the rigid etiquette structures the rakah peoples practiced, from the wizus tribe through the patrock, the harsh and war-like eagle-folk of the Isle of Foul southwest of the continent. When she had first come to the guild, Memnock had only an intermediate degree of magical knowledge, enough to pass as a caravan guard or an apprentice to a high-rank mage. Yet Rollins had identified potential in her right away, and in the first six months of her membership, the owl-woman had instilled in her more spellcraft than any college of magical education could have with years of study. Whenever she needed guidance, Rollins was her first go-to. In return for her kindness, Memnock had committed to learning the ways of all rakah.

"I come seeking clarification, my lady," she said, handing the form across the desk to her mentor, who briefly eyeballed the form before setting it down sideways between them. "We do not oft come upon such swift and high-level approval from the High Headmaster. Be there any reason to question his clearance in this regard?"

"I should think so, yes." Rollins rose from her seat and walked to one of her bookcases against the wall to Mem's left. She ran a single scaled finger along the spines of several tomes before plucking one free, bringing it over and paging through it at her seat. She finally located the page she was looking for, and turned the book to face Mem, her hooked claw tapping an artist's depiction of a rather brute looking renderman. "As you are aware, the metal men of the wilds are mostly pale imitations of humans in metallic form, little more than savage mockeries that slice and eat everything they come across, particularly if it is metal. Now, you know the standard Order of Metals, yes?"

"I remember the concept, but I forget what it's based on," Mem confessed.

"The Order is ranked based on the known and estimated quantities of each material in Tamalaria and Tallowmere. It goes bronze, copper, tin, iron, nickel, silver, gold, platinum, titanite, mythril, and adamantite. The rendermen populate the wilds in approximately the same concentrations, comparatively. They're already uncommon, making the last three sorts extremely rare."

"I've never even heard of a mythril or adamantite renderman," Memnock admitted, leaning forward to look at the picture Rollins was pointing to. The image showed a terrifying creature that looked not like a man, but rather like a demonic metal humanoid with a wolf's head, gnashing fangs clamped between curled lips. Shown in profile, it was drawn with a hand in the shape of an axe head, while the other held what was clearly supposed to be a minotaur by the throat, the victim's hoofed feet dangling a good two feet off the ground. "Is this supposed to be one?"

"Yes, an adamantite one. The picture may seem skewed, but it is my understanding this image was based off of a Mage's Eye pressing," said Rollins.

A knot of dread cramped Mem's stomach at the notion.

"You mean, something akin to a photograph in modern parlance?" Mem asked, incredulous.

"Aye, it is just so. This contract you've signed on to with the fox is well-known to many of us in the higher ranks, as the potential danger involved is extreme. We would have happily allowed it to lapse, but I personally suspect High Headmaster Tennison still holds a grudge against monsignor Delpa for besting him at the last guild open arms competition."

Memnock felt her hands balling into fists on her lap, incensed at the idea that the guild's overall commander would allow his own bruised ego to shove members of his organization into a likely lethal scenario.

"We even have it on good authority from a rashum hunter that this specific clutch is led by an intelligent and ruthless gold, one that has actively sent packs of his silvers and irons slashing and crushing into small towns and settlements. If the High Headmaster believes this savage renderman may end up in close quarters with the monsignor, well, the death of either works out for him. You know guild politics can be less than pleasant."

Memnock took a deep, cleansing breath, put her hands flat together before her face and closed her eyes, a traditional wizun gesture to convey that the individual feared their emotions might overtly color their next statement or question. "I also know Master Tennison can be a pernicious fuckwit when it comes to such things," she said, holding the gesture. She winced a little at the 'tch-tch' sound that immediately came from Rollins, but when she opened her eyes and lowered her hands, she saw that the owl-woman wore a wry smile on her beak, a playful gleam in her eyes.

"Such language, lovely Memnock. It is hardly becoming of you," Rollins chided amiably. "Master Tennison probably assumes that any personnel or gear is forfeit in the case of this contract, and is willing to absorb the loss in exchange for seeing the dwarven battle priest in his grave. Now," she said, handing Memnock the form back and closing the tome, sliding it across for Memnock to take as well. "Is there anything else?"

"No, my lady," said Mem as she rose and once more curtsied. She plucked up the form, tucked it in her sleeve, and slid the tome into her sling bag. "Pleasure and peace to you, lady Rollins."

"Pleasure and peace to you as well, lady Halcesh," the wizun replied.

Chapter Five

When Biff woke up, bleary-eyed and mumbling under his breath from dreams, his arms hosted traces of the tingling he'd worked up in them the day before. Though Memnock had returned to fetch him after only a short time, he had opted to stay at the forge and shovel coals for several hours, earning himself a whole gold coin for his efforts. Not knowing that his labors had actually been worth at least four times that, he'd considered himself quite fortunate, and finally walked away at sundown with a broad smile on his face.

When at last he ambled back into the guildhall, he had to reference his field journal to remind himself how to get down to the barracks chambers. Once downstairs, he removed his armor, pulling out the care kit his papa had taught him to use on his equipment whenever he'd gone a few days without tending to his gear. He methodically oiled his leathers, buffed the metal studs laced throughout the cuirass, and tightened the chain links on his leggings with a pair of pliers designed just for the task. He didn't much enjoy the work, but it was part of the routine, as simple and natural to him now as clockwork to a gnome.

He paid no mind to the three other low-ranking members bunked down in the main chamber with him, all of whom paused now and then to observe the enormous human with his careful procedures of maintenance. So focused was he that Biff didn't even hear them talking among themselves about how they would convince the newbie to tend to their equipment as well. Finally, one of them, a narrow man perhaps a decade his senior with green field travel tunics and a ragged pair of brown trousers tied up with a rope about his waist, approached cautiously, a curved long knife held down by the tip.

"Excuse me, friend," the man said, his voice phlegmy, thick, his triangular goatee jutting from his chin like a speartip. "I was just admiring how well you move your whetstone on that big old blade of yours. I was wondering if you wouldn't mind, being a new recruit, sharpening up my own knife for me?"

Biff gave the man a blank, wide-eyed look, mouth drawn down.

"Um, is it kinda like the military here? I mean, am I supposed to do that because I'm new?" the big lummox asked innocently.

One of the other two men, an illeck with a ponytail down to the middle of his back, nudged his fellow with a smirk on his lips.

"Sort of, yeah." Spear-Beard, tossed his knife on Biff's cot. "Just set it over there on my trunk when you're done," he said, pointing over to the wall opposite one of the other cots. The illeck repeated the gesture with a pair of hand-scythes, and finally, a second human fellow deposited his long-handled war axe on the barbarian's cot as well, gesturing wordlessly toward his own trunk.

Biff hitched a sigh, shook his head, and set to the task at hand, finishing up his own backup weapon, a simple hunting knife, before moving on to the weapons of his superiors.

Now, with his efforts still mumbling at him in the morning, he found himself looking up at the vulpesin, Digby, as the fox-man nudged him gently. "Rise and shine, young Biff. It's time we got ready and had one last meal in the mess before we depart on our job."

Biff grunted, tossed back the sheets, and served up to Digby and anybody else nearby a perfect view of his naked frame. "Oh, well that's just not fair," Digby muttered darkly, yanking his gaze away from the barbarian's groin.

Biff stretched as Digby departed, then got dressed and geared up, rolling his shoulders to eliminate the last of the vestiges of his previous night's work. The hand-scythes had been difficult to sharpen properly, given the curve of their cutting edges. Still, he had made fine work of it, he surmised, given how the illeck smiled like the cat with the veritable canary a few yards away, twirling them in the empty air. "Hope they're okay," he said offhandedly to the man.

The illeck paused, then turned and set his weapons on the foot of his bed, approaching Biff.

"Listen, friend, I'd like to know your name," said the illeck.

Biff had been warned about the grayish-skinned dark elves often by his papa, but he'd never actually met one until now. *You can choose to believe the best of people, Biff,* his mother's voice echoed in his mind, a rare speaker in that vacuous space. *Your papa doesn't know everything.*

"I'm Biff. Biff Mclargehuge," the barbarian said, offering his massive hand.

The illeck took it gingerly, shaking hands with the big man.

"I'm Davik. Look, you don't have to do that if you don't want to," Davik said, dipping his head back toward his cot. "Billy thought you looked a simpleton, and took advantage. Truth be told, I feel a tad shamed about doing it myself. It's a natural inclination, given my lineage, but I want you to know that you never have to do something for any of us that you don't actually want to, all right?"

Biff nodded, then patted Davik on the shoulder.

"Thanks," he said, then turned and headed out of the barracks, leaving a guilt-cleared and sore-shouldered Davik behind.

***

Digby walked around the chargers, carefully inspecting the horses visually, sniffing for any hint of illness in them. While not as sharp as that of a werewolf or a cuyotai, he nevertheless had a keen sense of smell, one which at the moment informed him that the four specimens milling about the ready yard were one and all healthy as could be. "I don't get it," he said finally, giving one of the stablehands a quick hand gesture to indicate the man could hitch the beasts to the traces and prepare the wagon. "These are some of the finest examples of horseflesh we've got. Why would Tennison approve of this?"

"Are you complaining?" Memnock countered, hands folded into the sleeves of her cloak a few yards away. Sirock and Biff were busy loading up the group's collective gear into the back of the wagon, the dwarf up in the wagon itself while Biff handed their bags and trunks up to him.

"What? Gods, no, this is fantastic," Digby said, hands on his hips as he watched the animals passively allow themselves to be harnessed. "Still, I would have assumed that, given his history with the preacher, we'd be up shit's creek for requisition approval. I was going to forge the forms, myself."

"Yet more reason to entrust the paperwork to me."

"You'd be surprised," Digby said. "There only a couple of folks whose handwriting I can't get down with enough practice. Well, in the common tongue, anyway. Sirock's is difficult, though, he uses some dwarvish symbols in place of common letters, kind of a bastardized script, so I can't really carry it off."

"Yes, because forging the signature of a priest is a worthy goal to attain," she said, slapping his arm with a light backhand.

"A man has to have a hobby, yes?" Digby shook his head and called out to the other men, "You gents about got it all loaded up?"

"Yes sir, Mr. Digby sir," Biff called back. "One more bag, that's it, sir."

The vulpesin pinched the bridge of his snout between his dark eyes, then started walking toward the back of the wagon.

"You don't have to call me 'sir', Biff," Digby said, coming around to find Biff handing Sirock the last of the luggage.

The big barbarian brushed his hands together, then hooked his thumbs through his belt. "Well, you outrank me, don't you?"

"That's as may be, but this is not a militia," said Digby. "You can just call me Digby, or Digs. My friends I let get away with calling me fox, or sometimes my enemies, since I know that familiarity breeds contempt," he added with a roll of his wrist. "Try to relax, Biff. We're about to do the meat-and-potatoes of our jobs as members of the guild; we're off to adventure!" With the wagon packed, the yard gates open, and Sirock and Mem in the back of the wagon, Digby clambered up onto the driver's bench behind the horses, motioning for Biff to join him up front. Hands on the reins, the vulpesin steered the horses toward the open gates, and soon enough the four animals were trotting along at a brisk, bouncy canter.

"So, where are we going?" Biff asked.

"Well, generally speaking, east and south," Memnock said from a couple of feet behind him. She had managed to wedge herself somewhat comfortably between one of her bags of spare clothes and a long bundle of rope coils that Sirock usually kept on his person when traveling. "The best lead we have for right now on where the shield could be is somewhere in the Ja-Wen territories. It could be in the wilds, it could be in some private collector's home, we just won't have a better idea until we actually get into the country."

"Isn't Ja-Wen pretty far away?" Biff asked Digby quietly.

"If we don't push the horses above a trot, about a week and a half," Digby replied. "If we run them about a third of the day and walk them the other third that they're not asleep, five or six days at best. That's if we're able to cut to the quick and avoid distractions, detours, or disasters that would force us off course for more than a couple of hours. Bear in mind, that trip time is to get us to the political terrain, not the metro itself," said Digby. "The city-state's political boundaries are actually only about half a day's travel east of the Allenian Hills. Mem?" Digby leaned back slightly, letting the reins go slack so he didn't rear up the horses accidentally. "Did you prepare an itinerary, or are we going to be stop points by committee?"

"Sort of a mix, like last time," she answered, taking out a faint red covered journal and handing it up to him.

Digby snagged it with his right hand, and offered the reins to Biff, who, though he had never once in his life held the reins for a team of horses, took them happily enough. Digby sat up and leafed through the journal until he reached the last page with fresh writing on it, perhaps halfway through. "Our first major point of interest might be in Faterin, about three days east. A traveling merchant named Cistek Montigan lives there, and it's said she too was in search of the shield until recent developments."

"What developments?" Digby asked.

"Mainly, that she had a child," Memnock said.

Digby handed the journal back, then took the reins once again from Biff.

"Sirock, what do you know of the Wayfarer troupe she's from, the Talford Family?"

The dwarven battle priest pulled his fingers through his beard for a few moments, then cleared his throat.

"Asked if any could be said to hold honor who did not engage in the glory of battle, blessed Reyko said unto the council of the gods, 'yea, there be such folken among the mortal kinds. They are those whose words are spoken in truth, and never in deception.' Does this satisfy?"

Memnock nodded, gleaning from his reply that the Talfords were a trusted Wayfarer company.

"And if she's not in Faterin, or we veer off course, we press on, yes?" Digby asked aloud, to which both Sirock and Memnock nodded dutifully.

For his part, Biff felt a queer pressure building inside his mind, a steady rise of tension as the chargers carried the group out beyond the last vestiges of Breck's outermost neighborhood and onto a broad, unpaved trade road leading east out of the city. They were now officially in the wilds and on their own. In most city-states or nations, they would still be under the legal jurisdiction and protection of military police patrols and other government officials; in the Freehold Territories, however, such niceties did not exist. When one left the comforts of Breck, Trios, Bios or Comel, they were pretty much on their own.

Biff wouldn't have said he was afraid, per se, but he had rarely spent much time outside of his hometown in the wilds, except while travelling to Breck from home. This was all new for him, and his eyes could not have been peeled more wide open unless he clipped off his eyelids. The plains swept out around them on either side of the road, verdant green for the most part, with distant fields of brown-gold wheat swaying gently in the breeze south of the road.

In the first two hours of travel, they passed by no fewer than four different farms, each a little different than the last. Biff, being curious, fired off questions to Digby about everything he saw, and to the vulpesin's credit, Digby didn't seem to mind answering. He didn't linger long on explanations about the things he named off for the young barbarian: doing so would have tested his knowledge and patience.

Sirock had his holy book of Reyko's teachings open, and was studiously reading as they trundled along at a fair pace, with Memnock charging several polished hematite stones with essential spells. Charging objects with spells had been developed in the early years of the Third Age, nearly three thousand years earlier. She had read various treatises focused on the initial investigations into the practice, which had developed quite by accident when several noted sorcerers of the time had been engaged in grand scale battles of magic against one another. Trying to destroy one another's staves or rods, or hurling focused spells at the weapons and armor of their enemies, several had inadvertently placed 'charged' spells on the objects targeted, allowing for a slightly weakened form of the spell to be focused into the objects like a trap.

Gemstones had become the favored materials for healing magics, and as such, Mem expended a considerable amount of her reserves of mana on charging spells of this nature into her small collection of hematites. She could ill afford the more expensive types of gemstone for her purposes, and the expenditure of mana to charge an object with a single spell was considerably more than that of casting the spell openly. After those first two hours, she was almost ready to lie down for a nap to recover her strength. Yet before she would curl up under one of her light blankets, she handed three of the stones to each of her comrades, explaining their function and how to access the power to heal themselves.

"Hold the stone between thumb and forefinger alone, and whisper the word, 'velin'," she instructed. "This will cast the spell from the stone upon you. I might not always be able to provide the aid of healing if we come across trouble," she added, then curled up for rest.

Biff, unused to magic to begin with, promptly stuck the stones in one of his spare hip pouches and returned his attentions to the reins as Digby continued teaching him the basics of driving the wagon.

At midday, the company pulled their wagon off to the north side of the trade road a hundred yards, keeping a safe distance from fast traveling groups along the main path through the territory while also keeping the roadway in sight. Sirock wordlessly prepared a simple stew for them all to partake of, grunting and pointing at various arranged ingredients to be added into the pot, Biff helping him without complaint or question. When they had all eaten a couple of bowls, Digby cleaned up, while Mem tended to the horses, releasing them from their traces one at a time and hobbling them to graze and stretch.

Biff, with nothing to do at the moment, found himself sauntering a short distance away from the group toward a lone sycamore standing about two score yards from the wagon, its branches beautifully still since the wind had died off in the area.

Digby watched him carefully as he scraped the last bowls dry with a towel, the battle priest seated on a large stone beside him, holy book in hand. "What do you suppose our big new friend is doing?" the vulpesin asked quietly, keeping his eyes trained on the barbarian. Biff appeared to have come to a stop at the base of the tree, staring up into its boughs.

Sirock peeked up from his book and grunted.

"You've gotten worse with this these last few months, Sir. I haven't heard more than 'does this satisfy' out of you without an attached quote from that book of yours in too long." Digby stacked the last bowl into the small wooden box their travel cutlery was kept in and shut the lid, then sighed, looking his companion right in the eyes. "What happened? Why the hardcore focus these days?"

Sirock shifted on his rock, looking away for a moment, and shook his head. "If a warrior struggles with his purpose, he should not be shamed, but nor should he be coddled," he said, quoting from the book yet again.

Digby didn't know Reyko's scripture by heart, but he could tell by the dwarf's tone and pattern that these words were not his own.

"Only by waging war against his own doubts may he rise victorious into the light of a new day, reborn."

The vulpesin rogue snorted derisively. "I suppose you'll explain all of this eventually," he said.

Sirock's gauntleted hand clamped down on Digby's shoulder, catching his attention. The intensity of Sirock's stare unnerved him.

"I will, my friend," Sirock said gravely, slowly releasing his grip on Digby and turning his eyes on Biff. "But I cannot explain that," he added, pointing to the barbarian.

Digby had no way of hearing the enormous human, but he could see what Sirock meant; it appeared as though Biff was *talking* to the tree.

"Fuck me running," Digby groused, then hopped up and jogged over to Memnock. The mage woman was just getting the last horse back in the traces as he approached, and the rogue whistled sharply to catch her attention. "Do you see this?" he asked, jabbing a finger toward Biff in the distance.

The mage woman looked, her initial reply just a raise of the eyebrow.

"Do you have any idea what he's on about?"

"I'm not entirely sure," she replied, watching the barbarian. "It could be he's of the Gaia faith. Many of her devoted speak with the trees, or to the stones of the earth. What do we really know about him, fox?"

"Not much, I realize," Digby said. They watched Biff for another couple of minutes, at which point the large warrior turned around and started back for the wagon. He didn't say anything right away, helping pack up the gear and getting back up on the bench seat in the front, with Memnock and Digby having swapped places for the next leg of the day. When they were a few minutes down the road once more, the sorceress spoke.

"Biff, were you talking to that tree back there?" she asked bluntly, but not unkindly.

Biff nodded.

"What about, dear?"

"His life, mostly," the barbarian answered with a shrug of his massive shoulders. "He's lonely now out there, used to be a whole bunch of trees around the area. I asked him what happened to the others."

"And?"

"And he said it was the meraks, about fifteen years ago. It's not much time for them," Biff said thoughtfully, pursing his lips. "I couldn't imagine living as long as a tree. Elves do. And dwarves, too, some of them. And jafts. But I think it would be just awful to outlive everyone you know and love, all because you can't get up and run when something comes to eat you."

Memnock, preconceived notions knocked off kilter, just faced forward once more, and hefted the reins to make the chargers pick up the pace.

I know what it's like, tree, she thought. *Even though there's people around me all the time in that guildhall, I know what it's like to be alone.*

***

Trouble finds its way into the lives of anyone who dares go more than half a day's ride from home. This folksy bit of doggerel, attributed to the gnomes of Tamalaria, frequently received scorn from the braver sorts of folk who spent much of their lives roaming the wilds in search of adventure or treasure. They tended to view the science-minded cousin race of the dwarves with disdain or mild annoyance. Yet the brutality of the world could not be denied, and Digby and his comrades received a reminder of this as they approached a major interchange in the trade route.

Perhaps three hundred yards from a massive intersection where the main trade road spanning east to west crossed paths with the artery that served to lead travelers into the north-central mountain or south toward Trapperstown in the Allenian Hills, the group saw a long, low building with smoke flitting out through a chimney in the roof. The Tesetrin Inn had been a common stop for many traveling parties for the better part of a century, and even Digby, Memnock and Sirock had stayed there before. Yet the battle priest drew the horses to a halt when they were still a good two hundred yards away, his brow furrowed, hand reaching to his hip for his battle axe.

"What's going on out there?" Digby poked his head out from the back between the armored shoulders of the other two men. He cast a look around as best he could, then asked softly, "Where are the guards?"

Sirock grunted, which, in this case, served as an answer and an explanation for drawing his weapon into his lap.

"Digby?" Biff asked.

"That's the Tesetrin Inn and Lodge," Digby said to him. "We've all been here on multiple occasions. The owners usually keep at least half a dozen guards in a perimeter around the property. One of them should have called us to a halt by now," the vulpesin explained. "Take us back about a quarter mile, Mem. There was an atoll we'll set the horses and wagon upon for now. Someone will have to stay with the wagon, though, while the other three check out the situation."

"I'll stay with the wagon," Memnock said as she got the chargers to wheel around and head back the way they'd come, soon leading them off the main road and up the slope onto the atoll Digby had mentioned. Before the three men clambered off, she chimed in briefly, "Don't forget your stones, if you should get hurt."

Moments later, Digby, Sirock and Biff were marching in a short line toward the Tesetrin, the rogue keeping a careful eye roaming in all directions while Sirock and Biff kept alert for immediate signs of incoming trouble.

As they came back to the point where they'd turned the wagon around, Digby put up a hand to stay them, motioning the other two to follow him over toward a clutch of trees with round, fuzzy green fruits of some sort blooming from their branches. As they placed the trees between themselves and the direct view of the hotel in the distance, the vulpesin took out his farviewer and used it to visually inspect the main area around the building.

As he'd feared, he spotted several brutish-looking men and women in full kit stalking the grounds, people who looked nothing like guards so much as highwaymen.

"Bandits." He collapsed the farviewer and tucked it away. "Five that I could see: who knows how many more? Odds are not in our favor by numbers."

"So, do we tell them to go away?" asked Biff innocently.

"Diplomacy is not usually the strong suit of highwaymen, young Biff," Digby said, crouching down and pulling open his gear bag. "Wait here, gents. I'm going to see if I can't catch their attention and draw them out." Taking out a variety of tools and bits of what looked like scrap, Digby disappeared into the trees for a few minutes, then came back with a smile on his face. "All right, hang tight here, and I'll be back shortly," he said, taking a sling from his bag.

"You a pretty good shot," Biff asked.

"Not at all," Digby replied. "As a fellow who practices the arts of a rogue, I'm unusually poor at ranged combat. No, this is not for hitting any of them, just getting their attention. Stay here, and watch," he said, darting through the trees once more. Digby carefully avoided the simple traps he'd set amid the trees, coming out the other side cautiously, creeping across the open fields between the trees and the hotel until he was close enough to achieve his aims. He loaded a small iron ball into the cup of the sling, drew back for a high, lobbing arc, and released the ball when he could see all five of the previously spotted bandits clustered fairly close together.

To his mild surprise and delight, he heard a metal 'thwong', and watched one of the men flail his arms about, one hand to his iron half plate cuirass. Five sets of eyes lanced out toward him, and the vulpesin rogue in his green tunics waved a jolly hello to them, loaded and quick-fired a wild shot, then turned and fled, five angry highwaymen in hot pursuit.

As he entered the trees in a bee line toward the first of the snares, he hopped to one side of the path, weaving his way back toward Biff and Sirock. As he neared another trap, he spiraled aside, then leapt over the last one he'd set, tumbling out of the thicket between the dwarven battle priest and human barbarian. He came up in a half-crouch, drawing his long knives to either side, and said, "Be ready, boys."

From within the trees, they heard a snap and whir, accompanied by a "Fucking hells!" Next, only a few moments later, they heard a metallic scrape and a crunching sound, which birthed wordless screaming of an unimaginable agony. More rushing through the brush, then a soft 'whup', followed by the crash of something onto the ground. When at last someone came out of the thicket before them, it was a pair of bandits in boiled leather armor with bastard swords in hand, looking terrified.

"Hello there, lads," Digby said calmly, twirling his knives. "Now, there *were* five of you a minute ago. There's two of you, and there are three of us. What do you suppose your chances are?"

The bandits looked to one another, screwed up their faces into sneers, and howled as they charged the trio with weapons held high. The man on the right, his beard ragged and hair flying wild behind him, manged only two steps before Sirock's axe flew from the dwarf's hands and planted itself in his face, cleaving his head nearly in half and felling him in a gory mess from the neck up. His fellow bandit managed an extra step or two before his overhead hack was blocked by Biff's broadsword, allowing Digby to roll forward and rapidly jab his blades up into the man's unarmored groin from underneath, finishing off with a carefully aimed stab to the femoral artery.

The man was dead in seconds, twitching lamely as he fell down, hands reaching futilely down for his perforated testicles and leg just before the last of his life fled him. Digby sheathed one of his blades and rummaged through the bandits' pouches, taking several of them filled with coin and depositing them in his gear bag. He then motioned for Biff and Sirock to follow him, and they came upon the nearest of his traps' victims. She was a fine-looking human woman, or would have been, were it not for the effect of the toxins that had taken their toll on her. Lying on her side with a dart sticking out of her neck, the woman's skin had gone waxy gray, her veins standing out in stark black lines of corruption. The tripwire had been snapped, the trigger blowdart gun fired when she'd come trundling through. Digby tried not to feel any remorse for the woman, reasoning that if she had survived his traps, she would have tried to kill him. Either way, this bandit had been dead from the start.

The second trap victim lay in a torpor, nearly dead from blood loss. His leg had been destroyed by what looked like a bear trap, the jagged teeth piercing the man's chain leggings, flesh and muscle. His bones had been cracked horrifically, uneven segments poking out of the skin, glistening with slick crimson blood.

Biff shook his head. "Is he still alive?"

"Barely," Digby said. "And at this rate, it'll be a slow death."

"Move, then." Biff gently nudged Digby aside with one heavy leather boot and rammed the wide point of his broadsword through the bandit's face, cleaving his head neatly in half to kill him instantly. "Better this way," the barbarian said.

When the trio came upon the third bandit, another of the women in the highwaymen's group, she was dangling from a rope about nine feet off the ground upside down, her face flushed with the blood going to her head.

"I don't suppose this ends well for me," she quipped with an effort, arms dangling down over her head.

Digby spotted a shortbow and a dozen arrows on the ground beneath her, her empty quiver also dangling down. The vulpesin pointed at the weapon and arrows, which Sirock dutifully gathered up before he cut the rope holding the woman overhead.

She yelped as she fell, landing awkwardly on her shoulder and rolling around a moment in pain.

Digby took his time approaching her, and when she rolled onto her stomach, he sat down with an indelicate drop, kicking his legs out as he was right over the middle of her back, knocking the remaining wind out of her. He then poised his dagger right at the base of her skull, and the bandit women went shock still.

"That really depends on how cooperative you are," Digby said amiably, as if he were sharing a pint with an old friend. "Five of you came up here after me. How many did you leave behind?"

"Seven," she replied quickly, no hesitation.

"And the Tesetrin family?"

"Owners we killed, sent the oldest daughter and two little boys packing on a donkey due south toward Felrop. It's a day's travel, they'll survive with the food and water we gave them," she replied, again with no hesitation.

"And the guards they usually employ?"

"Paid them off three days back to not be here this morning," the woman said.

Biff noticed something shiny down by her left ankle, and after sheathing his sword on his back, he knelt down and snagged out a wonderfully polished boot knife with a line of green gems set in the hilt.

"Hey, give that back," the woman snarled immediately, forcing Digby to draw back his weapon so she didn't impale herself on it. To remind her of her placement, he waggled his own knife tip inches from her eye, and she paled, going limp. "Sorry. I just, I paid good coin for that knife."

"Consider it, and the information, the cost of keeping your life today," Digby said, getting up off of the woman. Just from that small buck, he could tell she was strong, far more fit than he. If she had put even a little more effort into reacting to Biff taking her weapon, he would have been thrown off, and the situation might have grown bloody. He sheathed his dagger and reached down, helping the woman to her feet. She limped a little on her left foot, where the noose trap had snagged her and held her aloft.

"You are free to go, miss, without further incident. If you go back west, the way we've come, you'll spot a wagon with four horses. The woman tending it is our friend, Miss Memnock Halcesh. She is a mage of no small talent, so if you wish to continue drawing breath, avoid her. Widely."

The woman bandit sneered at him and took off, running west through the brush and out of their lives.

Biff held the dagger out to Digby, handle-first. "It's pretty nice-looking, but a little small for my hands," the barbarian said.

Digby took the handle, briefly glanced at the gems, and smiled. He rolled his gear bag off of his back, took out a spare knife sheath, tied the blade in, and tucked it away before standing up again.

"What now, Digby?"

"Now, we consider our options," the vulpesin said. "She says there's seven more of her fellows down at the inn. Now, these ones didn't make much noise before tearing off after me through the thicket, but the ones still there no doubt will be wondering where their comrades got off to if they don't see or hear from them soon. We could always hoof it back to the wagon and skirt the area, keep a safe distance."

Sirock snorted at this, shaking his head.

Biff folded his arms over his broad chest, pulling thoughtfully on his hairless chin in contemplation. "Could we maybe trick them into the same traps these ones fell for?"

"Unlikely," said Digby. "Besides which, I need at least half an hour to reset the springs on the cruncher, and that's if I don't clean if off first, which I fully intend to do. Sirock? Any ideas?"

The dwarf battle priest looked back toward the west, in Mem's direction, and a savage smile spread across his face when he eyed the vulpesin rogue and human barbarian once more.

"Care to share?"

Chapter Six

Grisham had never been a man given to panic since becoming an acknowledged outlaw. He'd been at it for about thirty years, robbing hundreds of people in his time. He tried not to murder people when it could be avoided, but he never let anything get between himself and a profit, especially not the moral codes of other people. No matter what outfit he aligned himself with, he always let it be plainly known that he would do anything, *anything*, to make some extra coin. A few of them had taken exception when that included turning his own colleagues over to bounty hunters for a share of the purse.

Most highwaymen lived short, brutal lives that ended in overwhelming agony at the tip of a sword. They romanticized the nature of their struggle against the major societies of the realms, styling themselves audacious contrarians who could not be bargained with or swayed from their course. This, and a colossally short-sighted view of the experience known as life led most to be killed in routine combat with travelers or lawmen who were simply vastly superior as warriors.

Yet Grisham had survived as long as he had for two primary reasons. Firstly, he knew when he was beaten, and could throw himself on the mercies of his targets with a gusto that always left his foes with a healthy respect for his reasonability. Yes, he had lost plenty of battles, and would do for all the days of his life. Some you win, and some you lose, simple as that. Sure, he had played right into the tricks and traps of men and women far more clever than himself. Two of his years as an outlaw had been spent serving a complete prison term in the city of Kai-Fen in the Fiefdom of Lomago in the south-central plains and grasslands after he'd been caught red-handed robbing a man along the road between Kai-Fen and Lom Jik. Guardsmen from Kai-Fen had been receiving reports from locals that a group of armed bandits had been ambushing short-travel merchants around the fiefdom, and the Kai Lom Road had been the most frequently hit area. Grisham and his cronies had been caught in a trap, and he had immediately confessed to partaking in many of the robberies.

His comrades tried to deny the claims, and when they were all found guilty in a regional court, his four cohorts had been executed for trying to lie their way out of it, while he was put in a short-term prison lockup for his acts. He'd been spared a much worse sentence because he had possessed the courage to speak truly of his misdeeds, something the justiciars of the fiefdom valued highly.

And so it came to pass that the moment the powerfully built jaft outlaw saw a bolt of magical lightning fling one of his men back into the inn's main room from his spot in the doorway with a shriek, his cigarette somehow still dangling at the corner of his mouth as he hit the floor groaning, Grisham's first thought was, *Well, here goes another surrender.* It had taken nearly three decades to finally have his own gang, and he wasn't going to get them all killed. As he brought his coffee mug calmly to his lips once again, the other three men and two women of his crew leaping to their feet, he used his other hand to signal them to hold position.

"Boss, what the hell was that," one of them barked, a terrified young illeck man with curved long blades in hand.

"That, my boy, was magic. Stay away from the windows, and very calmly, very slowly, put your weapons away," Grisham said. "Just stay put." He finished his coffee in one long pull, then sighed and hitched himself up to his feet. He kept his empty hands out in front of himself, and walked over to the doorway, slowly, making himself visible to whoever might be outside. The smell of charred leather and flesh from his fallen man caught his nostrils just right, and without even looking, he could tell the fellow was badly wounded, but likely not dead. He'd be in a great deal of pain, probably for days yet, but at least he might live. Grisham turned to look outside, and what he spotted just confirmed what he'd been thinking; this was not a fight he and his men could win.

A group of three men, a vulpesin, a dwarf, and a huge human, stood in a line behind a broad, robed woman with her hands swirling with magical energy, her hand outstretched and crackling with more lightning magic at the ready. Behind them stood a covered wagon bearing markings of the Ja-Wen City-State Militia, and arranged around the wagon, armed like a blitz battalion, dozens of soldiers trained bows on the inn.

"I believe this is the point where we come out and lay down our weapons, right?" Grisham asked with a smile. So grateful were his men to be offered their lives that they didn't question it when they were merely asked to disarm and leave by the sorceress. The jaft bandit alone was cuffed and trussed up to one of the wagon's rear wheels.

Digby suspected they all had at least one concealed weapon, but with two of them carrying their wounded comrade and the other four running well ahead, it didn't matter.

A few minutes later, as soon as the highwaymen were out of eyesight, Memnock nearly collapsed as she released the illusions, each soldier fading from the world. Grisham just laughed out loud and shook his head, sniffing. "By the gods, well played, folks," he said, looking up at Sirock as the dwarf stepped over to him. "So, what happened to my other people?"

"We killed four of them," said Digby bluntly. "One we let go after she told us how many were left here at the inn. Now, you came out and talked your people into surrender, so I'm assuming you were in charge of this group."

"That's right. Stongarick Grisham is my name. You bounty hunters?"

Digby shook his head.

"We're passing through on a job for the Freelance Adventurers Guild," Mem said breathily as she sat nearby, sipping water from one of her canteens. "We only came upon you by happenstance."

The jaft bandit pursed his lips and nodded.

"Is there a bounty out for you?"

"A couple that I know of," Grisham said, trying to adjust himself on the ground, limited in his movements thanks to being bound to the wagon wheel. "Big money's on a contract out of Palen. There's a fellow there who's offering a thousand coin to bring me in for a bit of payback."

"What did you do to him," Digby asked.

"Recruited his son," Grisham replied conversationally. "Hey, big guy, can you reach into my leg pouch here, grab me one of my smokes? It's been a while, and I'm fiending right about now."

Biff looked back and forth from Digby to Sirock, shrugging his shoulders.

Sirock knelt by the jaft, located the packet of cigarettes, and stuck one in the corner of the man's mouth, lighting it for him a moment later. Grisham raised an eyebrow at Biff and said, "Never seen a man smoke before, kid?"

"No sir," said Biff politely. "I've heard of it, but nobody where I'm from does stuff like that. They say it's bad for your health."

"I'm a jaft, kid. I ain't worried about no black lung," Grisham replied with a shit-eating grin that was tight enough to keep the cigarette in his lips. "The son's the one you hit with that spell, lady," he said to Memnock. "Lucky thing you didn't kill him."

"It should have done," she replied, taking another sip of her water. "I suspect he has natural magical talent of his own. Only an involuntary mana reflex to counter the spell I used could have kept him alive." She was feeling better by small degrees, but she would need to eat, and soon, to help speed up the process of recovering her natural stores of mana. "What do you gentlemen think we should do with him?"

"He's nothing to do with the job," Digby said. "I say we give it another twenty minutes for his people to get distance, then let him go."

"Sirock?" Mem asked, eyebrow raised.

The dwarven battle priest ran his fingers through his massive beard, thoughtful, then cleared his throat.

"A warrior's blade is not always his final recourse. Mercy is also a choice, and it is sometimes the right one. So said blessed Reyko to Phillistares, the first of her shepherds," the dwarf replied, a rare quote from the last chapter of his holy scripture.

"Biff?"

"Yeah, I'm with you guys," said the barbarian. "He surrendered fair and clean, and a good man honors his promises."

Grisham finished his cigarette and waited silently until finally Digby uncuffed him from the wagon wheel, then rubbed his wrists as he got to his feet.

"Thanks, fellahs," said the jaft, a confused crease in his forehead, eyes drawn down. "You know, I have to say, I'm grateful, but a little surprised," he said, speaking directly to Digby. "I've only met one of your kind before, and she was a nightmare. Lied, cheated, stole, and would've sold her mother for a few coin."

"Some of us are like that," Digby answered with a shrug. "And some of us are like me, go for the bigger stake and ignore the small fry if they're no trouble. Can you do us a favor, though?"

"Sure, what'd you have in mind?"

"Don't let us see you again," Digby said with a playful smile. "Because the next time, we just wipe you out. Ta." And with that said, he climbed up in the wagon's bench next to Sirock, while Biff helped Mem get up in the back before following her up himself. They left the dumbstruck jaft outlaw, the inn, and their trip's first hiccup behind, happy to be on the proper course once more.

***

Mem tugged gently on Digby's shoulder, and the vulpesin rogue looked up, then followed the path of her finger as she pointed off out into the dark. They'd run into no more trouble since the inn and Grisham's bandits and now found themselves situated about fifty yards off of the main trade road, encamped. About twenty yards from the fire pit, holding a torch against the moonless darkness of a new lunar cycle's start, he spotted Biff, once more standing before a tree, the barest trace of his voice carrying back to the camp.

"I really hope you were right about it being a faith thing," Digby said, trying to brush it off. "We can't afford to be dragging a madman around with us if it turns out he's just touched in the head."

"Particularly given how big he is," Memnock said in a whisper. "But I don't sense any malice about him. He seems almost child-like, in his way."

Digby scoffed, stirring the pot over the cook fire.

"Well, I'll be back. I have to make my necessary before we eat."

Mem ducked off into the dark, and Digby kept his eyes on the pot, occasionally peeking over at the young barbarian. Given how matronly Mem was with him and Sirock, he supposed it was only natural that she would see Biff as a potential little brother sort to the two men of the company. But if she were the mother hen of the group, then who played the part of father figure? *Couldn't be me*, Digby thought acidly, *I'm not precisely someone to look up to. And Sirock's a religious nutter, more like the weird uncle nobody mentions except at holiday dinners. Where does that leave us?*

As the food finished cooking, Digby stood up to fetch Sirock and Mem from the back of the wagon, and realized that Biff was no longer by the tree. "Oh, shit," he muttered, dashing over to the preacher and mage. "Have either of you seen Biff in the last few minutes?" When they both shook their heads, he cursed softly and planted his hands on his hips. "I only looked away for a few minutes, and he was just gone. Should we split up and find him?"

Sirock put up one wide hand and shook his head, silently walking away from his friends, ambling toward the tree where Biff had been standing. The dwarven battle priest needn't hear words to learn a story: like most dwarves, he could track a man through even the worst terrain.

Sirock kept his ears tuned for any oddment he might hear, keen to keep himself ready for any threat. Capable as he was in his own way, Digby could not be trusted to track down Biff, as far as Sir was concerned. The vulpesin had never been a very good hunter, and on his own, would have to rely on stealth entirely to deal with unknown threats out here in the wilds. Sirock had his axe, his hammer, his armor, and his wealth of techniques at hand if something nasty had taken their newest crew member.

Not that any plan or prep is perfect, he thought, following Biff's footsteps around the tree and then on to the north. *But I have something the fox lacks,* he added with a grin, pressing his palms together and uttering the arcane words in a whisper. Though it was limited in scope due to his nature as a dwarf, Sirock had access to some little magic as a priest, and he called upon it now to try and sense how far away the young human barbarian was. Pulling his hands apart, a whirling ball of umber light pulsing between them, Sirock said the last word. The ball floated up between his eyes, and appeared to press into his face, filling his eyes with the light.

The world around him swirled with strange energies, and it was two in particular that drew his attention. Perhaps only thirty yards away, he spotted Biff, his nigh-boundless energy and passion blazing around him like a corona of pure force. Standing on all fours perhaps five feet away from Biff, however, was something that gave Sirock pause: a chimera. The lion-goat-serpent headed monstrosity stood nearly as tall as Biff from paw to shoulder, and its lethal scorpion stinger waggled back and forth like a tail at its back end, tracing lazy arcs in the air and along the ground.

And just as he had been speaking to the tree earlier, Biff was now talking to the chimera. Sirock couldn't get close enough to make out what the big man was saying, but Biff's enormous broadsword remained on his back, and his body language appeared relaxed. His energies possessed a sense of calm, as though the barbarian had no cause to fear the rashum right before him. The creature made a bizarre, guttural response of some sort, and Biff nodded, hands now on his hips.

Whatever this is, it is meant to be private, else he would already have told us about it, Sirock thought, turning away and heading back for the camp. As he came back within view of Digby and Memnock, he just put his hands out in front of him and made a downward easing motion, then hooked a thumb back over his shoulder to indicate where Biff was.

"Is he all right?" Mem asked.

Sirock nodded, and almost as if on cue, Biff came whistling back toward them out of the dark.

"Biff," the mage woman called, hands on her broad hips, eyebrows knitted down angrily. "What were you thinking, wandering off like that at night? These wilds aren't always the safest, you know."

"I know. I'm sorry." Biff looked pleased with himself despite Memnock's suddenly matronly turn. "I just wanted to take a little walk, is all. Is the food ready?" And without another word exchanged about his absence, the company gathered round the fire to eat and set up the watch. Digby and Mem cleaned up and headed into their separate tents, while Biff made himself comfortable in the back of the wagon. Sirock, axe in hand, made a slow circuit around the camp, pausing at one point to glare out into the darkness in the direction Biff had gone to talk to the chimera.

With a brief use of his aura sight, the dwarven battle priest spotted the beast, itself laid down and sleeping only a hundred yards away from the group. He didn't like its proximity, but whatever oddity was going on here with Biff, he would leave it well enough alone for now.

***

Digby tapped ashes into the low grass and ambled along slowly, now and then stopping to stare out into the distance. It had been a quiet watch, though he'd had one hell of a scare about an hour and a half into his shift, spotting what he believed was a chimera prowling about twenty yards beyond the perimeter, stalking a blue-furred elkorn. The moment he'd seen the beast, the vulpesin rogue had dropped to his belly on the grass, terrified that he'd be caught out before getting back to the others for help.

As soon as the chimera was past, Digby set up several of his more lethal traps around the perimeter, wanting to take no chances. None of them had been sprung by the time the sun started to rise for the day, and he swiftly disassembled them and got breakfast going. The smell of cooking bacon and eggs served as enough of an alarm to bring Mem, Biff and Sirock out of slumber and around the cook fire, each darting away before the meal was done to do their necessary.

With breakfast eaten and the camp packed up, the quartet once more clambered aboard the wagon and headed to the main trade road, continuing heading east and slightly south. The early hours of the day passed without much in the way of incident, their only real moment of note when a scarlet dragon flew past high overhead, heading north toward the North-Central Mountains. Biff had moved from the bench through to the back of the wagon, propping himself up in the arched back by hanging onto the cover frame and leaning out, watching it go until he could no longer see it.

As he resumed his seat, Memnock, reins in her hands, snickered. "Like dragons, do you, Biff?"

"Oh yeah, they're awesome," Biff said with a broad smile, eyes still gleaming with wonder. "They're like, really strong." He drummed his fists lightly off of his knees. "I've never seen one up close, though. I think it'd be pretty neat to see one, maybe in its cave or something."

"If you saw one in its cave, it would likely be the last thing you ever saw," Mem replied. "Here, take the reins, Biff." She handed the straps over to the young barbarian and signaled for Sirock to switch places with her. She wormed her way to the rear of the wagon, easing down next to Digby and dangling her legs over the back with the rogue. She leaned toward him and whispered, "There's a chimera strafing us. I'm not sure how long it's been there."

"Since morning," Digby said back with a nod. "I caught the scent off of him about an hour back, when he got close enough. Doesn't seem too ready to come after us while we're moving, but it might make a jump at us when we stop for lunch. Suggestions?"

"I can throw up a barrier when we stop, make it a repulsor if we don't stay halted for long," she replied. "It's strange, though. A short while back I felt a pulse of dead energy, and the chimera veered off briefly before coming near again."

"Dead energy? What's that about?"

"Likely some kind of undead," Mem commented. "The Echo Woods are north of us now, lousy with zombies and skull warriors, that sort of thing. Not a major threat in small numbers, but sometimes a horde roams the area, and we'd have trouble then. If a chimera came too close to them, it'd have to defend itself. Those things will attack anything living."

Digby snorted, then turned about and scuttled toward the front bench.

"Right, gents. Mem says we're being paralleled by a chimera," Digby said to the dwarf and human. "We'll be stopping for lunch in about ten, fifteen minutes, and when we stop, it may come at us if for no other reason than to range away from the Echo Woods."

Biff visibly shuddered, shaking his head.

"You know about the Echo Woods?"

"My pops told me about them, couple of years back," the brawny young man said with another shake of his head. "Said there's all kinds of not-really-dead things there."

"Right. Well, the chimera is, for right now, between us and the woods, but we're on a slightly southward angle, so we're getting farther from the undead roaming there with each passing minute. Sirock, I want you to get these horses up to a full run and let them put space between us until I give you a hold call, understood?"

The dwarven battle priest grunted, snapping the reins in response.

The chargers took their cue immediately, bucking the entire wagon hard enough as they accelerated to throw Digby back into the wagon's main interior. The vulpesin landed with a 'hooof!' of air being knocked from his lungs, blinking dumbly up at Memnock's pretty smile and laughing eyes. "Stow it, witch," he managed breathlessly.

"Didn't say a word," she replied as the company bolted down the road with their chargers.

Digby managed to sit up and pull out his pocket watch, keeping track of how long they'd been coursing along at the horse team's maximum pace. He occasionally peeked out through the back of the wagon, trying to get a sense of how much extra road they were covering this way. When they'd been on pace for nearly ten minutes, he called out, "Whoa up, Sirock!"

The dwarf, having more experience and sense than Digby most of the time, gently pulled on the reins, gradually reducing the horses' speed, safely pulling the wagon off the side of the main trade road toward a sparkling pond nestled in the dip of a hill. When Sirock finally got them stopped, Memnock made several arcane gestures with her hands, and a queer warbling sound wavered around them for a moment before being followed by a loud 'POP'.

"Wow, neat," Biff said from the driver's bench, surveying their surroundings.

Digby clambered out of the back and came around the side toward the front of the wagon and the pond, observing how Biff goggled at the translucent blue dome of magical force Memnock had erected around the area. It was a small dome, only about twenty yards in diameter, but that provided plenty of protection against incoming hostiles. The vulpesin paused to consider some of the symbols threaded throughout the dome's projected energy, recognizing a few of them as rakah words, terms used by the bird lycanthrope tribes of Tamalaria.

"This is something Rollins taught you, isn't it?" he asked Memnock as the sorceress came out of the wagon at last, wobbling a little at the expenditure of so much mana. She had spent a little more of her reserves than was necessary for the spell's basic protection, wanting a bit more padding against whatever may come. Still, she looked quite pleased that he should figure that much out.

"It is indeed, fox. How'd you know?"

He pointed to one of the symbols that had caught his notice, and she nodded. "Do you know what it means?"

"Not a clue," he confessed. "I've seen it a lot, though. It's embroidered on a couple of her dresses, and if I don't misremember, it's on the plaque next to her office door, just under her name. That's the only reason I know it."

Memnock approached the symbol and gently tapped it, sending the pulsing light spinning clockwise.

"It means 'balance'," she said. "This spell doesn't actually act as a barrier against threats, per se. It operates on the basis of the current amount of energy within its perimeter remaining in relatively the same constant state, with a few minor allowances. Air can permeate, coming in and going out, as can light, wind, heat. But any major change in the amount of mana, life force, or other energies will result in expulsion."

"Wait, does that mean you can't cast a spell within the dome," Digby asked as they walked over toward the back of the wagon, helping Sirock and Biff unload their meal supplies.

"Oh, I can, but if I do, the barrier will immediately be weakened. If I perform a spell that's too powerful, the barrier will snap apart entirely."

Biff gave her a thin-lipped look, eyes squeezed shut.

"Something wrong, Biff?"

"Um, what if we have to go to the bathroom?" the young barbarian asked. Memnock waved her free left hand toward the barrier, which parted in an arch just large enough for Biff to race through on his way behind a cluster of bushes.

He swiftly returned, and helped make the fire while Sirock tended to making their meal. Memnock herself headed up into the back of the wagon for a brief rest before their meal, and Digby tended to the horses, leaving the barbarian with the dwarven battle priest once more.

As he stirred another stew, Sirock looked up at Biff, noting the way the young man's attention kept shifting off north of their position, back toward the road and the Echo Woods. "You'd know if he was hurt or dead, I imagine," the dwarf said quietly.

Biff blinked rapidly at him, his expression otherwise locked in surprise. "Yes, sometimes I speak precisely what I mean to, Biff. I saw you talking to the chimera last night."

"Oh." Biff rubbed his huge left biceps and looked down into the fire. "Um, he seemed nice enough."

"Maybe so, but that's not the point," Sirock said quietly but sternly, stirring evenly. "Chimeras are rashum, monsters, pure and simple. Least, to most folks. You can talk to the wind for all I give a shit, but I ask you this question now and I ask it straight, Biff; do you think the beast will try to bring us harm?"

Biff's response was immediate, a fierce shaking of his head.

Sirock's glower softened a little, and he aimed his eyes back down into the black pot once again. "Good enough for me."

"Really? Okay. Um, Sirock?" Once more the flinty eyes raised up to Biff's face, scouring over him like a wire pad. "You, uh, won't tell the others, will you?"

"No, lad, I won't. You may lack wit and caution, but I suspect you're a good judge of character," said Sirock in his low, gruff rumble. "Now go ask Digby if he needs his blades sharpened. That layabout never cares for his gear proper-like."

Biff got up swiftly, and headed over to Digby, per the dwarf's recommendation.

Digby may be in charge, but Sirock's the one to listen to, he thought as he ran his whetstone over the vulpesin's shamefully blunted knives.

***

"Travelers, from the looks of it," said Digby as he peered through the farviewer, Sirock holding the reins on the bench seat beside him a few hours later. "They're not flying any sort of colors or banners. Three wagons, looks like some heavies in the drogue." He collapsed the device and tucked it back into its loop on his belt. "Fly our own," he asked of Sirock and Memnock.

"I say yes," said Mem, and Sirock grunted but nodded.

"Biff, under that blue blanket, there's a pole with a banner wrapped around it," Mem said.

The barbarian discovered the pole and took it in his hands.

"All right, hand that up to Digby."

The vulpesin planted the bottom of the pole in a bracket by his left foot, then turned a crank on the middle of the shaft and pulled a thin yellow cord. Atop the pole, a triangular banner unfurled, a field of mid-shade green with a picture of an open scroll in the middle. On the left side of the scroll was a sword, and on the right, a coiled rope.

Digby pulled out the farviewer once more, and watched for the other wagons, still nearly two miles distant and approaching slowly.

There came a little bit of commotion, and after a minute, the left-hand wagon's driver unfurled his own banner.

It was a triangular field of dark blue with a pair of crossed swords over top of a scroll. Digby groaned and tucked the farviewer away once again. "Hells, it's the United Freelancers," he muttered darkly.

"Is that bad," asked Biff.

"They're the biggest competition in the realms, young Biff, so yeah, it's a little bad," Digby said.

Biff started to reach for the hilt of his sword, but Memnock stayed his hand by grabbing his wrist. "Not *that* kind of bad, Biff."

"They're likely going to want to trade some barbs at our expense in a conversation," Memnock said, crossing her arms over her chest like a sullen child and slumping down and back against one of their supply chests. "We're going to probably come out looking like mummers."

Biff, as ever unable to conceal his naivete, just looked back and forth from her to the vulpesin rogue.

"Think of it like this, Biff; we're the kid brother who constantly has to live in the big brother's shadow, and those folks are the big brothers."

Biff snapped his fingers with a smile, which quickly faded. "Oh."

"Yeah, oh," said Digby. The United Freelancers' wagons gained speed again for a short burst, coming to a complete halt and blocking the trade road a hundred yards away from them. It would have been simple enough at this distance to go around, but Sirock just kept the reins loose in his hand, letting the chargers trot along down the road toward the impasse. Only when they were twenty yards away did the horses begin to slow themselves for a total halt, ending up merely six or seven yards away from the United mounts.

A lizardman in exquisite blue and gold enameled brigandine scale armor sat on the bench seat of the right-hand wagon by himself, and he smiled perhaps too amiably at Digby and Sirock. "Well, well, it's some members of the offshoot," said the lizardman in a tone that, in another universe, every outsider adolescent boy in high school recognized as belonging to the Cool Kids' Alpha Male Leader. It carried a note of false camaraderie and affection, as well as a trace of malice that landed on the ears of the aware as just somehow *off*. "Got yourselves a job in the area, boys?"

Snickers sounded from inside the lizardman's wagon, beyond a silkscreen flap between his bench seat and the interior of the wagon's cover. Digby didn't care for the sound of the laughter; *too many of them*, he thought. *Best to play this one cool.*

"Not really, no," the rogue answered. "We're a few days away at least, all the way in the Ja-Wen territories. What about yourselves?"

It wasn't the lizardman who answered Digby, but rather, a regal-looking elven gentleman in shining half-plate armor with a blue-and-gold stylized enamel on his cuirass that portrayed the animistic sigil of a falcon in black relief. He trotted over between the two wagons on an enormous stallion with deep umber hair and its own mount armor. The elf looked cut from the 'Stereotype Lovers Home Order Catalogue', all pointed ears, long silvery hair halfway down his back, and an almost androgynous, effeminate beauty some might have called ethereal. Digby thought of it as 'Classic Fey Douche'.

"We have been beseeched by the Lord Governor of Halfelden to seek out and destroy a vampire taking refuge in the Echo Woods to the north," said the elf, his enunciation crisp and dignified.

Digby felt the insane urge to leap from his bench onto the prig's chest and punch him in the face until all that physical perfection lay ruined and bloodied beyond recognition as anything other than ground beef. Yet the vulpesin held himself in check: it wouldn't do to start a fight with these people.

Memnock poked her head out between the rogue and battle priest, eyebrows raised.

"Halfelden? That's only a day east of here. Why wouldn't he have come to us instead? Isn't your nearest branch all the way in Selstheim?"

"Indeed, good lady, and that is whence from we dispatch," replied the elf. "Have you met anyone on the roads that might have mentioned this creature? We have only a general idea of where it resides, and any information would be welcome among... colleagues."

"I thought that was supposed to be a good word," Biff whispered to Memnock. She ducked back to find herself nose-to-nose with the barbarian.

"It *is* supposed to be," she said.

"Then how come when that guy said it, it sounded like he was saying 'poo'?" Biff asked.

"I'll explain later, sweetie." She patted him on the leg. "Now hush a minute." She turned her attention back up front as Digby answered the elven warrior.

"Well, we haven't come across anybody sane, if that's what you mean," the vulpesin said, folding his arms over his chest.

The elf raised an eyebrow, and Digby went on. "About an hour ago, we spotted a guy fleeing south, looked like he'd been kitted up for a military march. So I head off the wagon to flag him down, and he comes screaming our way, babbling some nonsense about how all his brothers were slaughtered, that there was a clutch of ghouls roaming the Echo Woods not a mile from the road north of this pond we were drawing past. Sounded like a loon, if you ask me." The vulpesin flapped his hands dismissively. "I wouldn't put much stock in it."

Biff looked to Memnock with confusion in his eyes, but before he could open his mouth to pose any question, the sorceress put a hand out over it and drew her other hand up in front of her lips in a pointed shushing gesture. For the rogue's part, he knew full well the glare the elf was giving him, a scowl of skepticism mixed with curiosity. He very nearly had the poser convinced that he should check into this madman.

"Did this man actually use that word, fox? Ghouls, I mean," asked the United Freelancer.

"Well, maybe I misheard him, or he used the wrong word. That's just a word for undead, ain't it," Digby asked with the confident shrugged shoulders of the blissfully and willfully uninformed. As he relaxed, the vulpesin spotted the fleeting glint of certainty wash over the elf's eyes and thought, *Got him.*

"It is indeed, fox," said the elf. "Very well. Come along, men," he called back to his fellows, leading his group around Digby's company.

When a few minutes had passed, Sirock got the horses moving forward again. Though he didn't think the dwarf would ever admit it later, Biff could not help noticing the rumble of a brief chuckling coming from behind his thick beard.

Chapter Seven

"**I** don't understand how this helps," Biff said as Digby balanced himself carefully with his feet on the barbarian's shoulders, hands darting into the branches to snatch several of the fat dark blue fruits, tossing them down blindly to Sirock and Memnock below. It had been two days since their encounter with the United Freelancers, and though they still had plenty of supplies, the sight of a grove of varalow trees had prompted Memnock to take them off track for an indulgence.

The group hadn't encountered anything else extraordinary in the interim, other than passing by other groups of travelers along the main trade road. However, they would be leaving this common track in a short while, venturing into lesser-passed roads and paths as they angled more south-by-southeast since they were now past the easternmost reaches of the Allenian Hills. The odds of coming upon dangerous rashum would be a great sight higher then, and any travelers they came across would have to be initially viewed with suspicion and with guards raised.

Memnock not only had a weakness for varalow fruit, but she knew the journey was about to get a lot more fraught. Biff had proven to be a simple young man, but pleasant and possessed of an odd charm. His naiveté acted as a balm for the near constant cynicism of Digby and the inscrutable stoicism of Sirock. The mystery surrounding his interactions with various flora and fauna intrigued her to no end. The night before, all three of the veteran freelancers had watched in silence as, off in the distance from their camp, the burly human knelt before a clutch of bushes and carried on a conversation, seemingly with no response. There had been no fluctuation of magical energies from the plants that Memnock could detect, though unbeknownst to her, Sirock had at the same time been using his own divinity-based powers to observe the way life force energy tendrils seemed to waver back and forth from the bushes to Biff when the young barbarian ceased speaking, and instead listened.

"It helps because it stretches our own supplies further," Digby said, tossing down a few more to Mem and Sir, who had only dropped a couple of the fist-sized blue fruits overall. The vulpesin then gave a sharp whistle, and as previously instructed, Biff shrugged his body upward and took half a step back, sticking his arms out with the palms up, elbows slightly bent. He caught the vulpesin rogue like a thrown sack, and Digby crossed his legs and threw his head back, the back of one hand draped dramatically over his forehead. "Oh, Biff, I didn't know you cared," he quipped.

Biff giggled and set him down, then joined the three veteran adventurers at the back of the wagon with their basket of varalows.

"When we turn into the wilds in a short bit," Digby said, "we're going to be at least a solid day and a half, two days from the nearest village. If something should happen that we need to abandon the wagon, we won't be able to carry much on our persons, so we'll only be able to keep the best supplies. I'd prefer we not eat into them just yet."

Biff, having never even seen a varalow, was about to bite into the blue orb when Sirock tapped him on the leg and reached for the fruit.

Biff watched as the dwarf pulled a crimson protrusion from the varalow's skin, then slipped a finger deftly into the consequent hole, pulling it in half with a clean, crisp ripping sound. He then worked up the edge of the skin, and handed it back to Biff.

"You can't eat the skin, Biff," Memnock said as she began peeling her first fruit. "It's mildly toxic to humanoids. Lycanthropes can eat them, though."

Biff cocked an eyebrow at Digby as the vulpesin rogue peeled his, pausing under Biff's inquisitive glance. "Digby's not a lycanthrope, Biff. Vulpesins are bestials, like lizardmen and minotaurs."

Biff nodded, then started eating the varalow proper. After a single bite, letting the flavor dash around in his mouth like a wild thing, he devoured the rest of it, barely pausing before tearing into the next one.

"You must be careful not to eat them too fast, Biff. They're a lot more filling than they may at first seem."

But the young barbarian heard her about as well as a wall might under the same circumstances, because he mowed through a total of three varalows before excusing himself to take his necessary. Sirock ate just the one, taking his time, savoring every bit of the texture and taste on his tongue. Digby made a brief perimeter sweep around the camp stop, farviewer in hand as he needed it to check into several movements around them he thought deserved further inspection. Only one such gave him pause, and when he watched for a minute, he returned to the others promptly.

"We may have a problem," he said, hands on his hips.

Mem wiped her hands on a simple white cloth before tucking it back into her robe pocket, causing the grass around them to flutter as she conjured environmental mana from around them.

"There's another camp about a mile directly south of us, on a lake. Looks like orcs and goblins from what I could tell."

"What colors are they flying," Sirock asked.

The dwarf brought his gear bag down off the back end of the wagon and pulled it open, rummaging through it.

"No flags that I could see, no pennants," Digby replied. "Does it matter? They're greenskins. They spot us, it isn't likely anything good will come of it."

"Now that's just prejudiced thinking." Memnock snorted. "Both orcs and goblins have made great strides toward integrating with humanoid societies, Digby. I should think you'd be a touch more empathetic toward them."

The vulpesin gave her a dour look, folding his arms over his chest.

"Mem, these folks are encamped in the wilds, like one of their traditional tribes," Digby countered. "If they were progressive thinkers, they might be fixed up in the Greenskin Nation or another major metro. Greenskins living in the wilds being civilized by your or my standards is extremely rare." He turned to Biff, who was inspecting his gear. "What about you, young Biff? Any experience with goblins or orcs, ogres or trolls? Kobolds, perhaps, or hobgoblins?"

Biff paused, then nodded.

"Yeah, I met a goblin once, when I was a kid," Biff said at last. "Seemed okay. Said he was in town to trade for his pack or something. I didn't really get it. But they're not all bad, right? I mean, maybe we can just get going again and not have to worry."

Digby scoffed, hands on his hips.

"Goblins and kobolds on their own, yeah, they can be okay. But I spotted orcs and hobgoblins out there, and those things have never come within shouting distance of what I'd call 'civilized'. I think we should head back to the main road and follow it east a little farther, give that camp a wide berth. What say you, Sirock?"

The dwarf made no sound, offered no reply, merely indicating Memnock with a dip of his head in her direction.

"Mem?"

"Well, if we've seen them, the chances are good that they might have already seen us," said the mage reasonably. "I say we skirt their camp, but not by miles. I think if we maintain a couple of hundred yards' distance, we should be able to pass unmolested."

"Can you put one of those barrier things up around us when we do," Biff asked.

"A rolling bubble big enough for the horse and wagons? Not really, Biff," she confessed. "Making a stationary barrier dome is one thing, but making one that's mobile would be too taxing, and it wouldn't even be a guaranteed thing. Other sorcerers have tried in the past to make moving barriers, but the same problem always comes around: it drains a mage's mana reserves too quickly to be practical. I can project a wide shield for us, maybe a partial dome, but that would be it."

"So we're hoping that they decide to be non-confrontational?" Digby asked, his voice incredulous. "I don't think so. Hey, Biff," Digby said, as the young barbarian turned and began stalking due south, toward the greenskin encampment. "Hey, what are you doing?"

"I'm gonna go ask them if they're gonna try to hurt us," Biff said, as if this were the most reasonable thing in the world to do.

"Aaaaaaand, you think they might just tell you the truth?" Digby skipped ahead of Biff and stood in his path, walking backwards with his hands up to stop the towering human. "Do you figure if you ask real nice and they promise, cross their hearts and hope to die, they won't just go back on their word? Wake up, sunshine, these are greenskins we're talking about," the vulpesin said with a snort, slowing down his backwards march until his hands pressed uselessly against Biff's armored chest. "You said yourself that you've only ever dealt with a single goblin, once, right?"

Biff stopped his forward progress, a helpful pause for Digby, whose boots for the last ten paces had done little more than create a twin track of ruts in the rich grassland soil as Biff pushed him along like a plow.

"Right. So?"

"So I've dealt with goblins, and orcs, and ogres, Biff. Hobgoblins and trolls too, okay?"

"And kobolds?"

"Well yeah, but those little guys are never really a threat to anybody but themselves," Digby said with a flap of his hand. "The point is, I have experience with their kind, man, and it never goes well when they're in numbers. That camp isn't a pack, or even a group, it's a *tribe*, Biff. You have to trust me, we should leave them alone."

Biff cocked his head curiously to one side, a soft grin slipping over his lips.

"I *do* trust you, Digby," Biff said, putting one massive hand on Digby's shoulder. "But I don't think they're a threat," he added, then shoved Digby roughly aside, and the rogue barely managed to catch himself from tripping over his own feet.

With a snarled curse under his breath, Digby sprinted back toward Mem and Sirock, waving his arms over his head as he drew near to them.

"Pack the gear, he wants to talk to them, the fucking simpleton," the vulpesin barked when he was in earshot. "His pace, we should be able to cut him off before they spot him."

"Too late." Sirock pointed with the wedge of his axe back the way Biff had gone. The barbarian, Digby saw, was now jogging toward the greenskin encampment, waving one hand overhead at them.

Digby swiftly extended his farviewer and saw a couple of massive brownish-green arms waving back, ogres standing as perimeter guards on the outer fringe of the camp.

"Shit!" He slammed the farviewer back into its loop, hastily tossed their cooking gear into the back of the wagon, and hopped around to the driver's bench. "Get in, get in, get in," he yelled at Sirock and Mem, barely waiting long enough for her to clamber up over the wagon's rear gate before he got the horses going at nearly full tilt toward Biff and the greenskin camp.

Mem clambered up toward the front, moving cautiously so as to get herself seated up next to the vulpesin without getting thrown either forward onto the backs of the horses' traces or off the side to be tumbled on the ground.

"Digs, keep left of him and stay calm," she said, hoping he could hear her over his own panting and the clamour of the horses' hooves. "Sirock, give me one of your stones," she called back over her shoulder, thrusting one hand back toward the dwarf.

In less than four breaths, she felt the smooth surface of one of Sirock's hematite's in her hand, and she clapped it between her palms, undoing the spell she'd locked within it in order to release the pent up mana into a new spell, one she began weaving as the wagon bore down toward Biff.

Ahead, Digby saw two of the ogres approaching Biff from the camp, still perhaps a hundred yards away from the young barbarian, enormous clubs in their hands. Tall and thick, the ogres looked less humanoid than their smaller cousin races, their triangular ears jutting out to the sides of their heads, animal pelts draped over them like primitives. Either Biff had realized that they were a threat, or he'd heard the rumble of the horses behind him, because suddenly he stood locked in place, hands hitched up on the straps of his pack.

When they were perhaps twenty yards away, Memnock stood on the bench seat and whipped her hands out toward Biff, loosing a warbling shriek from her mouth.

As the sound blasted forth, Digby watched a column of translucent green and yellow swirling power form in the air between her mouth and Biff, ending in an enormous hand. It wrapped around the barbarian and hoisted him in the air, pulling him back toward where Memnock stood.

"Oh, fuck," Digby managed as the barbarian crashed into Memnock, and the two of them fell into the back of the wagon on top of Sirock, whose only addition to the proceedings at this juncture was to fart loudly as they pressed down on top of him.

The ogres still came on, waving their clubs in circles over their heads as they jabbed big, gnarled fingers at the horses and wagon.

"Next stop, housewares," Digby quipped as he yanked on the reins to get the horses to veer hard left, heading almost directly east.

After much grunting and jostling, Biff sat up with his back against a trunk and gave Memnock a sullen look, shaking his head. "They weren't going to hurt me," he said crossly, like a child who has been stopped from doing something that would likely have gotten him killed. "They were just coming out to talk." He turned his head to the side, looking out of the wagon's back.

Memnock was about to say something when an enormous rock came crashing through the tarp and bracings overhead, collapsing half of the cover down on top of the three seated in the back.

Very faintly through the wind whipping through the gash in the canvas, the barbarian heard Digby up front saying, "Yeah, this is about how their conversations tend to go."

***

Sirock secured the last band bracer in place, then came down off of the little step stool, collapsing it and tucking it away amid their gear. "How's the boy?" he asked Digby as the vulpesin gathered their cooking gear. They had waited to repair the wagon until they finally stopped to make camp for the night, a risky delay given that they were now truly traversing the wilds. They'd gotten lucky thus far, but Digby had insisted they repair the wagon first thing when they stopped for the evening, and it had fallen to him and the dwarven battle priest to make the repairs.

"His pride's wounded, but otherwise I think he's fine," Digby said, helping Sirock down off the back of the wagon. "Mem's leg got a pretty good gash from the rock, but she already healed it while we were going. How about you?"

Sirock lifted his left leg, showing Digby where the rock the ogres had thrown came to rest—a hefty dent in his plate legging.

Digby whistled, shook his head. "Good thing you weren't just sporting chain or it'd be crushed pretty bad."

Sirock grunted, then started to arrange the cooking pit.

"Of course, none of that would've happened if the boy would've just listened to me."

"And the captain said unto his troops, who here has known battle?" Sirock said, once more lapsing into quotations, Digby could tell by the tone, the quality of his voice. The dwarf sounded more lively when quoting his scripture. "And among them, a single man stepped forth. I have known battle, said this young man, and I believe we should not charge the flank. The captain asked of this young recruit, why is that? And the recruit said, Because I don't think we need to hurt anyone today." The dwarf smiled to himself, struck the kindling alight, then put the racks down in the dirt to warm up.

"And what is the message of this little homily, if I might ask?" Digby mused with a sneer.

Sirock turned his smile on Digby, and eased back onto his own rear end. "The captain spake thusly to his other troops: 'Hear this boy's words? Are they not foolish? No, my boy, we must do this, for it is war, and that is what happens in war. And so the battalion marched on the Falsterans, a great battle pitched. When it was over, the battalion had won the day, and several prisoners of war were captured after their surrender. As the battalion prepared to sup and scour the town for supplies, a lieutenant brought a list of the fallen. Upon it was the name of the boy who had spoken out." Sirock took out from one of his pouches a flask made of faded copper, one Digby rarely saw him take into hand. The battle priest sipped from it, and the smoke coming from the cookfire quickly concealed his hand as it vanished into his pouch again. The smell of the fire played tricks on Digby's mind, and he found himself envisioning that captain in Sirock's parable sitting across the fire from him, right then and there. He saw an older human man staring at a tattered parchment with names hastily scrawled down in coal.

"What happened then?" Digby whispered toward the apparition, though it was Sirock who gave answer.

"Another of his lieutenants brought over a man from the township they had sacked, telling the captain that this elder had asked to speak directly to him, and to nobody else. The captain agreed, and the elder was put down next to him at the fire. 'What do you want?' the captain asked. And the elder, he shook his head and said, 'We were going to ask that exact question when you attacked us. We would have given you what you wanted.'"

Digby sat in stupefied silence for a couple of minutes, watching the phantom captain from the story weep into his own upturned hands before the image faded in his mind's eye. Had he been wrong? Would the ogres have left Biff unharmed if he had only been allowed the chance to speak directly to them? The vulpesin rogue shook his head, patted Sirock on the shoulder, and walked over toward Memnock.

The husky mage woman was focused on putting a fresh healing spell on Sirock's hematite stone as he approached, quietly chanting the spell under her breath, plainly visible orange light flowing from her chest down her arm, into the stone in her hand. He looked around, spotted Biff at the edge of their main campfire light, fidgeting with his chain link leggings in silence, a stern glower on his face.

"He's rather cross with you," Mem said as she stood up beside Digby, brushing her robes off and pocketing the hematite.

"Yeah?"

"Yeah, he is," Memnock said. "He wouldn't tell me why, just that he was mad at you and me both. Of course, he accepted my apology on the spot, even gave me a hug," she said with a sigh, folding her arms over her chest. "He's a very sweet young man, even if he is a bit, well, dense."

Digby rubbed the bridge of his snout between his eyes and snorted, uncomfortably aware of what was being unsaid, but what she likely expected from him. *Her and Sirock both,* he mentally amended.

"He could have gotten himself killed," Digby said quietly in his own defense.

"He didn't know that, fox," she replied, reaching over and turning him towards her, a hand on each of his shoulders. She had nearly half a foot on him, and it always made him self-conscious. She slid her hands to the sides of his face gently, giving him that look, the one that always made him think of his mother when she was trying to convey some lesson in a stern but loving way. "Talk to him, won't you?" The way the fire's distant light touched her auburn hair, the resemblance to his own mother only needed Memnock's face to suddenly elongate into a snout, and it would be nearly perfect.

Well, that, and maybe if she was as small-framed as me, he thought. "Okay," he said, and she let him go, mercifully. "But after him and I talk, you and I have to have a little tete-a-tete of our own, Mem, okay?"

She let out a small chuckle and patted him on the back as he started over toward the main fire and Biff.

The young barbarian gave him the stink-eye the moment Digby came close and seated himself nearby. "Whatcha workin' on, friend?" Digby opened.

Biff just grunted at him, then used a pair of pliers and a crimping tool to readjust a couple of links.

"Look, Sirock does the whole 'grunting quiet type' well enough for the group, so unless you can fart the common alphabet, we've got non-verbal communications taken care of in our little family."

Biff paused for a moment, and the vulpesin could see him struggling to hold in a smirk. It took an effort, but the barbarian managed to keep his mirth to himself.

"What do you want, sir?" Biff asked, snipping off another link that was too bent to be salvaged. He began rummaging in a smaller green pouch he'd pulled out of his main bag.

"I want to tell you I'm sorry, kiddo," Digby said, softening his tone a touch. "I'm sorry I didn't try to give your idea a shot, okay?"

"So you think it would have worked?" Biff asked, pulling out a replacement link and getting it put into position before grabbing up his crimping tool again.

"Not a snowball's chance in the seven Hells, no, but that doesn't mean I had any right to stop you from learning that yourself first-hand," Digby said. He took one of his canteens off of his hip and took a swig of water, offering it to Biff.

The barbarian hesitated a second, took a sip, and handed it back. "I imagine you could've handled those two uglies for a minute until we caught up to help out, and you'd have learned for yourself what greenskins are actually like."

"Or they would have talked to me," Biff countered, standing up and sliding his legs into the chain armor. "Do you really think they would have attacked me on my own, sir? They saw me coming, and then a great big wagon with a mage standing on the bench, casting a spell, with a fox-man driving the horses like a crazy person. Wouldn't that spook you?" Without waiting for a response, Biff set about angrily throwing his tools in his bag and marched off to his tent without another word, leaving Digby standing there with nothing to say.

Before he knew it, Mem was there, her hands wrapped around his arm, guiding him back slowly over toward the cook fire.

"Didn't go over too well, I see," she commented in the deepening dark.

"No, it did not. I don't get it, Mem. I apologized," he said.

"And then you tried to justify when he asked you a simple question," she said. He looked at her, and she sighed. "I used an aural funneling spell to eavesdrop."

"Really wish you wouldn't do that kind of stuff."

"Please, you know me, fox, I'm not much good at minding my own business," she replied. The pair had arrived at the cook fire, and found Sirock spearing a mid-sized steak onto a plate, then spooning out some baked beans next to it. He put up a finger to his comrades, then walked off toward Biff's tent. "Have you noticed, by the way?"

"What's that?"

"Sirock has spoken more of his own words and been more present on this trip than he has on the last four or five jobs we've all taken together," Memnock said. "It's nice to see." She readied her own plate, then waited to speak again until Digby had grabbed his own food, by which time Sirock had returned to grab a plate. "Anyway, what I was saying before, you were doing well until you tried justifying your fears to him. Biff may have the body and physique of a man well grown and built, but he has the mind of a child."

"Kids need tough love," the rogue countered snippily.

"Well bless the gods you haven't got any children," she said.

"Hey, we don't know if that's true," Digby said around half a mouth of beans. "I'm not always playing it safe with the ladies, if you know what I mean. For all I know, I could have half a dozen little bastard pups running around out there," he japed, snickering. Sirock and Memnock share a look, then turned quietly to their meals. There wasn't much more conversation before Digby and Mem headed toward their own tents, leaving Sirock with the first watch, and that suited the dwarven battle priest just fine.

There had been entirely too much talking for his liking the last few days anyhow.

Before sliding out of sight for much-needed rest, however, Digby stayed Memnock for a moment with a light touch of the arm. "Tell me something," he said quietly.

"Certainly."

"The three of us, you, me, Sirock, we've been working together pretty regularly for about a year and a half, two years, right?"

She nodded, casting a quick look over to the dwarf.

"And what do we do after each contract, or in between the ones we work together?"

"Well, mostly, we all do our own thing, tend to personal matters, pick up chores around the guild hall," she replied, folding her arms over her chest. "Why?"

Digby looked at his tent, a smallish contraption meant only for function, never for comfort.

"Well, it puts me in mind of your little jab there, about having kids," Digby said with a sigh. "Didn't you ever, since joining the guild, wonder if maybe we could all have it better?"

Memnock patted his arm and sighed.

"I just take it one day at a time, Digs," she said, crouching down to crawl into her tent. "That's all any of us can do."

But Digby wondered for a while, even after tucking into his bedroll inside the tent, if that were necessarily so.

Chapter Eight

Biff ran Hell-for-leather alongside Digby until the vulpesin yelled, "Break!" Then, the two men turned at opposing 90 degree angles and bolted apart, a pair of corruscating fireballs exploding in the earth where they had been moments before. Digby located a boulder to duck behind for a moment, taking the opportunity to breath.

The morning after the greenskin encampment incident, the company had been rolling along just fine through the wilds when Memnock had detected something massive, powerful and approaching them fast. Digby had spotted what she was sensing with the use of his farviewer, and had nearly screamed. Coming due north toward them was a pair of creatures he had heard much of, and even seen once, at a great distance. Seeing them now coming right for him and his friends flooded him with terror in a way few things could.

The creatures stood approximately ten feet tall, with dark brown flesh and ungodly musculature where it was visible. Their left legs appeared to be made of vines and sections of wood while their right legs were composed entirely of a warbling column of flames that did not burn their own earthen appendage. Their left arms were ghostly white ice, and gnashing, razor-toothed mouths yawned wide with a wet growl on their chests, below powerful shoulders. Atop those shoulders rested not heads, but rather, there floated an inch or two above them what looked, for all the world, like sloshing fishbowls.

They were known in the realms of Tamalaria as bladerons, a kind of superior rashum that most folks thought had gone extinct at some point or another. The creatures had never been well-documented, since most people who encountered them didn't live to tell of it later. Memnock, thankfully, had knowledge about their lore from someone who had come across bladerons, someone who had in fact studied them for a brief time.

"We need to leave the wagon, and the horses," she had commanded the others as she snatched the reins from Digby's lap and guided the horses toward a pond. "Bladerons don't pay any attention to creatures with four legs unless said creatures try to attack them.

They won't be interested in any of our gear, so leave what we don't need behind until we can come back for it!"

"What is she talking about," Biff asked Sirock, but the dwarf cut him off with a solid finger over his lips to shush the young barbarian.

"They'll go after the largest of us first, and Biff, that means you and I." Memnock drew the wagon to a final halt, clambered back over the bench and snatched her staff from its spot amid her belongings. It wasn't a necessary tool for mages, but it helped them focus and cast spells with greater force, though it traded off by making some spells take a little longer to cast. She reached into her robes and found the narrow wand that could offset the staff, since they could be used to enhance casting speed in exchange for a reduction in spell power. "Bladerons are a nearly perfect balance of magical and physical energies and power. If they get close, go after the earthen leg first, and whatever you do, don't let them grab you with their ice hand. Now come on," she barked, hopping down off of the wagon and running back in the direction they had come and slightly east.

Biff jumped down next, helping Sirock down, then Digby last.

The vulpesin risked a quick glance south, and found the enormous creatures had already halved the distance between them, stomping along toward them with pure malice, the air shimmering around them as the bladerons gathered environmental mana from around them in preparation to attack. He put on an extra burst of speed with an effort, and soon he and Biff had passed Memnock, who hung back to let the shorter Sirock catch her up.

Digby spotted the first fireball coming at them, and reached out for Biff's collar, drawing them both up short with a yank. The ball of flame crashed into the ground a mere three yards ahead of them, hurling soil and rocks everywhere, pelting them as they turned course and ran again. Less than twenty second later, spotting a rock outcropping to the left and right of their current course, Digby yelled, "Break!" Another fireball blasted the area they'd occupied only moments before, and he took a moment to breathe.

For Mem and Sirock, the situation was similarly intense, but not as deadly, at least for the moment. The two bladerons had, as she hoped, split off from one another, one pursuing the human and vulpesin, and the other herself and the preacher. She kept the head of her staff aimed back at the bladeron pursuing her and Sirock, a dark blue shield of magical force held up between them.

The creature flung several fireballs at it, then a spear of ice, and lastly, with a rotation of its hips, it threw a vicious side kick with its earthen leg at the shield. The impact flung Memnock through the air dozens of yards, and she landed in a heap among the tall grass. She managed to get up onto her knees in time to watch as Sirock danced nimbly around the ridiculously larger creature's feet, dodging its kicks and hammerfist blows with strange ease for a man wearing such heavy armor.

Meanwhile, Digby watched in horror as Biff shot out from around his meager cover with a battle cry that would probably have caused most mortal men to consider their approach to life, and how little of it they likely had left. With his broadsword gripped high in both hands, the barbarian charged the bladeron, and Digby had a single moment to rise to his feet and call out, "Biff, no!" But the barbarian heard nothing, it seemed, and the bladeron shifted its hips and flung another huge fireball at Biff.

What happened then struck Digby as simultaneously beautiful, impossible, and mystifying. As the swirling ball of lethal magical fire bolted toward Biff, the barbarian took a subtle hop-step to the side, squared himself up, and swung his blade like a baseball bat at the fireball. As his weapon connected, the fireball let out a 'thud', and streaked right back at the bladeron, blasting it full on the chest, knocking it back, arms flailing, stutter-stepping to remain upright.

And now Biff came on, snarling and grunting, hacking at the creature without pause. The bladeron managed to keep blocking and parrying Biff's attacks with its frosted left arm, but it was losing ground, being pressed back toward a small stand of wild apple trees nearby. Biff had the creature pushed back almost right against one, when the bladeron slipped out a stiff front kick with its flaming leg, which knocked Biff back and to the ground. The bladeron stood tall, arms stretched out to its sides as its monstrous mouth yawned wide with a roar of predatory triumph—

And that's when the tree *moved*. A single branch, without the aid of any kind of wind or breeze to explain it, swung down and knocked the fishbowl-head away from the bladeron's shoulders.

The beast wobbled, unbalanced without its strange head over its body, and Biff launched up from the ground with his broadsword, plunging it deep into the horror's chest-mouth. He rammed the weapon in and out several times, and as the bladeron dropped to its knees, he began hacking away at it savagely, all sense of self-control seemingly lost.

Too stunned and fascinated to do otherwise, Digby just watched.

Around the moment Biff knocked the fireball back, Sirock was dodging attempts to be grabbed by the other bladeron's icy fingers. Despite his superior conditioning, the dwarven battle priest was flagging inside his heavy armor, though he could see with a mute satisfaction that he had nearly managed to hack through the creature's wood-and-vine leg. He used the flat of his axe head to block another grab attempt as he came around the front of the creature and he thanked blessed Reyko when Memnock launched a lime-green lasso of energy around the creature's flaming leg, stopping it mid-swing as it tried to kick the dwarf aside. He never would have been able to block the majority of the blow's force, and was too tired now to fully dodge it.

Sirock bounced back away from the bladeron as it struggled to free itself of Mem's lasso, grabbing the magical cord with both of its hands and straining to break it. "Throw me at the bowl," the dwarf shouted at her. Without hesitating to question his idea, Memnock used her free hand to conjure pressurized air magic around Sirock's feet, and a moment later, the dwarf launched himself through the air like a rocket at the bladeron's fishbowl head.

Before he'd asked her to throw him, Sirock had drawn out a simple cat's-eye marble, one he'd gotten from Mem months and months earlier. With the marble in his right hand and his axe in his left, he'd flown at the bladeron. As expected, it released the lasso as he drew closer to his target through the air, the frost-magic arm reaching up in a looping grab at him. At the apex of his flight he released the marble toward the creature's shoulder, and the simple fireball spell Memnock had locked on it months before snapped into life in a hellish conflagration ring as Sirock swung his axe into the fishbowl, smashing it apart.

The severed arm and Sirock landed with separate thuds at about the same moment, and the bladeron managed to stumble about a dozen yards away before it fell dead to the grass.

The dwarf groaned loudly, having landed on his shoulder, where the armor did little good. It had been a calculated risk, but his maneuver worked out beautifully.

Reyko blessed me with vision in battle, and has guided me safely through, he thought. *Now if only she could bless me with a loss of feeling in my arm, sweet gods this hurts,* he added as he tried to sit up.

Memnock was soon at his side, joined by Digby and Biff, and all four companions enjoyed a nervous laughter as they huddled together.

That was, until Biff, adrenaline now worn off, turned aside to vomit.

***

The village was a much-welcome sight for the company as the sun dipped ever-closer to the horizon. Though it meant going nearly a full day's ride out of their way, and that they would have to alter their course when they left, Digby, Memnock, Sirock and Biff were all in agreement that they had earned a break from their travels in some modicum of comfort.

When they had stabled the horses and parked their wagon for a modest fee on the edge of the village, the quartet made a few inquiries of locals and found their way to the village's lone inn, which doubled as one of three pubs in the small hamlet. All four agreed to meet in the pub of the inn after settling into their separate rooms and getting bathed and perhaps changed into lighter garments, then they split apart to their own rooms.

The moment Digby had closed his hotel room door behind him, he hitched a heavy sigh of relief. "Showed a superb lack of ability out there today, big guy," he grumbled at himself, thinking back on how he had remained cowering behind that rock outcropping while Biff had risked life and limb to assault the monstrous bladeron in the wilds. The vulpesin had ridden along in a near catatonic state after they'd returned to the wagon and got going again, replaying the battle in his mind over and over again. For all of his skills as a sneak thief, his traps, his talent with a knife in close combat, his lethality in the shadows, he never would have been able to stand against rashums like bladerons on his own. Not the way Biff had, no. Digby undid his light armoring and stripped down out of his clothes, sauntering into the bathroom and running the shower for a moment before stepping in, letting the blissfully warm water sluice the dirt and debris of travel from his fur and skin.

How does that old expression go? he thought to himself. *About as useless as tits on a boar? Yes, I think that's it, and that's what you were, old boy.* He tried to ignore this inner admonition, but could not deny the hard, simple truth of it. He hadn't been able to help at all, crouched away from the conflict while his friends took up the task of protecting them all from the powerful rashum. *That boy had never left his village until a couple of weeks ago, and he's got more stones than you'll ever have in a lifetime.*

Digby sat down in the tub, and allowed himself a short, good cry.

***

Sirock peeled the armor off, 'hrrrm'ing at each wound he spotted as the armor and underclothes came away. The bladeron's leg-vines had lacerated him in several places where his heavy armor was creased and joined to allow him maneuverability. Had it been any other normal, mortal creature, the damage might have been much less severe, but bladerons were among the deadliest creatures to roam the wilds. They'd gotten fortunate to survive not one, but two of the beasts.

By the time he was as naked as the day he was born, Sirock's head swam from the blood loss that he'd suffered, both in the battle and throughout the day. He had made no outward mention of discomfort or injury, especially since everyone seemed rattled enough from the experience. Memnock had been sore from bruised ribs and muscle spasms from when the bladeron had blasted her and her shield aside, but the mage woman had seen to her own wounds with healing spells as they rode along. She would be fine. Biff's outer leathers had been ruined and a patch of links on his cuirass shirt melted together when the bladeron he'd squared off with kicked him with its flaming foot, but he otherwise seemed none the worse for wear.

As for Digby, well, the fox had been smart enough to know his limitations, Reyko bless him. Sirock looked down at his body, a brief, flitting memory passing through his mind's eye as he gazed at each scar that crisscrossed his flesh. Most dwarves could grow hair out of even scar tissue, if the damage hadn't been too severe in the first place: unfortunately for the battle priest, wide swaths of his flesh were bare. He ran a rough finger over one particular line, which traveled from his left hip up at an angle across most of his torso, hooking sharply up toward his neck, terminating at the clavicle. He would never forget that wound, not as long as he lived.

But I can see my scars, he thought. *How deep run those of the fox, the mage, or our new friend? What guidance can I give them? I beseech thee, Reyko, give me wisdom before the battles ahead, that we may prevail.* He clenched his hands into fists, pressing the knuckles gently together in prayer, and knelt to meditate and pray on the teachings of his deity.

***

Biff wrenched off his cuirass with an effort, tossing the armor on his rented bed with a grunt. He already knew he'd have to scrap at least half of the chain links on the lower half's overlay, blasted as they were. The leather covering would have to be cut away to clean lines and replaced, a task he wasn't sure he had the spare material for at the moment. *Might have to just go bare,* he thought. *But poppa would not approve, no. Looks matter too, he always said so.* Rather than dwell on it, Biff finished getting stripped down, then hopped in the shower. It felt brilliant to get cleaned up, and since he wasn't at his father's house, where the worry was always that there might not be enough hot water if he kept the temperature maxed out for more than a couple of minutes, he cranked it as high as he could and hummed to himself contentedly, scrubbing the dust and grime and sweat from the road.

Biff considered himself immensely lucky that he'd survived the battle with the bladeron with as little damage as he had. After all, if the wind hadn't knocked that tree branch around to disorient the weird creature, it might have gotten in at least one more clean attack on him before he could put paid to it. He supposed fortune had smiled on him, though, and that was good enough for his liking.

It never crossed his mind that the morning had been completely windless.

***

The trip thus far had been rough for Memnock, who'd had to rely on her magic on an almost daily basis. Sure, most mages became accustomed to using simple cantrips and domestic spells, but she'd rarely been prone to relying on magic when simple, everyday solutions were available. As such, she found the use of such spells as camp barriers, lighting fires, or scanning her surroundings using mana-infused vision more taxing on her physically and magically than most. The trade-off, she supposed, was an increased raw strength and accuracy in her combat spells.

She laid back in the tub, soaking in the steaming hot water, her every muscle crying out in worn relief from the hardships of their trip. The worst part of it all for her was the absolute certainty that they had at least another four or five days' travel before they were even in the right region to start tracking down the shield that was their quarry. Even then, the quartet would have to find a likely town to situate themselves in as a kind of temporary base of operations. "Could be worse,"she mused aloud. "At least it wouldn't be communal showers." The lack of privacy had been one of the more glaring cons about living in the guild hall, especially for a woman as self-conscious about her size compared to the other women of the guild as she. This, or any other rented room for that matter, offered a respite of sorts.

Her research months before, back when she first thought they'd be dispatching to come searching for the last masterwork of Jayen the Hammer, had pointed out several candidates, none of them particularly better suited than the other. One of the towns was a hamlet inhabited entirely by lizardmen, who did not take kindly to long-term guests or visitors; another town required all visiting mages to serve a term of no less than four hours of guard duty on the perimeter of town each day, since it was routinely attacked by rashum that wandered the region. A third town, while having neither such shortcoming, was nonetheless rumored to be under the tyrannical governance of a mayor whose use of his own hand-selected guardsmen had people wondering where he'd originally come from, and why so many of those guards carried on like little more than a glorified street gang.

The fourth and final option she'd come across was not really a township, per se, but a Ja-Wen military outpost that occasionally allowed small, private groups of travelers to stay within its patrolled walls for a few nights before pressing them on to other climes. Of the places to go when they first got to the area, this seemed like the best choice initially. "I'll have to do a warrant check first, though, won't I," she muttered to herself as she lifted her left leg slightly out of the steaming water, flexing her foot back as far as she could to stretch the tendons in her ankle. "Never know if Digs might be asked to spend a few extra days in a lockup," she mused with a sigh.

She didn't allow herself too much extra time to soak, though she did take the opportunity after toweling off to run a little extra heat down over her legs. The magical energies, a much-subdued fire shielding spell cast directly on her skin, left her legs both warm and smooth, one of the few nods she gave to femininity on a regular basis. A quick towel down and burst of warm air to dry her hair, then she changed into one of her more civilian dresses and cloaks and prepared to meet her comrades down at the inn's pub.

***

Biff never would have passed for a bright young man, though he at least had native wisdom to recognize this shortcoming of his own intellectual prowess and capacity. Part of being a simple fellow, however, and one brought up the way he had been, put him into a state of sheer mental chaos when he saw Memnock stride into the pub on the first floor of the inn. He felt the urge to smile, to laugh, to clench the table hard enough to break a chunk out of the edge, to howl like an animal, and for reasons he only understood in the abstract, he wanted to be alone with her in a dark place. *Preferably with a soft floor,* he thought.

The dress was not revealing in the sense commonly understood among many young women in the more modern city-states throughout the realms, but it did have a slight plunge to the neckline to accentuate her already ample assets, and it flowed along the curvature of her frame in a way that complimented her well. Digby, seated to Biff's right at the round table they'd claimed when they bumped into each other passing through the pub's entry arch from the check-in lobby, gave her a playful whistle.

"My goodness, Mem, you actually look like a lady," he said. She smiled at his jape, though only for the second before Biff backhanded the vulpesin's biceps with an admonishing scowl.

"What?" Digby snapped, rubbing his arm. "I was paying her a compliment, Biff."

"Oh," said the barbarian, overcome by a moment of awkwardness. He scratched his head and sighed. "I sometimes don't get any of this stuff about 'tone'," he offered weakly.

Mem lowered herself into one of the two seats available at the table, on Biff's other side, and put a hand gently on his forearm.

"That's all right, dear," she said soothingly. "It'll come with time." She cast a look around the pub for a moment, then turned a curious look to the rogue. "Where's Sirock?"

"He'll be here," Digby assured her.

A moment later, a petite human woman in a ruffled white blouse and layered skirts approached with a tray bearing three glass mugs and a pitcher of ale, gently prodding them about ordering food. "We've got a fourth coming, dear, and he's a dwarf," the vulpesin said.

The waitress nodded, and returned less than a minute later with another pitcher, setting it by itself at the empty spot at the table just in time for the dwarven battle priest to enter the room. He was not dressed in his usual heavy armor, which still needed repair, but rather in the hardened leathers that, while presentable, still left no mistake about his status as a warrior. While he didn't wear his larger battle axe on his hip, Sirock had a small hatchet hanging plainly where it would be.

"You look smaller without your armor," Biff commented as the battle priest took a long swig of his ale.

Sirock grunted, but with a grin.

"So, now that we're here, how long are we staying?" Biff asked openly.

"Well, we're not exactly racing anyone else to get the shield," Memnock answered thoughtfully. "It might be nice to spend a couple of nights in a row in a bed. It's well within our budget, and we can talk to people around town, try to get more leads if anyone local knows anything about it. Biff, what do you think?" She took a sip of her drink, waiting for the barbarian to respond in some way, but he just remained silent, staring at her. "Biff?"

"Huh? Oh, um, yeah, I think it'd be good if we stayed here a day or two," he said, blinking rapidly. "Sorry, my mind was, uh, wandering," he stammered. "Digby?"

"I'm game to hang about for a couple of days, sure. But we've all got things to work on, so let's not just treat this as a relaxation period. I, for one, am going to find out in the morning if there's a machinist in this village. While I'm off taking care of that, could you sharpen my blades for me, Biff?"

"Yeah, not a problem," said the barbarian.

Their waitress came over to them and offered a short, simple menu of food offerings from the pub's kitchen, jotting down their orders on a pad which she deftly tucked into her blouse before taking away the empty pitcher and replacing it with a full one.

"Sirock? Did you want me to work on your gear?"

The dwarven battle priest made a sour face, squinting at Biff as if he was looking at a new and disgusting kind of insect.

"If he shall follow the ways of blessed battle, he shall labor to his own benefit unless wounded too much to care for his tools of combat," Sirock rumbled, shaking his head as he quoted Reyko's scripture once more. His eyes met Biff's, and the dwarf visibly softened with a sigh. "I mean no offense, lad, but no. It is my way. Nothing is keeping me from doing it myself, so I must do so."

Shortly after this, the food was delivered, and the company shared their meal in companionable quiet, only occasionally pausing to ask one another for salt, pepper, or a napkin.

When the meal was finished, Biff excused himself to bed for the night, as did Sirock, leaving Digby and Memnock alone, still nursing their ale. When another guest left, presumably to retire for the night herself, Mem raised an eyebrow at the vulpesin rogue.

"Why are you looking for a machinist, Digs?" she asked quietly, though she already had her suspicions. "We don't have any complicated equipment or technology with us, except maybe for that radio in your bag that you've been talking about getting fixed for, well, ever." She sipped her ale, and the rogue gave her a defeated glance.

"I'm going to get a firearm," he confessed. "You know, I'm probably the only thief in all of Tamalaria who can't use a bow, or even a fucking crossbow, properly. It's embarrassing," he grumbled.

"It's never bothered you before," she pointed out. "You've always gotten by with your traps and your wits, and you're quite skilled in close quarters. I've seen you work the knives, you're very capable."

"Yeah, well, there's times when that's not going to be good enough," he snapped. "Look at what happened with those bladerons, Mem. I was less than useless," he said more quietly, swigging more of his ale.

"In that moment, yes, you were," Memnock supplied evenly.

"Thanks a bunch for that."

"Now hear me out, fox," she continued, talking right over the tail end of his words as if he hadn't spoken. "In that instance, you couldn't help. But there have been many times over the last couple of years, working together with you, when I can think back to how badly things could have gone if you weren't there, being, well, *you*," she said. "The Tescaners Wayfarer Troupe ring any bells?"

Despite his inclination toward self-pity for the moment, Digby smiled warmly at the memory, how he had bested the patriarch of that traveling community in a test of wits. It had pushed him to the edge of his ability to be clever without turning to violence in combination, but sure enough, he had managed to do what no amount of fighting would have.

"Sirock and I would have botched that, and Biff may be a tender soul at his core, but he's a barbarian, Digby. He can rule the battlefield, but not everything ends on the field of conflict in this world. You're the best at what you do, and you should be proud of that."

The vulpesin reached out his hand and took hers, squeezing her fingers briefly.

"Thank you," he said, then tipped back the rest of his drink.

"Still getting a gun, aren't you?"

"First thing in the morning," he replied before getting up and putting a few coins on the table to pay their bill.

Chapter Nine

The following morning, just before the village's lone market street really came fully alive as farmers from the nearby fields brought their rolling storefronts to set up, Digby stood wide-eyed before a long, dusty countertop. The gnome engineer on the other side of the counter did not seem in the least concerned or surprised at just how bug-eyed the vulpesin was, even as he verged on looking like something out of a newspaper comic strip.

"Can you run by me just briefly why these little things are so expensive," the vulpesin asked as he held up a slender copper tube, its head steel-colored and nearly perfectly rounded.

"Gunpowder ain't cheap, sunshine," the gnome said in his thick west-regions' accent. The fellow wore a wrinkled cream colored tunic top with crossing bandoliers, different tools looped into place for easy access and to make him easily identified by his trade. His beard was well cropped, and even had streaks of black colored in, further making him stand out for a member of a race that usually considered such ostentatious self-decoration to be pointless, if not downright vulgar. "And not a whole lot of blokes or lasses the world 'round can even make bullets. It's a fine thing, requires a lot of attention to detail, and plenty of resources."

"I appreciate that, I do, but two hundred coin for a box of twenty of these things," Digby asked, holding up and rattling the box of ammunition. "That's ten coin for a single bullet!"

"Makes you appreciate the cost of such easy killin' then, don't it?" the gnome countered. "Now shit or get off the pot, lad, there'll be real customers comin' along soon, an' they might likes to have me full attention when they do."

Digby grumbled, but he ended up handing over one of his money pouches and asking the gnome for a demonstration on the firearm's breakdown, maintenance, and use. It seemed a simple enough little device, at first, but as the gnome walked him through the disassembly and cleaning ritual, Digby wondered if he would have the diligence to properly maintain the weapon. However, when he thought about the firearm in terms of his various traps, both pre-made and his personally crafted contraptions, he realized it wasn't really all that complicated after all. At least, not for him.

With the firearm and ammunition purchased, Digby then procured a holster of a variety the gnome told him was called a 'docker's clutch', a rig that would seat the gun up under his armpit. It was as he was standing before a fitting mirror in the shop's main room that he had a thought that might normally cause him to slap his own forehead for not having considered it earlier. The Last Shield was rumored, according to Memnock's information, to be in the possession of rendermen. The metallic humanoid-shaped creatures came in several varieties, from bronze to copper to iron, to a handful that were even said to have flesh of gold, mythril or adamantite. The bullets he'd just purchased might do some damage to the lower forms of the creatures, but if they should come upon any of the sturdier variety, he was going to find his new toy to be worth little more than a fart in the wind.

"'Scuse me again, sir," he said to the shopkeeper as he brought out another pouch of coin from his duffel. "I just realized that I might need to purchase some specialized rounds."

The gnome's face broke out in a beaming, 'Gotcha' smile, and Digby mentally groaned.

***

Sirock read over the passage for the third time since waking up an hour earlier, uncertain of why, precisely, it was vexing him so much. It wasn't a long or complicated bit of the scripture of Reyko, but it was one he realized he hadn't spent much time thinking over. Like much of the first half of the holy book of his sect, it took place during Reyko's time spent as a mortal dwarven woman, back in the days before the acknowledged histories of the First Age. She was passing with her clan out of a ruins seated in the middle of an island off the west coast of what would come to be known as Tamalaria, and had taken the time to write down an observation in her journal. It was this journal that, according to the lore of his faith, served as the fundamental basis for much of the early writings of the scripture.

'And lo, blessed Reyko saw among her kinsmen a man whose prowess had put to shame that of his peers. He did not brag of his skill, but used it for the betterment of his clan. What pain could there be, she reasoned, in asking this warrior to share with his kin his secrets, his skills? And when she spake thus to him, and asked if he would impart his knowledge to his kin, the great warrior said, 'No, I shall not, for what if some day my brothers should turn on me?' And so she smote him in singular combat, and taught her kin how she had done so, but sorrow weighed upon her, for secrets had died with her foe, secrets that still may have benefitted her kin.'

He had never shied away from brutality when it was necessary, which seemed perfectly in keeping with this passage. More than this, he knew for certain he'd read it numerous times before. *So why am I obsessing over this now?* he wondered, scratching his head. He read through it again, and paused his internal narration when he came to the part about Reyko asking if the warrior would impart his knowledge to his kin. He clapped the book shut and got up off the chair by the little card table in the corner of his rented room.

"But wait," he said to himself, hesitating yet again. "What in the seven Hells can any of us teach each other?" He had worked with Digby and Memnock on several occasions over the last few years, and not once in all of that time had any of them stopped to try to teach each other anything from their own personal skill sets. Memnock couldn't very well teach him any magic: dwarves didn't take well to using magic, and as a priest of Reyko, he was forbidden from wielding any magic that could not be sourced from his deity or divine powers. Digby couldn't teach him any of his particular skills, as they were distinctly lacking in honor. Followers of Reyko could be thieves, if they so chose, but priests were explicitly forbidden from using skills or techniques that could be construed as dishonorable, no matter how noble the end cause.

But Biff, well, he was a barbarian. Such warriors possessed skills that he *could* pick up, if Biff could focus long enough to teach him. And Digby's skills could be taught to Memnock, if she proved nimble enough. Yet, what could Digby learn from any of them?

"What can a vulpesin do, though?" he asked himself aloud, pacing the room. He didn't know the answer for sure, but he knew where he could find answers. He finished buttoning up his casual tunic, grabbed one of his journal books (mostly empty, a kind of travel log he'd started when they'd left Breck since his previous one had only two pages left blank before they left town) and a couple of pens, and headed down to the hotel lobby. A cheerful-looking human woman was sitting the check-in desk, and he steered himself over toward her and tried to return her inviting smile. He could tell from her reaction that whatever he was giving her, it wasn't exactly what most folks would call a 'smile'. It certainly didn't feel like one; it felt like the grimace of a man who has to defecate but who has to have a polite verbal exchange first.

"How can I help you, sir?" she asked cautiously.

"Library," he replied simply.

"About a five minute walk east of here, over on Tayak Street," she said. "Open all hours."

Sirock raised an eyebrow at her, and she cleared her throat, clearly feeling a little awkward. "Um, well, some folks are a little put off by the librarian here."

"Any particular reason?"

"Well, he's a ghost," said the young woman.

Sirock managed this time to keep a straight face, and perhaps his lack of reaction put the clerk at ease, because she continued after a notable sigh of relief. "Most passersby that hear about him get a little freaked out. Tell the truth, I guess I shouldn't be surprised you're not. I mean, the dwarves I've known, most of them weren't exactly superstitious."

"So, how exactly does a ghost serve as a librarian," Sirock asked, opening his journal and jotting down some new notes.

"Well, my brother, he's an elementalist, so he's studied lots of magic, he knows a lot about this stuff, anyways he says he's not really a ghost, but a specter," she said in a rush.

"A *specter*? You're sure that's what he said," he asked, scribbling.

"Yeah, a specter. Michael says there's a few different kinds of, um, what'd he call them?" She quirked up her face, thinking, tapping the counter with one long pointer finger. She finally slapped the countertop and proclaimed, "Phantasms! Yeah, he said there's ghosts, specters, poltergeists, spirits and something he called, um shades."

"Strictly speaking, shades aren't considered phantasms anymore, since they spend half of their time in corporeal form," Sirock corrected out of habit. The girl blinked at him, and he clarified with, "I'm a priest."

"Oh." She bit her lip and looked away, murmuring softly, "Awkward."

"Not for me, miss. Not all priests try to cast out phantasms, and not all phantasms are harmful," he finished, shutting his journal and tucking his pen in a pocket. "Tayak Street?"

"Mm-hmm. Cheery-bye, then," she added as the dwarven battle priest tromped out of the inn and down the street toward the library.

The township they had stopped in wasn't much to look at, not even compared to a small city like Breck. The streets were hardpack earth, easily wide enough to accommodate the passage of three full-sized wagons abreast, most of the buildings were rustic wooden structures that had taken on the dark gray of old construction that had seen many winters, and the citizenry was largely cooped up indoors. As Sirock turned at an intersection onto Tayak, he could see from the angled deck roofs that most of the village's market was along this street, a row of nearly identical shops whose primary identifiers were hanging signs bearing a simple pictogram and the name of the store. Even the town smithy had an identical setup, which told Sirock the smith inside was most likely of a race other than dwarf, minotaur or jaft.

The library stood alone on the left side of the street as he walked along, a buffer of dead grass lawns on the near and far side, and what looked at a distance like a caretaker's shack in the rear. Said shack, when he took a moment to give it a harder look, appeared to have partially collapsed in on itself. He drew his lips into a thin line and shook his head, but then carried on up the steps and through the tall, white door into the library's entry vestibule.

The difference from being outside to passing over the threshold could only have been missed by a blind man with no tactile sensation. The moment the dwarf stepped inside, his eyes could make out only blurs as they adjusted to the sudden darkness within, and the temperature drop would have shocked most folk. Where the sunny morning walk had been warm bordering on hot, he could now make out the plume of his own breath in front of his face. "Brisk," he said to himself, his voice bouncing back to his own ears in the narrow, short chamber. Coat hooks studded the wall to his right, and a dusty bench offered a place for patient caretakers or companions to wait while someone else pursued the tomes of their choice.

Through the open doorway at the back of the vestibule he then trod, his softened leather casual boots making only a faint scraping sound as he went along into the central library space. Wide steps circled a lowered area in the middle of the main chamber where stood a circular oak counter with a pair of ancient rolling desk chairs. Four different register books sat at even intervals around the countertops. The dusky aroma of cinnamon, so common to old parchment, hung pleasantly in the darkened space, not overpowering, but not teasing just under the normal range of detection. The space had a cozy quality to it.

This, despite the fact that a lime-green apparition, looking vaguely like a lizardman in a plain hooded robe, stood off to one side of the counter, a heavy-looking volume in his hand. This creature was looking directly at the battle priest, and the shadows cast by its luminous form wavered slightly as it shifted its body to face Sirock squarely.

"You're not here to perform an exorcism, I hope," the specter said, snapping the book shut and letting it go. As its arm drooped to the apparition's side, the book continued to hover in mid-air beside it. At a distance still of about twenty feet, Sirock could not quite make out the specter's facial features, but his divine senses were not catching hostility so much as worry and fear. "I've become quite comfortable here these last nine years."

Sirock held his hands up before him, fingers splayed as wide as he could make them.

"I mean you no harm, specter," he replied, consciously forgoing quotation from his scripture. *It'd probably make him feel a little uncomfortable,* he thought. "I am indeed a priest, as you no doubt sensed the moment I walked inside."

"I felt you from up the street. It's impressive, your righteousness."

"Is that a compliment?"

"It should be."

"Thank you, then," Sirock said with a nod, taking a slow step down to the next ring around the central book check counter. "I wonder if you might be able to help me do some research, actually."

The ethereal light coming off of the creature briefly flashed brighter, then settled back to its usual hum. It approached him then, walking along the floor as though gravity still had any kind of hold on it. As it drew close, Sirock could see a smile that was so delighted, it wrinkled the scales on what had obviously been an older lizardman's face, when the mortal form had been alive and well.

"How delightful! Yes, yes, of course I can help! Such is the very purpose of my, er, being, I suppose would be the proper term these days, yes?" The specter patted Sirock on the arm, and the priest's shoulder went almost completely numb with cold from the contact, but the specter seemed not to notice as it wheeled about and led him toward a tall card catalogue cabinet. "Come along, now, my friend! And by the way," it said as it turned and held out a hand toward Sirock. "I am Dolzen."

Sirock took the hand offered, and shook briefly.

"Sirock."

"Well, Sirock, what is it you're looking to learn more about?" asked Dolzen, running his phantasm hand over the small drawers.

"Vulpesins," the dwarf replied.

Dolzen pulled open one of the lower drawers, walking his fingers along the tops of the cards within until he finally made a little 'ah-ha' noise under his breath.

"Found something, I assume?"

"Yes, just a moment." Dolzen walked over to the counter and passed through it to the inner area. The specter's body disappeared where it contacted the desk, accompanied by a peculiar warbling noise that set Sirock's teeth on edge.

Dolzen grabbed up a small notepad and pen from a desk drawer, came back to the card catalog, and jotted down a couple of quick notes on the top page. "Come with me," he said, sliding the drawer shut.

Sirock followed the specter down a long aisle of bookshelves to a section of wall-mounted racks, benefitting from the light given off by its phantasmal form.

Dolzen hunched his head down and forward, scanning the racks, snapping up a thin book with a bright yellow cover embossed with curling blue script on the front which read, 'Vulpesin, the Fox-Men of Tallowmere'. He turned and handed the volume to Sirock, then started back toward the main area.

"Wait, is this all there is?" Sirock asked, incredulous.

"Unfortunately, yes," Dolzen replied over his shoulder as he stalked along ahead of the dwarven battle priest. "At least, at this library. It's really sort of a pity I'm bound here, and not in some grander locale. I'm sure the Coreth Library in Ja-Wen or perhaps Eldred Library in Palen would have more for you." The specter passed through the counter once again and opened one of the book registries. He jotted down the name of the book and its reference number, then looked up at the dwarf. "Your full name, township of residence, and nations of citizenship, sir?"

"Sirock Delpa, Breck, Freehold States and the Northwestron Nation," the battle priest answered. His eyes narrowed, cheeks rose up, and chin waggled as he contemplated an odd notion. "Dolzen, you said you're bound here, right?"

"That is correct," the lizardman-specter said. "It's interesting, actually. The moment I re-formed here, I expected to just *know* how to go about being a phantasm, the whole spiel. But I had no idea," he said, closing the register with a thud. "I was clueless. However," he continued, pointing over his shoulder in the direction opposite of where he'd led Sirock for his book, "there's an entire phantasm section over there in one of the shelves. I had nothing else to do with myself, and couldn't leave the library grounds, so I just did some reading."

"Interesting." Sirock tucked the book under his arm. "So, do you know what's got you bound here?"

"My reading glasses," said Dolzen. "They're in one of these top drawers, somewhere." He indicated the counter interior with a vague wave of his hands. Suddenly, Dolzen flinched backward, hands up defensively. "Wait, I thought you weren't going to—"

"I'm not," said Sirock. "But I do have an idea." Sirock laid out the notion that had been playing through his mind, and Dolzen, reiterating that he had nothing to lose at that juncture, agreed to his suggestion.

Sirock Delpa, high priest of Reyko, left the library with a book, a pair of reading glasses, and an unseen passenger.

***

Locating a fellow mage was not something that came automatically to most magic-wielders in the realms of Tamalaria, but Memnock had been so practiced at manipulating her own mana reserves to seek out other concentrations of magical energies that she never had to look long. As Sirock was on his way to the library and Digby was haggling over the cost of special ammunition for his new weapon, the tall, broad mage woman made her way toward a simple little brick hut near the southern edge of the village, her vision locked on a small vortex of magic surrounding the building.

The brightness of the day had a natural side effect of improving her mood all on its own, something for which she was exceedingly grateful. Despite her attempts to reassure Digby and restore his self-confidence, he'd gone off to a machinist's anyway, as if to say her perspective was appreciated but ultimately not worth listening to. It might have stung a little less if the vulpesin rogue weren't her best friend.

That does not speak well to my social skills, she mused, moving a stray lock of hair out of her face as she came up to the porch fronting the hut. A simple wooden sign hung from two eye-hooks over the door, reading, 'Muffin Stuff'. She pulled the simple blue-painted panel door open, and the moment she did, Mem's entire body quivered with simple delight. The blended aromas of baking sweets, spices, and undoubtedly unhealthy treats flowed over her, a tide of comfort in olfactory form, calling out to the simpler times of her childhood when her own Gran had practically forced pastries of every sort down her and her brother's throats. Her eyes slipped shut, standing in the doorway with one hand on the doorway, the other on her chest just below her throat as her mind raced through those memories of Ago.

"You're letting the heat out, ma'am," a voice cut through her reverie, and with a flutter of her eyes and a snap of her jaws, lips thinning out in embarrassment, Memnock spied a stout gnome woman on the other side of a short, rounded countertop fronted with a display case of baked goods. A narrow passage behind the counter in the back wall led back to a gaggle of ovens, one of which she had open, a thick black oven mitt covering one hand as she looked out at Mem. Like most gnome women, her beard was short and neatly trimmed, and her hair was a slightly darker shade of gray than the males of their race.

"Please do step in," she said.

Memnock stepped inside and let the door shut behind her, then watched, fascinated, as the gnome baker set a tray of muffins on the cooling board and waved one hand over them, a faint orange light washing from her fingertips downward. She tossed the mitt casually next to the tray and sauntered out of the kitchen to the area behind the display counter, peeking around quickly at the few tables to see if there were any present customers, of which there were none. Like most such small eateries, there were only three booth-style tables on either side of the shop's main room, and another narrow passage on the left side leading to what Mem assumed was a restroom.

"I'm sorry to trouble you, miss, but what sort of magic are you employing here?" Memnock asked, once again brushing her bangs back out of her face.

The baker lifted her head, jaw set.

"Why would you want to know?" the gnome woman asked suspiciously.

"Just curious. I'm a sorceress myself, and I sensed rather a great deal of mana cycling around the building. I'm traveling with a group towards the wilds around Ja-Wen in search of something, and I just thought it might be helpful, given the nature of what we're looking for, if I was able to speak to someone local with a bit of magical knowledge."

The baker folded her arms over her chest, nodding, lips pursed. "I'm surprised you didn't head to the library, then, to chat up the ghost what serves as librarian," the baker replied. Her eyes flashed wide for a second and she gave a little derisive chuckle. "Sorry, *specter*, not ghost, though what the real difference is I never could tell. S'just creepy all round, having some spook holing up like a proper person, you know?"

Memnock had known plenty of mages in her time who would have loved the opportunity to speak to such a librarian, but she also recalled from her studies of the various races in Tamalaria that gnomes were not fond of any sort of phantasm.

"That must be, interesting," Memnock said, doing a little eyebrow-raise that would, she hoped, convey subtle disapproval. A quick glance at the baker's own expression in response told her it had paid off, as the gnome's posture relaxed. "My company is with the Freelance Adventurers Guild of Tamalaria, and we're in search of the last shield crafted by Jayen, the Hammer. Have you ever heard of it?"

"I have done, yes," said the baker, leaning forward on the countertop. "Must've been about half a year back I heard tell of it, as there was this fellow coming round asking about it himself. I think his name was Toto, or summat like that."

"Toro the Bold. He used to be Jayen's apprentice," Memnock supplied. "If you remember him, I imagine he made quite an impression."

"I'd say yes, that he did, miss," said the baker as she opened one of the sliding doors at the back of a display rack and pulled out a cruller, munching thoughtfully on it. "Bloke outfitted all seven of our constables with new gear in exchange for some free room and board at the hotel, and quite timely too, I might add. We're technically a protectorate of Ja-Wen, but quartermasters don't get out this far west too often."

"How long had it been," Mem asked casually as she plopped a few copper coins on the countertop and pointed out an apple fritter in the display, which the baker placed on a small paper plate for her.

"Four years. Poor old Billy Norbett had been without a fresh axe for nearly three years, having blunted the crap out of his own when a bladeron wandered into town. Took all seven of the lads and meself to take the beastie down, and it weren't pretty." The baker paused mid-bite, seeing Memnock flinch. "What?"

"Well, it's just that, my friends and I, we came upon a pair of bladerons only half a day outside of the village. Are they common in this region?"

"There used to be a breeding pit about three days south of us here," the baker answered, shaking her head. "Militia cleared it out some four years back, but I think the offspring wander back now and then as some kind of memory thing. I've never been entirely sure, and there's not a lot of good literature out there about them, except maybe in Palen. You can find out just about anything about rashum or magic there. Anyhow, what's your interest in this last shield?"

"Toro commissioned our guild to fetch it," Memnock said, taking a bite of her fritter finally. She moaned with delight, shutting her eyes, relishing the tart but sweet flavor. "This, is incredible," she said, her taste buds singing of rapture in her mouth. "I can taste *everything* you put in here! How do you do that?"

The baker gave her a wide smile and twitched her fingers, which once again gave off a little shimmer of orange light. "It's a minor enchantment I picked up from me mum. Four generations we've had this bakery, and me own daughter'll be picking up the trade soon's she's grown. The spell's a wonky little thing, created by her grandmother originally as something of a gaff."

"It's worked well, considering. What was her original aim with it?"

"Well, she were trying to make a little trick that could be used to bring out a singular flavor in healthy but largely unpleasant foods and the like, for the militiamen out of Ja-Wen. She figured the lads and lasses what have to settle for those packet meals in a pinch usually complained they were rubbish, and as a ranked officer in the mages' division, she set on the task for her comrades. Spell went a bit off, but the result was so useful, she kept it and made a go of her own business here."

Memnock nodded as she chewed, thinking clearly on her next question. "Ma'am, is there anybody here in town you'd say could be considered a rashum expert? Perhaps a scholar of some kind, or another mage who focuses in that area who isn't this librarian you mentioned?"

The gnome woman folded her arms and ran a thumb back and forth under her wide chin, thinking hard for a minute.

"Well, there's Bannon, the git what owns and runs the pub," she finally said. "He used to be a ranger, made his riches back in the day selling rare monster bits about. 'Is place is locked up tight until nooners, but when it opens, you may want to give him a talk. Just mind he don't veer you down a path to one of his tales of glory. He gets started on that, you'll want to get knackered on his cheapest gut rot just to drown out the sound of his voice."

Memnock snickered, accidentally spraying sugary flakes onto the floor. "Well, thank you, ma'am. I think I'll take a walk around a bit until noon, then, and speak with this Bannon character. Be well," she said, heading for the door.

"Ta," the baker replied.

As Memnock stepped back out into the sunlit street, the warmth and pleasant aura of the bakery's interior faded, replaced with the more mundane heat of the sun beating down unimpeded by cloud cover.

Striding slowly back toward the inn to wait for the pub to open, Memnock considered that some magic had nothing at all to do with spells and invocations; some folk, like the gnome baker, just had a way of making a person tingle from pleasant conversation.

***

Biff thanked the elven gentleman for the cup and saucer, then scooted a few inches aside so the slender fellow could sit down next to him. The barbarian had done his gear touchups early, and not wanting to bother any of his new friends since they'd all be traveling together again in another day or so, he'd decided to take a walk around town. During this excursion, he'd heard singing and followed the beautiful chorus to this odd little glass hut situated behind a house on the northern edge of town.

The roof of the hut was arched, with clear glass paneling that allowed the sunlight to stream right inside onto scores of beautiful plants, all arranged in neat little orange clay pots and green potters lining tables, hung from hooks or raised on pedestals. The outer door had been secured with an Ironfist brand lock, but Biff had found that the 'Biff Plus Rock Equals Open Door' equation had worked just fine once more. When he'd opened the door, the music filled him with so much joy that he'd been shocked to feel tears streaming from the corners of his eyes.

When he wandered inside, slowly stalking between two rows of the old tables, Biff had tried to crunch his bulky frame inward, to avoid touching any of the gorgeous greenery. It was a subtle thing, but he'd noticed over the few years of his young life that the smell of some plants changed when they were touched, and they withdrew from the outer world as well. Not wanting to risk this, he had finally stopped walking and just sat down in the middle of the aisle, gaping at everything.

He wasn't sure how long he'd been sitting like that when the elf came crashing in and yelling about idiot kids and their total disrespect for a man's property or privacy. He was stopped short by the brilliant, exuberant look on Biff's face, and the barbarian's question: "Isn't their song lovely?"

The elf had been holding a rather fierce-looking cudgel overhead, but it quickly lowered at this question, and his face went from stern disapproval to cautious curiosity.

The elf had a saucer and cup of his own as well, and as he sat down nimbly beside the bigger man, Biff finally took him in a bit more carefully. His ears were lot sharply pointed like a southlands elf, but more sort of rounded along the bottom, something Biff had been taught by his father was indicative of westernland elves. The beginnings of a beard had taken residence on the man's chin and cheeks, indicating he was at least two-hundred years old: elves didn't grow facial hair at all until about that point.

The homeowner's features were altogether soft and plain, unremarkable but for his eyes being different colors, the left one green and the right one brown. He wore a simple brown sleeveless vest over an off-white long-sleeved shirt, farmer's brown trousers, and a pair of workman's slippers on his small feet. "So, you hear them singing, do you?" asked the elf after he and Biff clinked glasses like proper company.

"I did, yeah. That's why I had to come here. I heard them out on the street. They sounded just gorgeous," said the barbarian.

"I can imagine. I'm Neville, by the way, Neville Huff," said the elf, offering Biff his hand.

The barbarian took it with gusto and pumped the man's arm, grimacing apologetically when he heard Neville's knuckles pop in his grip. "Biff," the young barbarian replied.

"Well, Biff, I'm sure you can appreciate it isn't everyday someone breaks into my property and a constable isn't sought," said Neville in a friendly but disapproving manner.

"Yeah, sorry about that. I can pay you for the lock, if you like."

Neville flapped a hand to wave this offer aside, and sipped his tea.

"Where'd you get all these plants?"

"From seed, actually. These are all third or fourth generation now," the elven gent responded. "I'm an herbalist, you see. I grow the plants here for use by alchemists, druggists, mages and the like. Of course, it's easy for me to tend to them; I'm a gaiamancer."

Biff raised an eyebrow, unsure of what this meant.

Reading the look, Neville went on, "It means I specialize in magic that uses earthen powers and energies."

"Oh, okay. You're a mage, then. My friend Memnock's a mage, too, except she makes things blow up, or makes things appear to be there that aren't really there, not when you look real close. She's also very pretty," he said, then stopped himself abruptly, pulling a face. "I'm not sure why I've said that."

Neville laughed, shook his head, and sipped his tea once more. "So, you heard my plants singing, and just decided to come check them out, Biff? Had no other nefarious intentions or aims?" Neville asked.

Biff still heard the plants around them, though their volume was now reduced to a dull hum. It was always like this when there were other people around, he'd noticed. It was as though the plants wanted to be mum unless he was alone with them. But through their hum, and perhaps thanks to the reduced volume, he began thinking on the very careful way Neville was enunciating his every word. There was a word for it, one that just escaped his grasp.

"No other bad intentions, no. I sometimes just do things without thinking about the consequences," Biff said, taking another sip of his tea and sighing. "My pop says it's because I'm a simpleton, but my mom says it's because men don't have any impulse control whatsoever, no matter how bright they are." An unfamiliar tingle started just under the skin on Biff's hands, and he now realized the buzzing hum was not coming from the plants at all; it was in his own head.

Something is wrong here, he thought. *I'm not sure what, though.* "I don't know why I told you those things my folks said."

"You said them because that's what benadaren extract does," said Neville, getting to his feet with a grunt. "It's one of the plants I grow here. The extract acts as a natural truth serum in humanoid subjects. The other side effect is that it paralyzes the extremities, though you're still holding your cup, which is, I must say, somewhat remarkable," the herbalist remarked as he walked away from Biff toward the greenhouse door, shutting it firmly. "Just a small precaution, and I am very sorry about it, but I've a competitor closer to Ja-Wen who's had some folks come through to try and steal some of my rarer samples. I had to be sure you weren't one of his boys."

"Oh. Well, I suppose that's okay, then," Biff said, popping up to his own feet. As he did so, the crestfallen, terrified look on Neville's face alarmed him, and Biff looked around himself quickly. "What is it? What's wrong?"

"You're standing," Neville half-choked. "Holding the cup, that's one thing, but the legs are supposed to go completely to rubber after a single sip! How is this possible?" the elf stammered, shaking his head. "Um, you're all right, then? Are you feeling wobbly at all?"

"Not really, no, but the singing's gone, and there's a slight tingle in my hands. I sometimes talk to animals and monsters too, but they don't always talk back, though some do," Biff continued, unable to stop himself now from talking. "It's always been like this with me, since I was little. I once accidentally drank a quart of fire starter thinking it was some weird juice my pop had bought, and even though everyone thought I was going to be sick or possibly die, I was just fine."

Neville's ears twitched as he shook his head, and he snapped his fingers. "Antidote. Come into the house with me now, I'll give you the antidote," he said in a rush, stepping forward and taking Biff firmly by the wrist, leading the great lumbering brute behind him out of the greenhouse, through a meticulously maintained back lawn, then up a set of rickety steps and into a small cottage house that appeared to be little more than a single oversized room with a separated washroom. He guided Biff over to a wide, long gray couch in the darkened room and led him down onto it. "Sit here, don't move a muscle," Neville said, and Biff just nodded mutely. The herbalist then dashed over to a cutting board by his sink and began rummaging through a rack of thin glass vials, muttering to himself.

"I met my second goblin a few days ago, out on the road," Biff said loudly, the hum starting to rise in pitch in his ears. He let his eyes roam about the large, rounded chamber. Various herbs and gourds were hung from bits of twine and rope from the low, domed ceiling, and a few charts and diagrams that he couldn't read were pinned to the walls. "And I killed a bladeron before my friends and I came here yesterday. It was scary, that thing, but I had no choice."

"I'm sure you didn't," rasped Neville, scurrying back over toward him with a vial filled with a cloudy pink liquid. "Now just drink this, friend, and I am *so* sorry I was a paranoid, it's just that I've got to think of my business, you know? Go on, then," he said, pressing the vial into Biff's hand.

Biff drank the stuff, which tasted as sweet as it looked, and he let out a little burp afterward, covering his mouth with one thick hand before giving the vial back.

"It'll take a minute or two to take hold, all right?"

"I met a chimera the other day, too," Biff said, and Neville stopped walking halfway back to his vials, spinning on his heels to stare in wonder at the barbarian. "Yeah. Says his name is Charlie. Well, that's not his name exactly, but it's the closest thing in the common tongue. I wonder if Charlie's staying close to the town while we're here?"

Neville grabbed a plain wooden chair from its spot at a small, two-person table and brought it over to sit in front of Biff, putting his hands up as if to stay the younger man from speaking any further. "Biff? I want you to count to ten, okay? Slowly, one number at a time, all right? By the time you're done, the antidote should have finished working, okay?"

"Okay," Biff said, then slowly began counting aloud. As he went along, the ringing in his ears subsided, and he could once again make out the music in the greenhouse outside. It was more muffled now than before, but still quite beautiful. By the time he got to 'ten', his eyes had shut, and he was humming along to the tune.

When he opened his eyes, he frowned, for Neville had a single tear track running down his cheek. "Hey, what's wrong?"

"That tune, where'd you hear it," the herbalist asked.

Biff pointed toward the greenhouse, and Neville sniffled, then nodded. "My wife used to sing that song when she was alive."

"It's pretty," Biff said. He recalled something then, an incident that had happened when he was still just a boy. He'd wanted his father to hear a couple of trees near the town talking to one another since the old man wouldn't believe him. The barbarian quickly stood up, took Neville by the hand, and half-dragged him through the hut, through the yard once more, and into the greenhouse. Once inside, he twined his fingers with Neville's, who stood staring at him for a moment before he gasped, gaping around at the plants around them.

The elven herbalist dropped to his knees, weeping, and Biff the barbarian knelt beside him, letting him listen as long as he wanted. It just seemed the nice thing to do, seeing as he'd broken the poor man's lock and upset him.

Chapter Ten

Digby nabbed another chip from the plate, dipped it in ketchup, and popped it in his mouth as Mem came back from the bathroom and reclaimed her seat. "So, what precisely did the blowhard manage to tell you? Anything you didn't already know?"

"Well, he did confirm something for me I'd heard a few times before, read in a book somewhere along the line too," the husky mage woman said with a sigh, taking a swig of her ale. "Rendermen aren't solid metal: at least most of them aren't. Solid metal ones are called 'alphas', and they're the rarest of the rare, even if they're of a common metal. Most rendermen are squishy things inside of an inch-thick outer layer of metal. Part of the reason they consume metal is to replenish their outer coating, which is why the solid ones don't come out of their nests for years at a time; they don't need it as often."

"Interesting." The vulpesin rogue rubbed his hands together expectantly as the waitress brought out their main courses, a fat, juicy burger for him, a meatloaf section and mashed potatoes for her. Sirock had begged off of dinner, and they hadn't yet seen Biff since the day before. "Anything else?"

"Well, rendermen often take on the outer physical shape of one of the first few organics they see, which is why they so often seem to take on a generally humanoid shape, though obviously the ones that wander the Allenian Hills area look a lot like either simpa or khan," she added as Digby took his first bite and grunted with satisfaction, chewing. "And though it's rare, some of them do this thing called a melding. It's where a clutch of them will just sort of press into one another and become one huge renderman-thing. It's irreversible, though."

"Surely our barman didn't witness such a thing himself," Digby asked sardonically.

"No, he says he heard about it from an expert in Palen, which seems credible enough," Mem replied. She tucked in, and for a minute, the two enjoyed their meals in comfortable silence. A brief hurly-burly of motion soon drew both of their attentions from their plates as Biff came into the inn's diner with a flustered-looking elven gentleman beside him, positively radiating excited nervousness. The two adventurers stood up quickly, but Biff calmed them with a smile.

"Hey guys, this is Neville." Biff waved a hand to the elf. "Oooh, that looks good," the barbarian added, staring laserbeams at Digby's plate. "I'm gonna go order one of those. Neville, this is Digby, and this is Memnock."

Neville offered his hand to Digby first, then Mem, and as he shook her hand, he leaned toward Biff.

"You're right, she is pretty," the elf said quietly, though not so much that the rogue and mage couldn't hear him.

Mem felt a sharp pain in her cheeks as she blushed, and Biff scampered away to approach the counter and place an order.

"Neville Huff, herbalist. Um, could I talk to you two, then, about Biff?"

"What's he done?" Digby asked sharply, smelling trouble.

"Nothing, nothing at all," Neville said in a rush, stooping closer to the two of them, peeking over his shoulder toward Biff. "Well, nothing much. He broke into my greenhouse, but that's fine, it worked out quite well, actually, but look, I need to recommend you get him to Palen at some point, and sooner rather than later."

"What? Why?" Memnock asked, skipping beyond the part about Biff breaking into this elf's greenhouse.

"Because someone has to *study* him, Miss Memnock," Neville rasped. "Did you know he talks to plants?"

Both guildmates nodded and shrugged their shoulders as if to say, 'yes, and?'

"Well all right, but did you know he also talks to some animals, and rashum?"

Here both of them blinked at the elf silently, sharing a quick look with one another.

"I thought not."

"How do you know all of this, then?" Digby asked. He put up one finger to stay a response, swigged down his ale, and looped it up over Neville's head and took a half step toward Biff, who was returning to their table at that moment. Ever the rogue, he'd been keeping an eye on the big fellow in his peripheral, since Huff here seemed to want to speak without Biff on hand. "Be a good friend and get me a refill, Biff?"

The big lunk smiled and nodded, then bustled away with the mug back toward the counter.

"When I found him in my greenhouse, I offered him some tea. I spiked it with benedaren extract."

"For questioning, then," Digby said as Memnock raised an eyebrow. "It's a toxin, works like truth serum on humanoids. Paralyzes the arms and legs."

"Are you a herbalist too, then, Mr. Digby?"

"No, but in my particular line of trade, one must know one's poisons and toxins," the vulpesin answered with an unpleasant grin that turned into a frown of confusion. "But wait, if you dosed him with that, how is he ambulatory? Did you give him an antidote right off when you realized he's no trouble?"

"No, and that's just another oddity, Mr. Digby. He didn't drop his cup, and he stood up on his own power, as if the paralysis effect didn't take. It's like he's got an ungodly tolerance of some sort. Like I said, he needs to be studied."

And here, finally, Memnock put into the dialogue, grabbing the narrow elven man by the front of his shirt and vest.

"He is our companion and our friend, Mr. Huff, not a curiosity to be poked and prodded," she snarled. "Now we thank you for looking after him and not pressing charges, but I think you should just go home now." She gave him a little shove.

Huff adjusted his vest, glowered at both of them, and stormed off, allowing the travelers to resume their seats just in time for Biff to come back with Digby's ale and one for himself. He pulled out one of the two empty chairs and seated himself, waiting for his own food now.

"Neville have to go?" he asked.

"Yeah, said he wanted to get back to his greenhouse," Digby lied smoothly, tipping his glass slightly toward Biff's, who clinked with him. "So, have you seen Sirock at all today, Biff?"

"Can't say as I have." Biff sipped his ale, then said, "Think he's all right?"

"Town this small, yeah, I figure our preacher's plenty fine," said Digby. "Think you'd be okay with heading out tomorrow morning, then, Biff? Mem?" The others nodded, and Digby then opened up the conversation to chat about the benefits of traveling in good company, relieving tension and keeping spirits up. Even when he spied Sirock darting through the inn's lobby about ten minutes later, he kept a happy face on, because appearances, for a rogue, were often more important than truths. At least, temporarily.

***

Sirock got up, pointed at the letter opener on his bedside table, and Dolzen's ethereal form evaporated, streaming into the blade with a faint 'shwoop' sound that made the dwarf flinch. Switching from the reading glasses to the opener had seemed sensible, since Sirock would not be able to easily explain the sudden need for them to anyone inquiring, and shifting the specter's host object had been a simple thing for a priest with the right spells such as he. He got to the door as his visitor knocked again, and when he opened it, Digby didn't even bother with a greeting, swooping around the battle priest like a vulture with a squirrel in its sights.

He paused as he looked at the dwarf's rented bed, planting his hands on his hips. "Well by the seven Hells, padre, how do you figure we're going to transport all of these," the vulpesin barked, holding his open hand toward the haphazard pile of books taking up most of the mattress space. "Were you planning to try and load them on the wagon without someone noticing?"

"I'm not one to obfuscate, fox: that's your habit," Sirock muttered darkly.

"Hey now, deflection is not your style, preacher, so don't stick me with any of that 'remove the rod from thy own eye' Man-Jesus bullshit. That otherworld nonsense is for the birds anyhow." The rogue stalked over to the books and began plucking through them, tossing them one by one toward the head of the bed. "And these subjects are all over the place. Some of these are even fiction, Sirock. What's going on with you?"

"It's nuffin," the priest said, folding his arms over his chest.

Digby pursed his lips, cleared a small space on the edge of the bed for himself, and sat. The rooms at the inn were cozy enough, but like the bed in his own room, the springs on this ancient piece of furniture groaned so loudly he wondered if they were now more rust than actual metal. Big as he was, Digby thought it might be a miracle if Biff's own rented mattress didn't end up on the floor before night's end.

"Folded arms, short, clipped response, won't meet my eyes. You're a shit liar, padre. It doesn't suit you, so quit trying. What's going on?"

Sirock took a deep breath, eyes closed, and appeared to center himself. Against the murky gray wallpaper backdrop, the dwarf seemed even more muted than usual to the naked eye, Digby observed.

"And yea, she didst say that no soldier owes another all that is in their heart, regardless of rank or file," he quoted.

Digby flapped his hands in the air in frustration, letting the palms smack against his thighs. "This little show once more, eh? Look, Sirock, I know we're not exactly friends, but please don't do that to me," Digby said, noticing the little flinch on the word 'friends'. "If you've got something private going on, that's fine, I'll leave it be. But just answer me this, please: are we trying to take all of these books with us?"

"No," Sirock said, much more gently. "Just a handful. I'll have the rest brought back to the library. I'll pay the clerk a few extra coin to make it happen once we've left tomorrow. We are leaving tomorrow, aren't we?"

"Yeah, that's the plan." Digby hitched up and returning to the doorway. "Just, be sure you're ready, all right?"

Sirock nodded mutely, and when Digby stepped out into the hallway, the priest latched and chained the door, pressing his ear to it until he heard the vulpesin's footsteps receding down the hallway. When he heard another door open, then close, he snapped his fingers, and the luminescent form of Dolzen fluttered out of the letter opener.

"Shall we continue the selection process, then," the specter asked.

***

Biff tossed the haunch of beef to Charlie, watching as the beast lunged and caught it at the apex of its arc in the pre-dawn darkness. The rashum devoured it, bone and all, in mere seconds, turning its shaggy heads toward the barbarian and making a rumbling noise in its central, leonine head. Biff sighed and shook his head. "No, I can't stick around. I've got to be back before Digby's up. He'll wonder where I've been at this hour."

Another noise from the monster, this time a series of hisses and rasps from the serpent head.

"He's not really that bad, I don't think. I mean, he's pretty nice to me most of the time. How's the roads southeast?"

The creature Biff thought of as 'Charlie' made an otherwise unintelligible series of sounds from its three heads then, rumbles, snarls and growls from the leonine, hisses and snaps from the serpent, and assorted grunts and baaas from the goat's head, which seemed to speak the least of the three.

The young barbarian listened intently, then whistled near the end. "I've never heard of those before. What do they look like?"

The beast gave a short reply, and Biff grimaced and shivered. The face of the chimera's lion's head took on a concerned aspect, and it reached out a paw toward him, setting it gently upon the armored shoulder plate.

"I'm sorry, I'm sorry, but those things have always freaked me out, you know? And a bigger version, the size of a dog? I think I should convince Digby to divert the wagon around that stretch."

Charlie made another noise, then departed quickly, charging off to the southeast, leaving Biff to sneak back into town, into the inn, then finally, back up to his room. He went about the business of packing up the last of his things, then made zero effort to cover his sounds and movements as he carried his bags out of the room and down to the lobby, heading for the stables.

The stablehands released the horses and wagon to Biff, and he double-checked to make sure the cargo they'd left with it was all still present and intact, referencing a list Memnock had written out for all of them and slipped under their doors the night before, so that whoever was up first could complete this task.

With the reins in hand, he walked the horses back to the front of the inn, where Sirock and Digby sat on the porch, each man enjoying a cup of coffee. "Oh, you guys're up," he said.

"Couldn't be much helped, what with you crashing about like an elephant with an itch on its scrotum," Digby grumbled. "Grab yourself a cuppa, and the plate of bacon should be ready by now if the desk man can be trusted."

Biff nipped up the steps and headed inside, veering right in the lobby, giving Memnock a smile as he met her at the counter. Dark rings under her eyes and a stiffness in her shoulders shone noticeable to the barbarian, and her hair was, well, 'scruffy' was the only word he could quickly think of, unkind though it was.

"Morning, Memnock," he said quietly.

She returned his smile, but also pulled the hood up over her head on the cloak. He presumed she was embarrassed to be seen so untidy, given the sudden blush in her cheeks as she half-turned away from him. "Um, cuppa, please," he asked the desk clerk as the gnome fellow came out of the kitchen in the back with a plate laden with sizzling strips of bacon.

The gnome prepared to cups of coffee, put a tiny pot of creamer and a container of sugar on the counter, then disappeared again mumbling into the kitchen.

"See you out there," he said to Mem, snagging the plate of meat and his coffee.

The big man was barely a step out the door onto the broad front porch of the inn when the vulpesin rogue liberated the plate of bacon from his hand so deftly done that Biff took another two steps before realizing that it was gone. As he looked back, he saw Digby holding the plate just up out of Sirock's reach.

"When a warrior has more than he needs, he is blessed who so shares with his fellows," the dwarven battle priest grunted as he tried hopping to get at the plate, Digby giving him a playful smile with his eyes half-lidded.

"Come on, now, you've almost got it," Digby teased.

After a brief pause, the fully armored dwarf stamped on one of Digby's feet, eliciting a yelp and lowering of the plate as the wounded rogue hopped about on his undamaged foot. "Loki's holy dagger, that fucking hurts!"

Memnock strode outside as Biff giggled at the fox's antics, giving Sirock and Digby a disapproving glower, her mouth a thin line.

"Are you boys quite finished being horrible to each other? We're not even on the road yet," she chided.

"Sorry, mother, but I was only having a bit of fun with shorty here when he decided to mash my toes into paste with his big honking boot," Digby whined.

"Don't call me 'mother', Digs," she warned, waggling a finger at her vulpesin companion as she took a pull of her coffee. "Makes it very strange thinking on those times you've peeped me in the shower."

"They were both drunken accidents, and you know it," Digby said sniffily, taking a seat on one of the low wooden lounge chairs on the inn's porch, propping his stepped-up foot on the opposite knee and pulling his boot off to inspect the toes, making sure they weren't actually damaged.

"That only makes it worse, seeing's it was only about eight in the morning each time," the mage woman muttered, stepping down off the porch toward the wagon to inspect their supplies in the back.

Biff followed her, handing her his own list with the neat little column of boxes he'd already ticked off.

"Oh, you already checked?"

He bobbed his head up and down, not trusting himself to speak. She'd put a little bit of makeup on, not much really, but the effect made her eyes simply pop out at him, and Biff found the overall effect both enchanting and stupefying. He'd always had trouble chatting up girls he thought were pretty, and at the moment, she was having the same effect on him.

She patted him on the biceps and peered into the back of the wagon again for a moment. "Thank you, Biff. Would you be a love and bring my bags out and set them in? They're at the foot of the steps in the lobby."

The barbarian didn't pause to respond verbally, pounding down the rest of his coffee and bolting inside, fetching her bags and rushing them back outside before she'd even returned to the porch proper. Biff hoisted her bags into the wagon, settled them into place, then hopped down to the street once more. To cover his eagerness to curry her favor, he did the same then for Digby's gear and Sirock's, though the dwarf now had an extra sack full of books in addition to his previous belongings.

Once everything was loaded, Biff stood at the back of the wagon, watching as the sun began to peek over the distant horizon.

"Quite pretty, isn't it?" Digby asked beside him as he watched.

"Yeah, it is," Biff replied.

"Well, we can watch it from the back," said the rogue, clambering up into the rear of the wagon. "Mem and Sir are on the bench to start us off. Come on, lad, let's shake a leg."

Biff hopped up onto the back of the wagon then, keeping the half-door open so his feet could dangle off the back. As the horses began drawing the wagon down the village's main street, the tiny burb soon became visible in its entirety as they picked up speed beyond the residential limits.

It had been a nice break from the road, but now it was back to business. *Too bad,* thought Biff as as he watched the town recede. *It's nice when we've got a roof over our heads together.*

***

Perhaps an hour and a half before noon, Digby drew the wagon off to the side of the seldom-used roadway, his and Memnock's curiosity piqued by the scene before them. The vulpesin heard a groan from behind him, and when he looked back, Biff had drawn his knees up to his chest and yanked the half-door at the rear shut. The smell of death hung heavy in the area, a shallow wetland where the road was bracketed on either side by half-foot shoot weeds and marsh, the brownish-green stalks grown in thick patches sporadically in all directions. Black-barked ironwood trees dotted the landscape here and there as well, typical of such wetlands, and the waviness of the terrain created an unbalanced, uncertain perspective of distances, distorting one's visual cues of the surroundings.

The environment interested Digby far less than Biff's current mood, however. "What's the matter, big guy?" the vulpesin asked as Sirock clambered up and over the rear gate and hopped down into the murky water. Biff had broken a near-instant cold sweat, and his head was locked in position, refusing to look outside of the wagon.

"C-c-crabs," Biff stammered, shaking his head. "They're g-g-giant crabs. I *hate* crabs."

Memnock was climbing into the back, and she sat down beside Biff and pulled his head gently down onto her shoulder, shushing him quietly and stroking his hair.

"I, I don't remember why, but I can't stand to look at them."

"Well, they're not technically crabs, these," Digby peeked around at the dozens of shredded creatures floating on the marsh's surface.

"These're rashum, a sort specifically called ganderclaws. Their meat's actually pretty good…" Digby trailed off at the daggers Memnock shot him with her eyes. "Right, sorry. Sir and I'll take a poke about and we'll get going again quick, promise."

Digby shook his head and hopped down into the murk himself, repressing a chuckle. *Of all the things that walking wall of muscle could be scared of,* he thought as he idly toed one of the floating carcasses with one boot. *Crabs.*

He wandered a little bit from the wagon into the wet, meeting up with Sirock about twenty yards from the wagon, well out of earshot. The dwarven battle priest had hoisted one of the carcasses up out of the marsh and was turning it over this way and that, inspecting it. He held it in one hand up toward the rogue, and pointed at the wide, vicious claw markings on its underbelly. Whatever had killed these creatures, it had done so with ruthless efficiency. Some of them that Digby had spied before approaching the preacher appeared to have been burned to death, fried in their own shells. He leaned down closer to the one Sirock held, and sniffed the wounds carefully.

The sour aroma of the shoot weeds couldn't cover what he scented on the ganderclaw. "Chimera. Same one that was strafing us before the village," he said quietly. "There's nearly four dozen of these laid out, it must've ambushed them, started with claws and teeth until they packed up on it, then used the fire breath." The rogue peeked back toward the wagon, then gave Sirock a questing look. "Coincidence?"

"Coincidence is divinity not recognized as such by the unfaithful," Sirock quoted, tossing the corpse back into the marsh with a splash.

"You know, one of these days, I'm going to find a question that you absolutely cannot answer with anymore of that holy book stuff, and you're going to either burst a blood vessel or use your own words again," Digby quipped, patting the dwarf on the arm and turning back toward the wagon.

A couple of minutes later, they were on the road once more, past the ganderclaw corpses and taking in the bleak stretch of the wetlands around them.

***

The sun was half down beyond the horizon before they had cleared the wetlands where they found the road broadened out and began a series of twists and turns through a range of low hills. Being as close as they were to the Allenians in the central region of the realms, Digby recommended they bring themselves to a halt off to the side of the road before passing into these, just to scout the area and ensure they weren't dealing with an offshoot of those much-embattled lands. "Wouldn't do to be woken up in the night by a khan's lance through the chest, would it," the vulpesin japed.

Memnock didn't care for the way Digby was carrying that new firearm of his in hand whilst looking about with his farviewer. She was not opposed to technology as a whole: she did enjoy radio, after all, and autocarts and trains, as well as home and residential lighting with electrical bulbs. But machines like the one in Digby's hand served only a singular purpose: to bring harm. Then again, she supposed, all of those little traps and riggings Digby used to prepare for enemies they could lure in served the exact same function. *Perhaps I should adjust my thinking a bit on it,* she mused as she used her magical senses to reach out around them for unseen threats.

The area where they'd come to a stop had all the hallmarks of a natural blight, the grasses short, dried and brown, a natural side effect one might associate with the borderlands surrounding a marshy stretch. What she felt coming back from her mana-based scouting said something quite different. The fouled soil in the area, the lack of vibrant plant life and animals, even insects, was a direct result of magical taint.

"There's been a necromancer here," she said loudly, so that the others could hear her clearly. The three men came back over toward her, Sirock's jaw clenched hard. "The energies aren't even that old, and it sapped everything in the area. Whoever they were, they were powerful, and whatever they raised, it took a tremendous amount of lifeforce to animate it. Couldn't have been more than five or six days ago."

"Necromancer?" asked Biff, hands on his hips. "What's that?"

"They raise the undead," Mem responded. "Zombies, skeletal warriors, revenants and the like. Some of them can raise liches, and the most powerful ones can turn certain humanoids into vampires."

"Can you tell what was raised hereabouts, then?" asked Digby. "And whether or not they're all gone? Bad enough we'll have to keep an eye out for khan and simpa wandering near, and rashum, we don't need to pile undead on top."

Memnock closed her eyes, concentrated, and began rotating her hands around one another, as if rolling a ball between her palms. Slowly, a humming globe of white energy formed between them, giving off a familiar warmth that she enjoyed, momentary though it was. Then she pushed the orb down into the ground, keeping her eyes shut.

In her mind's eye, she watched as a benighted field full of mossy stones and wetland flowers began to wither and shrivel, the thick, verdant grasses wilting around a tall, gorgeous illeck woman in a brilliant sapphire dress with her hands stretched toward the sky, a ring of black power circling her. Standing near her was a similarly tall, dark figure in a broad cloak, dark blue hair slicked back over his head, his skin paper-white, a fanged smile stretching his lips as dozens of revenants burst up out of the marsh nearby, ambling toward the pair.

Memnock broke the connection with a grunt, shook her head, and opened her eyes to gaze upon the fascinated stares of her compatriots. "Revenants, dozens of them. An illeck woman, necromancer, and she appeared to have been with a vampire. She had a mark on her neck, probably his familiar."

"Could have been the fang those United Freelancers were hunting for," Digby said. "But they're all gone, yeah?"

Memnock nodded. She felt a quick, sharp pain behind her left eye, a minor side-effect of scrying such a generalized patch of ground. Most mages could only scry specific objects, and even then, it took a tremendous deal of effort since the art had mostly been abandoned in favor of the newer sciences of forensics. Anybody, with the right tools and aptitude, could do forensics, leading fewer and fewer people in this glorious 'Age of Mecha' relying on the magical arts that didn't have to do with making things dead. *Of course, I and a certain baker I've just met might disagree with that perspective,* she thought as she moved off to help the gents set up camp for the evening.

She'd noticed something else during her search, though, something she was holding back on. She had detected the same chimera that had been strafing their wagon before stopping at the village, perhaps half a mile away, hiding in the foothills.

***

"Common thread," Memnock said after the meal, as Sirock disappeared into his tent and Biff informed them he'd be taking a little stroll. Digby poured a little more water into the pan and continued scrubbing, giving Mem a little nod to indicate she should explain. The moon overhead shone bright, as it was finally full, casting wondrous lunar light on the realms below. Even the murk of the nearby wetlands glistened prettily in that shine, though the bog stench was something the vulpesin's sensitive nose could have done without. "Secrets," the mage said.

"How d'you mean?"

"Well, we're all carrying secrets with us, that's a given," she replied, drying the pan as he passed it over the side of the fire to her. "Everyone has their own private spaces in their mind, where we keep memories that are just for us. But I mean right now, everyone in this company is keeping an active secret from the others, and I suspect it's only a matter of time before things come to a head and we have an argument."

"That's sort of gloomy to think, isn't it?" Willing one of his claws to extend a little, the rogue scraped a dried shred of pepper off of one of the bowls, then scrubbed it out and rinsed it, and passed it over to her. "Besides, Sirock's got nothing to hide from us, he's a priest. I've never known the preacher to keep anything from me unless it was absolutely none of my business."

Memnock snorted derisively, shaking her head. She never would have guessed Digby could be so naive about obfuscation, being the cynic that he was.

"What?"

"Digby, have you ever been around phantasms?" she asked abruptly.

"Not for a good long while, why?"

"So, you don't remember what they smell like, most of them? I mean, I know you're not a true lycanthrope, but it's my understanding that vulpesins have a strong sense of smell, almost equal to werewolves, right?"

"Nearly equal, yes. Again, why?"

"Because," she said with a sigh, wiping out the bowl and setting their cutlery and dishes into the burlap bag beside her, "ectoplasm has a very subtle odor, but it's there. It also carries a very specific mana signature, and I can detect it inside of Sirock's tent right now. He's got a ghost or something in there with him, and he's probably holding court with it. Why else set his tent so far from the wagon?"

Digby did a double-take, peering out into the darkness and just barely making out a faint, greenish tinge to the candlelight coming from Sirock's tent.

"Son of a bitch," he muttered, starting to stand up.

Memnock clamped a powerful hand on his slender wrist, and eased him back down onto the dried, brittle grass.

He yanked his hand away, then hung his head. "What else do you know, lady? Because I've always suspected you were a lot more shrewd than most of the folks I've worked with, mages included. I can only imagine what you've picked up on that I haven't."

"We're being strafed by a chimera," she said simply.

"Sirock and I already know about that: it left sign all over those ganderclaws," Digby replied with a flap of one hand. "Not sure why it would do that, though, such critters would likely have left it alone."

"It did it because Biff is clearly troubled by such things," Memnock observed. "He's not a beastmaster, we'd not be able to go twenty feet in any direction without the creature being right at his side if he were. He's a barbarian, by his own admission and skill set," she mused aloud.

"And he's no gaiamancer, but he talks to plants, too," said Digby. "And I am beginning to suspect they talk back. I'm not sure how it works, the boy's somewhat dim from all I can tell. I've never seen him crack the spine of a book this whole time we've been travelling with him, except to jot things down in that notebook of his." He leaned back on the palms of his hands, staring into the fire. "What else do you know?" And here, finally, there came a palpable feeling of awkwardness, of something that was being left alone quite on purpose. Sensing it, Digby slid along the ground, agile as a snake, until he was sitting right beside the mage woman, his canid jaw hovering half an inch over her shoulder, his lips pressed almost right against her drawn white robe hood. "What else, Mem?"

"I know about Vanessa," she gasped, unaware of his movements, so slickly he'd maneuvered. Shame bolted through her heart as she confessed, "I know about the Shadow Hands."

Digby felt his own hands clench and open rapidly with a blend of blank fury and terror, and he slid a couple of feet away from her, drawing his knees up under his chin and wrapping his arms around his legs, clasping his opposing wrists tightly.

"So, you know what I did," he said after an awkward minute's silence. "Or rather, what I *didn't* do."

"Yes."

"You know about the contract." He turned his head slightly, saw her nodding. "They won't risk sending more than one or two over here to Tamalaria. They don't know what name I'm going by, or the alterations I've made. There's only a few people who would ever make the connection. How did you find out?"

"I didn't," she said quietly. "It was Rollins. She has contacts in Tallowmere, colleagues who send her correspondence. When you and I started working jobs together, she took me aside and, well, warned me about you. About what you used to be," she amended.

"Yeah, well, they aren't all alike," Digby snapped, shuffling one foot back and forth in the dirt. Another stretch of silence passed between them before Memnock ventured a question of her own.

"So, whatever happened to her? Vanessa, I mean."

Digby hitched a sigh, loosened his grip on his arms, and sat crisscross, hands in his lap.

"They sent a second in to do the job," said the rogue. "Don-sar venom in her milk delivery. Very quick, almost painless. Same young woman found me on the wharfs, purchasing passage. We had a brief conversation which ended in my sending a little package to the chief."

"Dare I ask what was in the package?"

"The second's eyeballs," Digby said matter-of-factly. "The rest of her went into the ocean. Nocstra's a big port city, not a lot of sailors ask too many questions when a body is dumped in the water, so long's it isn't one of their number." Digby pointed toward the north at an approaching figure. "Let's drop it for now, eh?"

"Agreed." Memnock got to her feet, still slightly shaken by Digby's confirmation of the suspicion set in her mind by assistant-headmaster Rollins several years earlier. "Have a good walk, Biff?" she asked the lumbering form that approached the cook fire.

The young barbarian looked in good spirits, but quite tired. He yawned and stretched his massive arms, and nodded.

"Yeah, but I'm beat. Is it okay if I take second or last watch tonight?" he asked.

"You go ahead and catch some sleep, I'll stay up." Digby drew out his firearm and twirled it deftly by the trigger guard. "If anything gets nasty, you'll hear this thing in plenty of time to lend a hand."

Biff gave him a thumb's up, then ambled off to his tent and slipped inside, snoring inside of a minute.

"Well, he wasn't kidding," said the vulpesin, holstering the firearm once more. He walked over to Memnock and threw an arm around her waist, giving her a brief squeeze. "So, how do you feel now, knowing a man trained as an assassin is keeping watch over the group in the small hours of the night?"

"I'd feel a lot better if I didn't think it was too easy to misuse that thing and blow one of our heads off," she chided, returning the squeeze. "I'm sorry, Digs, I didn't mean to make things weird."

"You didn't, not really," he replied, slipping free of her. "But I would appreciate it if the boys didn't find out, all right? Especially Sirock. He's already suspicious of me most of the time and this information wouldn't exactly alleviate that situation."

Memnock promised not to breathe a word of it to the battle priest, and got herself up into the back of the wagon, tucked under her blankets.

Digby, meanwhile, began a looping circuit around the camp, scanning the surroundings for any sign of trouble. The only thing that stood out, for him, was his own shadow.

Chapter Eleven

Sirock had slowed the horses to a walking pace so that they could all catch a glimpse of the herd stampeding by through the hills on either side of the caravan path, the horses huge and wild and multi-hued. Biff stared in wonder as they charged along, some passing within scant yards of the company, nickering and whinnying at their own tressed chargers, as if to say, 'Hey, man, what're you doing letting these bipeds use you for travel labor?'

"They're gorgeous, aren't they," Mem commented as she stood behind Biff on the lowered rear gate, both of them with one hand on a secure handhold along the cover frame beam behind them.

"They're awesome," he yelled back as another rush of the animals roared by. "I've never seen this many horses in one area before!"

Memnock had seen such things a few times on the road, though it had been a while since the last time. The smell of them, all musk and sweat and the loosened soil as their unshod hooves pounded the earth into ribbons as they streaked by, was a heady mixture that filled her with an exuberance she quite enjoyed. These hills were on the fringe of the Allenians, though, so as much as she wanted to just enjoy the moment, the mage woman couldn't stop herself from scanning the throngs of these majestic beasts for the telltale flash of orange or golden fur that would indicate a simpa or khan in its animus form.

Her wariness proved fruitful, though not for the threat she had been expecting. Among the rear of the herd, she spotted a massive pack of plains wolves, huge, ferocious creatures with the sleek, thin gray-and-white fur common to their breed. Snarling and snapping at the slowest of the horses, she watched as they collectively took down nearly a dozen of the huge, proud creatures, leaving these behind for later consumption and taking after more. The closest wolf got to within a few yards of the wagon, and Mem sent a warning arc of lightning from one crooked finger in its direction, discouraging pursuit.

Thankfully for her, Sirock guided their own horses and wagon around a bend in the path and out of sight as the wolves strayed back with their kills to feast. She remained standing and staring behind them as Biff ducked down and returned to his seat on her trunk in the rear, watching the road go steadily by. When she finally resumed her place, she secured the gate back into position and took a drink from her waterskin.

"I sometimes forget how vicious nature can be," she murmured, wondering how many of those felled animals would be left largely to rot out in the open. The plains wolves hadn't looked like the sort of starving pack that would need to overdo a hunt, thick and muscular as they were. She planted her hand to her side suddenly as Sirock brought their horses to an abrupt halt, and she heard the dwarf utter what she assumed was a curse in his native tongue of dwarvish.

"What's wrong?" she called to the front of the wagon.

"Rashum," Digby snapped back, standing on the bench and drawing out his firearm. "We should be ready, just in case," he began, but before he could say anything more, a large wad of greenish bile flew toward them, splashing on the ground only a few feet away from the wagon. Steam hissed up into the air as the acidic fluid ate into the ground and Digby quickly unloaded two shots that tore the air like thunder.

Memnock and Biff jumped out of the back of the wagon in tandem, he whipping around the right side and she the left, coming to the horses as Sirock charged a small clutch of creatures that were blocking the path. There were four of them, lumbering things that looked to Mem like giant seed pods stood on end, the seam along their fronts split open into mouths with several rows of teeth. Each of the beasts stood nearly as tall as she, on six thick, slab-like legs. Vine-like protrusions sprang from their tops, their outer flesh bluish and scaled-looking.

"I've never seen such creatures," she mused aloud as one of them fell back under two more shots from Digby's machine weapon. Its body-length mouth split wide, loosing a high-pitched shriek before it toppled over, blood spraying from its wounds. Whatever they were, they appeared to die easily enough to physical weaponry, so she pressed forward just behind Biff, drawing her short sword from her left hip. When the barbarian and she were still ten yards away, Sirock was hacking into one of the three surviving creatures with his axe, mercilessly chopping at it in a frenzy of blows.

Biff darted right, launching himself at one of the rashum as, seemingly in a panic, it began attempting to escape the little rut that was the road between two of the steeper hills of the area. Mem had just enough time to see Biff jump up on the creature's side, though, savagely grasping the head-stalks in his empty hand and cleaving them off with his broadsword in one vicious blow. At this juncture, she was within striking range of the last surviving rashum.

It leaned forward and whipped its stalks down at her, an attack she barely managed to dodge, countering with a lunge-stab of her own. The blade pierced the beast's lower belly-mouth, and it let out a grunt and took a step backwards.

The rashum then opened its huge mouth, and she saw its forked tongue, dripping with some ochre-like liquid, begin spinning about in preparation for some assault. Before it or she could make a move, however, another shot rang out from Digby's firearm, hitting it in the soft pink gums.

It flinched back, and Sirock, having dispatched his own foe, leaped over and buried his bloodied axe squarely in the creature's tongue and body.

It thrashed for a moment, then fell over, dead.

With the immediacy of the threat passed, she could now smell the creatures, and their foulness nearly gagged her. They smelled like rotted vegetables, both sweet and rank, and she quickly backpedaled away from them.

"Wow, these things stink," Biff commented as he approached the others, wiping his blade on a filthy but dry rag, which he duly tossed aside before sheathing his weapon. "What are they?"

"Not a clue." Digby came up to them from the wagon, shaking out the emptied cartridges from his gun. "Just rashum of some kind. Mem, any ideas?"

"Nothing," she replied, holding back another gag reflex. "There have always been oddities, even among the monsters of the wilds. Whatever they are, they have very little mana about them."

"Watermelons with teeth," Biff commented. Now that they were lifeless, Memnock, Digby and Sirock all cocked their heads to one side or the other and contemplated the creatures. After a moment, they all three muttered a kind of mixed agreement with this observation.

"Well, it isn't exactly fine poetry, but good eyes on you, Biff," Digby said. "You and Sirock clear the road and we can get moving again."

Biff hopped to, walking back to the corpses with the dwarf beside him and swiftly dragging the creatures out of the way so that Memnock could steer the horses past them. When they were by, Sirock and Biff clambered up into the back of the wagon, and the company pressed onward.

It was several hours before they were clear of the hills entirely, coming out at the top of a miles-long gentle sloping field, one which terminated in woodlands that appeared practically virginal.

Memnock handed the reins over to Digby, performed a quick magical search of the area, and found that the wild fields of wheat they traveled through not only grew naturally, but that the area hadn't been touched by any other magic in a very long time. As her scouting energies neared the woods, however, she felt a tremble of resistance, as though something therein not only detected her search, but was actively repelling it.

"Careful now," she warned, and Digby held up on the reins to slow their stallions. "There's something in the woods ahead, something that doesn't want its privacy invaded."

"Well, we haven't got any real choice." Digby swept one hand around the area. The path out of the foothillls and into these fields was bracketed on both east and west by trees which, collectively, attached eventually to the woods ahead of them on the southeastern course. "Do you know what it is?"

"No, just that something's pushed away my scouting," she replied. "It doesn't necessarily have to be something hostile, or even living. Some life forms simply repel scouting magics by their very nature."

Digby let the chargers bring them to within thirty yards of where the path wound into the woods, then pulled up on the reins for them to halt.

"What are you doing?" Memnock asked as the vulpesin clambered over the back of the bench into the wagon's rear, nimbly scurrying around Sirock and Biff to fetch his trap gear box and taking it with him out of the back.

As Digby came around the side of the wagon, Memnock reached down from the bench for his shoulder, and he stopped when her fingers brushed his canine ear. He gave her one of his most dazzling smiles.

"Mem, don't worry about me. This is sort of my thing." He darted away in a half-crouch toward the woods.

She watched him go, vanishing beyond the foremost trees in the blink of an eye. After a couple of minutes, she felt hot breath on the left side of her neck and cheek, and she knew Biff was staring off into the woods with her.

"Think he's okay in there?" the barbarian whispered, his voice gravelly, mouth curled down and just visible in her peripheral vision.

"Yes, I think he'll be fine," she answered, reaching up and patting his cheek tenderly, letting her own head tilt ever-so-slightly so that their ears pressed together for just a moment. "But I think we should be ready if he comes running back with his tail tucked between his legs. Come along," she said with a sigh, pulling away despite how nice it felt to be so *close* to the young barbarian. She hopped down off of the bench to the ground, and drew up her mana reserves around her, preparing for anything she might need to shape her magic to do.

Forward of her and the horses, about ten yards along the path, Sirock stood ready with his axe in one hand, and one of his wood-and-steel band buckler shields strapped to his off-hand forearm. She hadn't seen him use one in a while: perhaps their run-in with the odd rashum in the hills had put him more on guard.

Biff took up a position to her right, his broadsword still on his back, arms folded over his chest, squinting off into the woods. A faint breeze stirred, carrying a distinct chill with it. Autumn had only just started in the realms of Tamalaria, but the season already carried hints of the coming winter with it. Scholarly and magical forecasters were calling for one of the worst, snowiest winters in recent memory, and letters from colleagues at Eldred University in Palen told Memnock that the city council had already approved adding a heating element to the magical dome of force that was ever-present over and around the city.

After what was beginning to feel like far too long, Memnock saw a flicker of movement in the woods, and moments later, Digby could be seen, hovering about eight inches off the ground, tightly gripping his trap gear box to his chest with one hand and swatting at the air around him with his free hand and feet. Something shimmered just out of reach over his head, and as he drew nearer, Memnock saw Sirock relax his posture and put his axe away. A glance over to Biff showed a very puzzled young man. But for Memnock, whose vision was presently influenced by the presence of so much mana, what they were witnessing was very clear, and somewhat amusing.

Digby was being 'carried' away from the woods by a trio of fae folk.

Until they were about five yards away, she and Biff strolling up to join the battle priest, she couldn't make out precisely what sort of fae. But upon closer inspection, Memnock made out the ethereal wings of fairies, their flowing, ornately patterned dresses beautiful to see. "We believe you dropped this," one of them said in a mildly annoyed voice, and the vulpesin dropped unceremoniously to the ground in a clatter of limbs, the contents of his box rattling around loudly. "And he had these with him," the same high, feminine voice added. Just behind the fairies, a pocket of air morphed into a short, swirling purple vortex, and from it popped several dozen bits of metal, leather, hank, blade, spikes and springs, as well as what looked to Memnock suspiciously like a ruby with some unknown spell locked within it.

"As I tried to explain, I was just looking out for my, and my companions', safety," the rogue grumbled as he collected his gear, surreptitiously slipping it all back into his curious little box. The black walnut box had mythril hinges and fine scrollwork, woven into patterns in a language Memnock had never learned. Despite having seen this box of his on numerous occasions, she realized that she never spent much time thinking about it. *In fact, unless it's in plain view, I* never *think about it,* she mused.

"We apologize for the intrusion, and for any insult borne with it," Memnock said, taking her eyes off of Digby and instantly forgetting about his trap gear box.

Sirock took a step back, as did Biff, both men clearly deferring to their more learned colleague to deal with the fae folken.

"We're merely passing through the area on our way towards the open wilds nearer Ja-Wen, and your woods are our only path through."

"There is no insult from you, good lady," said another of the fairies, this one with a slightly more human-like voice. This fairy floated a little closer, and Memnock could see that she was the eldest

of the three, with a few lines creasing her cheeks and forehead. The
fae did not age like most folk, living lives of great length. It was often
said that the elves had descended from fae, and that they had inherited
this long lifespan from their heritage. Here, on this woman, Memnock
saw signs that this might be true, including the knife-like ears
protruding from the sides of the fairy's head. "The vulpesin clearly
meant no insult or harm either, at least, not directly. But I assure you,
we have kept these woods safe for travelers for many generations; all
who pass through are guaranteed safety, from the strongest warrior to
the humblest fawn. I must warn you, however; some areas are outside
of our protection. The sorts of beasts you would run into in such
places should be avoided. Wild troke have taken to nesting in these
spots, and even as powerful as you four seem to be, a lone troke
would likely spell doom for at least one of your number."

Memnock gulped, hard. Troke were savage shapeshifters, rarer
even than bladerons in the wilds of Tamalaria. In their native form,
they looked like seven-foot-tall walking boulders, but could change
their shape at will into anything they had ever come in contact with,
in any assemlage they chose. If a troke had ever been struck with a
blade, it could turn its hand or entire arm, or even its whole body, into
an exact replica of that weapon, with no more effort than it took a
person to breathe. Similarly, the creatures could access spells and
powers they had survived as well, making them ever-evolving, living
weapons. Memnock had never heard of a wild troke being spotted in
the Ja-Wen city-state, but if the fairies said there was one nearby, she
was not going to ignore them.

"I see," said Memnock. "Is there any chance you might mark for us
the safest course through on a southeastern course? Preferably one
that will allow the passage of the wagon," she added, just to be safe.
Fairies were not as prone to tricks and pranks as their cousin fae, the
sprites, but nevertheless, it never hurt to use all the appropriate
precautions. Among the fae folken's favorite kinds of games to play
with humanoids and lycans both was taking *precisely* and *literally* at
their word. It often concluded in absurd situations.

"We can certainly do that for you, good traveler," the fairy woman
answered, and with a twirl of her tiny body, the company could now
see a shimmering kind of gold dust glittering along a path into the
woodlands. "Just stay within the stream, and you should be perfectly

fine. Fare thee well, large folken," said the fairy woman, and the company sauntered back to the wagon, with Memnock taking the reins beside Digby on the bench while Sirock and Biff clambered up into the back, the priest and barbarian preparing their weapons in the event something went awry.

"Well, here we go, along the Path of the Beam," said Memnock, urging the horses forward.

Digby took out his farviewer, and started polishing up the viewport glass, raising an eyebrow at her.

"What's that from?" he asked.

"An ancient text vice-headmaster Rollins picked up some years ago in Palen, pre-dates the First Age," Memnock replied. "She wasn't able to recover much of the printing that had been damaged, but she came across numerous references to the direction of southeast being called 'The Path of the Beam'. She's been obsessed for some years now with Pre-First Age relics and artifacts."

"Doesn't the Unified Scientific Front have ownership, or at least working claim, over most of the ancient ruins we've found in the last few hundred years, or re-discovered?" Digby asked as Mem led the horses at a slow canter into the woods proper. The scent and feel of the air changed instantly as they passed out of broad daylight and into the dappled shadows of the woods. What had before been the crisp, loamy scent of wild-grown wheat now turned to the unspoiled scent of woodland foliage, animal sweat, and something faintly minty. The vulpesin spied a few patches of the herb growing along the edge of their path.

"They do indeed. Rollins has a few friends there who enjoy debating with her about the advantages of science over magic, or vice-versa."

"Who would *enjoy* arguing with that woman?" Digby asked with a wry grin. "I've tried having a few conversations with her, and she is terrifyingly bright. Seems like it would be an exercise in futility."

"That's why they don't *argue*, they *debate*," Mem replied with emphasis. "First they give a brief explanation of their perspective with supporting evidence, then she gives a rebuttal with her own. Then she makes a statement, and they give their rebuttal. It's all very formal, highly structured." She twitched the reins a little to the left, guiding the horses to remain on the path of the shimmering golden dust the fairies had laid out for them. The track they were rolling along had narrowed and grown a touch bumpier, so she drew back on the straps faintly to signal the beasts to take their time moving ahead.

"Sounds rather boring, if you ask me," Digby commented.

Rustling movement in the brush to their left brought the rogue to his feet up on the bench, knife in hand, but a moment later, he spotted the prongs of a proud and sizable elk, bounding through the woods. He sat back down, and hitched a sigh. "Let's hope we're not in these woods too long. I prefer the plains, where we can see what's coming."

***

Because of the slowed pace of travel, it took the company nearly three hours to ride through the woods, coming out finally on the edge of another small settlement perhaps half the size of the last one they had stopped in. Sirock was now up on the bench with Memnock, and they halted the wagon so that the dwarf could use Digby's farviewer to take a peek into the village.

"Work camp," he finally muttered, handing the tool to Memnock.

She took a look through, and grunted agreement.

"Look like a mining operation," she added. "Shall we go around?"

The others were in agreement and they swung the horses due east, going entirely off any kind of roadway for the first time during their trip. The soil was soft and springy, and gave them little trouble, though there were noticeably more bumps and hitches as they regained their pre-woods pace.

Mem handed the reins over to Sirock and clambered in the back, switching spots with Digby, and nearly planted herself on Biff's lap as they rolled over a protruding stone half-hidden by wild moss. "Sorry," she stammered, blood rushing to her cheeks as she scurried to sit on the opposite side of the wagon's back from the young barbarian.

"Not a problem," he said, returning to his study of one of her maps. "So, I've been looking at this map, and I was wondering, are we actually going to be looking more in the Greenskin Regions than Ja-Wen? I mean, it looks here like there's an overlap."

"That, my dear friend, is an oft-raised argument in the territories," Digby said over his shoulder. "You see, no other established nation has as yet recognized the Greenskin Regions as a sovereign state of its own, not even the High Council of Ja-Wen. There's not a lot of folks who're exactly keen on the idea of greenskins getting their own country."

"Why not?" Biff asked innocently. "Isn't there an Elven Kingdom in the southwest?"

"Yes, there is, dear." Mem reached one hand over and pointing on her map to the forested terrain in the southwest. "Right here. But everybody knows the elves aren't the only denizens or people with influence there, and everyone is welcome within its borders. A lot of cuyotai, werewolves, illeck, jafts and humans make the kingdom their home as well, as do some lizardman tribes and a couple of minotaur clans, though they smartly tend to avoid each other."

"Why's that?" Biff asked.

Memnock blinked at him rapidly, having to remind herself that there was still a great deal about the world that Biff seemed not to know, despite his nineteen years of life.

"Well, lizardmen and minotaurs are sort of like cats and dogs: they just naturally don't get along. Both races are largely tribal, produce some truly fine artistry, and tend to be highly disciplined. They also both tend to distrust technology. Unfortunately, that's where the similarities pretty much end."

"How do you mean?" Biff rooted around in one of their bags for something and drawing out an orange, quickly peeled it with his thumbs.

"Well." Mem pressed her left pinky with her right pointer finger. "For starters, while minotaurs are patriarchal, meaning the eldest or strongest man is in charge, lizardmen are matriarchal, meaning the eldest woman or wisest woman is in charge. For some clans, it's *still* strongest, though their measure of strength is different. Minotaurs are primarily warriors, largely distrustful of magic, whereas lizardmen are highly capable in the magical arts, and rely on ranged fighting most times in physical combat. Lastly, where most lizardman clans align themselves with one of the known and more widely-worshipped gods, minotaurs almost entirely practice a form of ancestor worship.

"That isn't to say that minotaurs and lizardmen never get along, mind you, but for the most part, they can't stand one another," Memnock concluded. "Anyway, you were initially asking about the Greenskin Regions. Are you worried about them?"

"Well, I was just thinking, we don't know exactly where these rendermen are that we're looking for, right?" Biff asked.

Mem nodded.

"Well, why not ask somebody in the Greenskin Regions? They might have a better idea than folks in Ja-Wen."

There was an awkward silence then, which caused Biff to look back and forth between Memnock and Digby. "What?"

"Getting that kind of cooperation would require two things," the vulpesin rogue said from his seat on the wagon bench up front. "First, it would require that a greenskin in the area be willing to talk to us with his words, not his fists or club."

"Okay."

"Second, it would require they actually know what we're talking about," Digby said. "The likelihood of having those two things line up is fairly low."

For a moment, nobody said anything, until finally, Biff said something so obvious, yet dripping with saccharine-sweet naivety, that Digby thought he might go into diabetic shock.

"Sure, but if we don't even ask, the likelihood isn't even there, is it?"

***

Sirock sat in the low-slung chair by the campfire with the book open in his lap, finishing it at last and slipping it into one of his bags beside him. A journal on his left came up into his hands next, and he made a few quick notes, summarizing some of his findings. By the conclusion of the guide, he'd come to understand a few key points about his rogue friend, Digby.

For starters, Digby wasn't all that different from most vulpesin in his attitude. According to the guide Dolzen had plucked out for the battle priest, the fox-folk were, as a whole, largely sarcastic, cynical, and tricksy. Their affinity for pranks often got them compared to cuyotai, along with their canine similarities, but where the coyote-based lycanthropes were playful, vulpesin tended to be more vicious and vindictive.

Secondly, Sirock now understood Digby's tendency to occasionally go round barefoot through the lands, even when on the job. Vulpesins possessed highly sensitized nerves in their toes, which allowed them to pick up vibrations from movement for up to nearly a mile away. They could tell both the size and direction of those vibrations' source through those nerves, which would explain how Digby sometimes seemed to know when trouble was coming before seeing anything out of sorts.

His race also appeared to be largely nocturnal, according to the guide, which made a certain amount of sense. Digby, being a rogue and often taking jobs that skirted the line of legality for the guild, would usually benefit from working in the dark of night. If his own circadian rhythm kept him nimble, active and alert during the night, why not make the most of it?

But there had also been a few points the guide made that Sirock found either no sign of in Digby (because he'd never witnessed them or asked), and a couple that seemed like utter contradictions. One notable such contradiction he'd discovered was a passage in the guide that spoke of how most vulpesin found a mate young in life, and stayed with them for a long time, often for the remainder of their long years together. Reading this passage, Sirock realized two things about Digby: one, that he had no idea how old the rogue was, and two, that the man had never even once mentioned a girlfriend, let alone a mate or life partner. Sirock wrote in the next empty line, 'How old are you, Digby? Have you ever been married?' He left some empty space for these answers, then jotted down one more line at the top of the next page: 'I've known you four years. How did I not know any of this?'

The dwarven battle priest snapped the journal shut and tucked it away in his bag, then resumed a relaxed, lounging position on the chair. The others were already tucked into their sleeping rolls, and per his pattern, Sirock would give it another ten minutes before getting up to patrol the outer perimeter of the camp. There wasn't much out here to be worried about, though. The only thing that was off was, once again, the chimera.

He'd seen it prowling about a hundred yards south of their position when Biff, Mem and Digs had all sauntered off to their rolls, a bulky silhouette in the distance that swiftly hid around the opposite side of a hillock from the wagon. Sirock worried about the following day's travel, which, if memory served him correctly, would bring them into greenskin farmlands. Ogres and goblins didn't make very good farmers, but Sirock had known of a few orcs who had proven deft greenthumbs in his time. If the chimera continued to strafe the company, would it end up attacking the farmers' livestock to eat? Would they end up being asked by some poor sod-buster down the road to drive the creature off or kill it?

"Fascinating specimen," Dolzen said quietly beside him suddenly, and Sirock gave a little start as he jumped off of the lawn chair. He put a hand to his chest, rapped his fingers on his breastplate a moment, and sighed.

"What is?" he asked.

"The chimera over that way," said the spectral lizardman librarian, pointing off in the direction of the chimera. "He appears to be bonded to your young barbarian friend quite strongly. Yet he is not a beastmaster. There is also no mana link to indicate it's any sort of familiar. What do you know about the young man's background?"

"Precious little, though there's not much to know, really. He's only joined our guild after finally leaving home. He's had no world experience that we know of, unless he simply hasn't mentioned it. But Biff does not strike me as one to obfuscate," the battle priest replied. He snorted, shook his head. "He is the most honest member of this group, and that's including myself, a priest of all things. You would think that distinction should be mine to claim."

"I wouldn't be so quick to say that," Dolzen replied. "I've known plenty of religious folk, and many seemed caught up in some form of church politics. Frankly, politics of any sort tend to lead toward dishonesty or concealing of truths."

Sirock raised an eyebrow at the specter, who put his hands up defensively.

"I know, that view may seem cynical, but it's simply my observation."

Sirock nodded mutely, and made a slow circuit around the camp in search of anything untoward. Finding nothing, he returned to his chair, noting that the spectral librarian had returned to his letter opener for the time being. With the sounds of a light breeze and the crickets of the grasslands offering a peaceful setting, he took out his holy book, and turned to one of his favored sections, once more reading to memorize the teachings of blessed Reyko.

Chapter Twelve

The company's pace had, thus far, been about average, considering how heavily they were traveling. They'd all exercised caution to not labor the horses too hard throughout the trip, particularly given that they were two of the finer steeds their guildhall had at its disposal. Now, however, the stallions raced along as hard as they could, guided by the talented hands on the reins of Sirock.

Digby and Memnock stood near the back of the wagon, Biff kneeling behind them with one hand cinched on the back of their belts to help them stay steady, the vulpesin taking aim with his firearm while the mage channeled her mana for another fireball. They'd been riding along peacefully enough, having passed three farms worked by goblins and orcs with no trouble, when a volley of arrows had rained down out of the sky at them. Digby had one of the projectiles sticking out of his left leg at the moment, blood drenching his pants from the wound, and Biff had another wedged in the muscle of his shoulder, a lucky blow that had missed his armor plating by mere millimeters. Two more of the projectiles had been deflected by Sirock's armor, and Memnock had been fortunate beyond measure, escaping the ambush strike without trouble.

A patrolling pack of four hobgoblins chased after them, their umber-green faces fixed in hostile snarls under open-faced helms, modified armor leggings hooked into braces as they rode behind on harnessed stamprouses. The beasts looked like thick horse-lizard hybrids, beasts of burden that had remained popular among greenskins, lizardmen and minotaurs due to their sturdier frames as opposed to horses. High-polish recurve bows in hand, they notched arrows once more and took aim at the company's wagon.

Memnock thrust her hands up at an angle, unleashing a spell into the open air that caused the wagon to fill with the scent of lilacs, though no visible effect appeared. Just before the hobgoblins could shoot, Digby squeezed the trigger on his firearm, and with another explosive report, a burst of blood issued from the blunted snout of a stamprous, and it tumbled to the ground, taking its shrieking rider with it, the hobgoblin's arrow flying wide of them. The other three arrows hummed forth, but halfway along their course, a curvature of faint purple force flashed out, knocking all three straight up into the sky harmlessly.

Sirock guided the horses along a hard turn in their course, and Biff grunted painfully as he flexed every muscle he had to hold himself, Digby and Memnock in position. His left hand twinged, and he gasped, terrified that his fingers might slip free of the vulpesin's belt. "Digby, can you crouch," he called out over the noise of the wagon's rumbling wheels and the horses' hoofbeats. "I can't keep my grip!"

As Digby dropped down, he saw a curious thing; the remaining three hobgoblin riders veered off-course, turned about and rode away, breaking off their pursuit. Were they giving up already? A sudden "Whoa up," from Sirock up front kept his heartbeat racing, though, and the abrupt slowing as their mounts strained to halt themselves and their payload turned his thoughts and body around, wrenching Biff's arm even further. The barbarian growled with pain as he released Digby and Mem, reaching up for the arrow sticking up out of his shoulder.

Digby hobbled around Biff toward the bench, and saw what had caused Sirock to come up short: a curved line of fifteen or sixteen greenskins, goblins, orcs and two ogres among them, in heavy-duty combat armor. They all appeared to be wearing matching sleeveless vests over their armor, a dark green cloth with a crudely fashioned crimson fist in a circle over the chest.

An orc raised up one hand in the 'halt' fashion, and slowly stepped forth from the ranks, his protruding lower jaw clenched, bestial lower canines jutting up out between his lips.

"Hold, travelers," the orc called out in a gruff voice, of the sort Digby suspected fathers used when telling their children bedtime stories about talking bears and such. "Those highwaymen will trouble you no more. Are any of you injured?"

The dwarven battle priest, who'd been fixed on guiding the wagon around rough terrain and possible hazards, finally looked back into the wagon, and his gaze fixed on the vulpesin rogue's leg.

"We've got a man with an arrow in his leg," Sirock replied loudly, eyes roving over Memnock, and then finally Biff. "And another with one in his shoulder."

"I have a healer here in my unit whom I would like to attend them," the orc replied. "Will you all come out? We will give you no harm."

Digby snorted but began making his way painfully toward the rear of the wagon. Biff and Memnock lowered the gate, the mage woman slipping out first, followed by the muscular young barbarian. Biff then turned around, and as Digby eased himself with various sounds and twitches of discomfort to a sitting position on the lowered gate, Biff surprised him by scooping him up like a child being taken to bed. Biff carried him behind Memnock, his face fixed in a blank stare, the pain of his own shoulder showing not a bit on his features as Digby lay in his arms.

In the distance beyond the arrayed greenskin troopers, the vulpesin saw the cause of their presence. Perhaps half a mile off, there stood the outskirts of a village or township. *Guardsmen,* he thought. *Proper guardsmen, at that, uniforms and everything.* As Biff brought him closer to the orc officer (whose tunic had a pair of solid silver circles pinned at the shoulder, likely to denote rank), a goblin trooper wielding a gnarled black wooden staff came forward from his fellows, faint green mana visibly swirling around his feet.

Biff laid Digby down gently on the grass, and the officer roughly yanked the arrow from the vulpesin rogue's leg, doing the same to the one in Biff's shoulder. Digby bit his lip against a scream, and the goblin healer quickly set to hovering his staff's head over the wound in his leg.

Warmth spread immediately over the wound and in mere moments, it had closed, leaving only the sticky wetness of his blood matted in his fur and trousers. He winced when he sat up, a trace of discomfort shooting up and down his leg, which intensified as he got to his feet. Biff, he saw, had to kneel for the goblin to do his work. Meanwhile, the orc officer was speaking to Memnock, who had stepped up beside Sirock, who dutifully took a half-step back to indicate the officer should speak to the mage woman instead of himself.

"I am most sorry about your encounter," the officer said to Mem, who was herself finally drawing back her mana reserves out of the visible spectrum. "Those men you were fighting are part of a crew we have been attempting to crack down on along the borders of our territory, brutes who have not recognized that ours is a civilized nation, to be lived in like any other country, or traveled through. They cling to the old ways, when greenskins warred with all others."

"Your apology for their behavior is unnecessary, but much appreciated, master orc," Memnock replied formally, giving a little curtsy. Given how ruthlessly he'd seen her dispose of foes with arcane power over the years, Digby found the motion out-of-character, though charming. He could detect a hint of some kind of grease scent on the orc, which he'd noticed on the goblin healer as well. The armor plating visible on their arms and legs fairly shone in the early morning sun, and he surmised that what he had scented was metal polish. These men and women (two of the goblins, he noted, were clearly females of the race, their noses more human-like than the hooked bulbs of the men) had probably just arrived on the edge of town for a perimeter patrol after making themselves presentable to the public. Despite his misgivings about greenskins in general, it appeared that, perhaps, some in the Greenskin Nation really were ready to live in the modern age.

"What brings such a company to our fair nation, if I might ask?" the orc officer asked, and the other troopers began dispersing in clusters of five each, though the healer and one massive ogre remained with them. Two of the clusters moved off south while one headed north, confirming silently Digby's assessment of perimeter patrol.

"We are with the Freelance Adventurers Guild of Tamalaria." Mem produced her membership paperwork from one of the many pockets inside her white outer robe.

The orc took it, brow furrowed as he looked it over.

"We are in this region in search of an object we've been contracted to retrieve."

"I see," said the officer. "Memnock Halcesh," he read, handing the papers back. "And your companions?"

"This is master Sirock Delpa, battle priest of Reyko," she said, indicating the dwarf with a wave of her hand. "The vulpesin is Digby Narick, a man of, er, many talents." Mem offered with a winning smile.

The orc officer's lips pursed, eyes narrowed. "Mistress Halcesh, in my experience, such non-titles usually mean the man is a thief of some sort," the orc officer said bluntly. He held up a hand to stay any reaction from Digby, who felt one should be expected and was deserved. "We all have our talents, Master Narick. The title associated with one's skill set does not make them that title by nature. Have no worries."

Digby felt his words fade away; who was this orc that he was not only so well-spoken, but non-judgemental as well?

"And the human?"

"He is Biff, a young barbarian and the newest member of our guild," Memnock concluded, and Biff smiled broadly at the orc and waved. "This is his first contract. Who might you be yourself, master orc?"

The officer puffed up his chest and smiled, planting his fists on his hips. "I am Sergeant Ukball Draylo, of the Gruga Police Department," said the orc. He reached up with his left hand and thumbed one of the solid silver buttons on his shoulder. "Got the second circle filled in a couple of days ago. This is the first time I've been able to announce myself as 'sergeant' instead of 'corporal', heh."

"Well, congratulations on the promotion, sergeant Draylo," Mem said. "Tell me, do you get many reports from patrols sent out into the wilds?"

"No, mistress Halcesh, I do not. However, my unit only patrols the northwestern outer arc and the area between Zoak and Doeffer Streets. It's a fair-sized area, and we have two bars in our assigned territory, so there's always something to keep track of. Is there anything in particular you're wondering about?"

"We're looking for any highly concentrated gatherings or lairs of rendermen," she responded, noting the faint flinch in the sergeant's eyes. "You're familiar with them?"

"Yes, we know of those creatures," said Draylo. "Blissfully, we haven't had to deal with them here in quite some time. You may be best served heading further southeast, about another two days' travel, to the city of Duh."

Digby snorted a brief laugh, clamping one hand over his snout to cut it off. When the sergeant raised a thick eyebrow at him, the vulpesin shook his head.

"They really named a city 'Duh'?" he asked, incredulous.

The sergeant shrugged his shoulders with a half-grin. "Say what you want about ogres, you can't fault them for their honesty," the greenskin officer replied.

***

The trade roads that sergeant Draylo directed them toward turned out to be little more than wide dirt paths that had been worn down from dozens of years of heavy wagons rolling along, the most commonly-used spaces transformed into wheel ruts that made for a 'natural' fit. Digby wondered, however, just how wide an average greenskin cart or wagon had to be, since they would have had to lash a second identical wagon of their own to their sides in order to make the fit sound. As it was, he was able to lead the horses pretty much right down the middle of the path.

Biff bobbed his head along naturally to the bump and sway of the wagon now, a development that had taken him less time than Digby had seen other colleagues manage. Physically, the boy was simply gifted, superior genetics and the smiles of the gods shining down upon him. True, he had a mind that was simpler than a game of ball and jacks, but for all of that, Digby had begun to sense something more to the barbarian. He was coming to understand, bit by bit, why Mem and Sirock had become intrigued by the boy.

As they passed a stretch of orchard on their left, Biff swiveled his head that way and asked Digby, "So, we're in another country right now, right?"

"Yes, Biff," the vulpesin rogue replied. "We've actually passed through a couple of countries already. Well, maybe not 'countries', per se, but territories. Yes, that's the more accurate term, territories." He took a peek at Biff from the corner of his eye, saw the confusion on the lad's face, and let out a quiet sigh. "We started off in Breck, yeah?"

"Uh-huh." Biff wagged his head up and down.

"Well, Breck is what is known as a 'singular governance' city, meaning it owes no fealty or governmental allegiance to any other city or town or hamlet. All of the sizable cities around Breck are such places, because they're within the recognized borders of a territory known as The Freehold States."

"I've heard of that, but I'm not sure what it means," Biff commented.

"That's understandable," Digby said with a scoff. "Few people do anymore. It used to be, most city-states were freeholds, what are now singular governances. In Tallowmere, in fact, most places still are freeholds," he added dryly, eyeballing a pair of loose oxen ambling along in the open fields as they drew clear of the orchards. A brief scan showed him a goblin, dressed in a common farmer's singlet and worn work boots, bent half-over, hands on his knees, panting. Held against his leg in one hand was what appeared to be a broken yoke and lead.

"That's the other continent across the blue divide to the south, right?"

"Hmm?" Digby took his eyes off of the farmer, shook his head a little, then resumed watching the road ahead. "Yes, yes it is. That's where my people are originally from, actually. Vulpesins are not native to Tamalaria. Likewise, there's tens of thousands of lizardmen in Tallowmere now, but they're not native to the continent." He flapped one hand to dismiss this line of thought. "Beside the point. When we passed out of Breck, we came close enough to be considered within the boundaries of the singular governance of Bios, another Freehold State city. Then, for about half a day, we were in the territory known as Basaque, a stretch of the north-central mountains and hills, mostly minotaurs, jafts and gnomes as populace goes. Then we traveled for a few days in unincorporated terrains bordering the Allenian Hills. Now we're in the Greenskin Nation." With another peek out of the corner of his eye, Digby could see that Biff was once more taking notes in his little book, keeping along with what the rogue was telling him. "We're apt to find what we're looking for in this country, actually. At least, if Mem's right about interpreting the info she was able to gather together."

"I thought this shield was somewhere in the Ja-Wen city-state," Biff replied.

"Well, a lot of folks don't recognize the sovereignty or borders of the Greenskin Nation," Digby said. "So, you see, if the folks Mem talked to are among that crowd, they likely would label the terrain we're in right now as part of Ja-Wen's geographical claim. As such, if they said it'd be in Ja-Wen, they're both right and wrong. Do you follow?" He turned his head then to look Biff head-on, but the barbarian was staring straight ahead, brow furrowed, eyes blinking rapidly, lower lip twitching as he muttered to himself.

After a moment, Biff finally answered. "Not one bit," he said.

Digby snickered and gave the reins a flick to signal the horses to move a little faster, since it looked like they had a nice straightaway stretch for the next couple of miles.

"I mean, there's what's true, and what isn't, right?" Biff's words came slowly, clearly, like the inquiry of a very serious academic posing a question aloud to help their own thought process.

"Y-es," Digby replied, equally clear, but with some hesitation. "In this case, however, we encounter what is called a paradox, dear boy." *Scribble scribble, scratch scratch.*

"Ends with an 'x', darling," Memnock said quietly, her head poking out between the two men's shoulders as she watched Biff's pen at work before she slipped back to resume her less intrusive eavesdropping. *Rub, rub, wipe, scratch.*

"A paradox is when something *is* true, even when it *shouldn't* be," Digby said. "I can't really think of any other way to explain it, except to say this, Biff." Digby cleared his throat, and thought for a moment back on his past. His own life would never fit easily into shades of black and white, right and wrong, up and down. The ethical and moral choices of his path through the world left a tremendous amount of room for interpretation or error. "Life is not black and white alone, my boy. There are within it many, many shades of gray."

Biff stared at him hard for a moment, and then scratched away in his notebook, leaving Digby to wonder if what he'd just said would be beneficial or harmful to the boy's future.

***

Digby dropped the coins one at a time into the kobold's little wooden box. Standing just on the edge of the doorway, his whole frame stooped to avoid scraping his skull on the low-hanging overhang of the porch. "And thanks again, sir," the rogue said with his best 'win-em-over' smile, raising his voice to be heard over the thunder and downpour of the rain sheeting down.

Biff stood with an unseen cone of magical force shielding him from the rainfall just on the boundary of the light spilling out of the landholder's front door form his tiny living room, his huge sword drawn and ready in the event Digby might need help.

"Well, it's a lucky thing you spotted the barn from the road," the little rodent-like man said, setting the box off to one side out of eyesight. "Luckier still I used to be one of you folks. Let me ask you, though," the kobold said, leaning his head to one side to look at Biff with eyes filled with worry. "Does he really need a sword that big?"

"Well, no, but who ever heard of the Butter Knife of Doom, eh?" Digby patted the kobold on the shoulder companionably as the little man snickered. "We'll try to shove off in the morning if the weather's settled."

"I'll have our Maggie bring some tea out to the barn if you like."

"We've got our own, that's fine, but coffee in the morning would be a treat," the rogue said.

"That'll be arranged, then. She can bring you some bacon and beans and toast, too, gods know we've got plenty now young Fessing's given out so much pig," the kobold said as he gently shut the door. Digby neither knew nor cared who Fessing was; bacon in the morning would be even better than coffee. He wheeled about and jogged through the few feet of rainfall to share the magical shelter with Biff, who had already sheathed his blade. "Come along, then, my boy, to the barn with us."

The storm had broken open with fortunate timing, as the company had been only perhaps half an hour from pulling aside for the night as it was. Digby, at the first crack of thunder, had swept the area with his farviewer, and spotted the barn quickly. A turn off the road and a brief drenching later, they'd arrived at a farmhouse where he'd wheedled the kobold owner, himself a former Freelancer, into renting out his now-empty barn to them for the night.

As the rogue and barbarian passed through another barrier Memnock had erected with her magic, covering the open barn doorway, their personal shell fell away with a 'POP'. The smell of old hay and dust gave Digby an immediate hum behind his eyes, but this too passed within moments as he approached Sirock. The dwarf had set up a fire pit in the wide, open center of the barn, and Memnock was with the horses near the rear of the interior, brushing them down, cooing softly to them. Digby was about to sit on the floor when Biff unfolded one of their collapsible chairs next to him, then went around the fire with one for the dwarven battle priest.

"Does your goddess send any word about our finding the rendermen's lair in the next few days, padre," the vulpesin asked with a grunt as he lowered himself into the chair.

"Victory comes when the battle is ended, not when the forces meet," the preacher replied, quoting his scripture.

Feeling playful, Digby leaned back in his chair and let a serpent smile worm its way across his lips. "Yet the greatest general knows the outcome of the fray before the first boots march," he replied, quoting from the scripture of Marakesh, Tamalaria's Great God of War.

Sirock's eyes widened and a savage smile broke out across his own gruff features.

Uh-oh, Digby thought, *I've just engaged a theologian in scriptural debate. This might not be so funny after all.* Keeping his game face on, though, he retained his relaxed posture and awaited Sirock's retort.

"Schemes are the tools of politicians and aristocrats," the battle priest said, setting one of the pot rack struts in the dirt floor and tamping it down with a small rubber hammer. "A warrior needs only his weapon and his shield."

Digby had heard Sirock say this several times, usually when Headmaster Vikas made one of his infrequent strolls through the commons room at the guildhall. The quote didn't feel quite the same here, though, less barbed but more calculated.

"Yet without the order writ to equip him, what warrior can use these tools without first receiving his orders?" Digby knew this was a paraphrasing, but he wanted to try, at least at first, to maintain the approach from Marakesh's doctrine. He knew it wouldn't last long; he'd heard a couple of devout followers of the Great God of War try to debate Sirock in the commons room and the dwarf had trounced them all within mere minutes, relying on nothing more than quotations from the *Pronouncements of Blessed Reyko*.

"A warrior needs not always be a soldier, though every soldier begins as a warrior. Derivatives may improve in some ways, but at their core, will remain inferior to the purity of the prime state," Sirock said with a sigh, shaking his head. He seemed disappointed, some of the passion melting out of his gaze as he tamped in the second strut and slid the pot handle over the hang rod. Yet Digby quickly identified a segue in the last few words of Sirock's answer, as well as a burning sensation in his ears; the two men now had an audience, as Memnock and Biff sat nearby, knees drawn up, watching and listening to them intently.

"The acolyte may be versed in many fields, but failing mastery of any, shall always remain below her true potential," Digby said, quoting directly from *Passages of Power*, a well-known spiritualist guide for mages devoted to the worship of Manahan, also known as Power, a god of magic.

Sirock's mouth moved itself into a thin, hard line between his mustache and beard, eyes roving back and forth as he gathered a counter. After what felt like too long, the dwarf finally spoke, his every word delivered carefully and with several looks over at Memnock.

"While her company broke camp, one of her cohorts approached Blessed Reyko as she hammered out the last dent in her helmet. 'Reyko, why must we keep these sorcerers with us,' he asked of her. 'They are not like us. They wear no armor, wield no blades, and speak in the tongues of their forest lands. They are not even dwarves, let alone warriors.' And Blessed Reyko laughed at him, pointing to the corpse of one of the beasts they had felled the day before, a massive hole burned right through its center. 'Their swords are made of mana, my friend, their arrows flung with words and gestures. The armor they wear is their charm, and their friendship and bondage to us. We are their shields, their greaves, their breastplates. Call them sorcerers, call them mages, call them wizards or even, yes, elves, as most of them are. Yet make no mistake, my friend. In the end, they are warriors, and they are our kin.'"

Digby had never heard this passage in all his time around Sirock, and with nothing coming quickly to mind, he slipped down off of his chair and bowed theatrically to the battle priest. "Fuck all, my friend, you've got me on this one," he said, and Mem and Biff joined him in clapping for Sirock's victory. A smile more genuine than any he'd seen in a long time fixed on the preacher's face, and Digby clapped him on the back, fetching them a couple of bottles from their meager stock of ale, handing one over.

Mem headed back to tend to the horses once more, and Biff removed himself a few yards and started performing some stretches to keep himself limber.

After clinking bottlenecks with Sirock, Digby said, "That was an excellent passage, Sirock. I can't imagine there's often much use for it. That scripture of yours is pretty handy."

"It's not from the *Pronouncements,*" Sirock said evenly.

Digby stopped his bottle just short of his lips, slowly lowering it to rest on his thigh.

"Then where was that from?"

"*Twelve Tales of Lesser Gods, Volume III,*" Sirock said. "One of the Lenosian compilations. The Great God of Wisdom and Tales delivered the story to Quillmaster Stevenson mere days after the one-hundredth anniversary of Reyko's death. I may be a priest, fox," the dwarf said, taking a swig of his ale. "But I'm no fool."

***

Biff shook the last dribbles off his cock, tucked it back into his trousers, and turned around. "Okay, I'm done," he said, but the chimera remained seated facing away to the north, all three heads aimed skyward, gazing at the moon. "You gotta be more careful. The others might've heard you, and I'm not so sure they'd be friendly."

The snake head hissed for several seconds at him, then the beast flapped its wings once as a demonstration of sorts.

"I suppose I didn't really think about that. It was raining so bad before, I suppose I wasn't sure if that would've grounded you."

Another set of hisses, and Biff nodded, patting the lion head gently, ruffling its mane companionably. "Huh, I learn something new every day. What about birds and stuff, then?"

Here, the goat head made a few grunts and baas, which made Biff tilt his head to one side. He took out his little notebook and jotted down this information, intrigued.

The snake head hissed an inquiry.

"Oh, if I don't write it down, I'm more than likely to forget it. It's weird; if I write it down, I remember it better. Not absolutely, but more often than if I don't write it down." He was about to tuck the notebook away when he remembered the question he'd thought to ask before excusing himself to go a few yards from the back side of the barn to take a piss. "Hey, did you find the lair yet?"

The chimera's lion head purred, rumbled, and clacked its teeth.

"Aw, man," Biff said, flapping his hands defeatedly. "Well how're we gonna figure out which one it is?"

The beast then paused, one of its huge forepaws scratching thoughtfully under its goat chin. Finally, it snapped its thick fingers, and the snake head hissed for nearly a minute.

Biff scribbled away in his notebook, clapped it shut, and tucked it away. "I never would've thought of that. Thanks Charlie. You're the best." Biff leaned over and gave the neck under the lion's head a light hug, and the beast half-returned the gesture, one deadly foreleg coming up and patting the barbarian on the back. "Hey, you should get out of here before the sun comes up. I'll talk to you later."

The barbarian jogged away, leaving the chimera wondering why all humanoids couldn't be more like the simple-minded Biff.

***

"Father tells us you're looking for renderman nests," said the petite kobold girl as she set the tray of bacon, toast and baked beans in a bowl on the lowered back gate of the wagon with an effort. Being a kobold, the top of her head was a good three inches below its lip, but she seemed practiced at maneuvering around spaces not designed for the low stature of her race. Like many kobolds living in greenskin-dominant territories, she wore only a simple shift dress of a ruddy, brownish color, devoid of pattern or design, but her voice carried a hint of liveliness. "Not sure why you'd want to go looking for those horrible creatures but I know there's at least a couple of nests about a day's ride due south of here," she added, stepping away as Sirock and Biff bee-lined for the tray, each man snagging several crispy strips and eating greedily.

"Are they monochrome nests, or varied?" Memnock asked, pouring herself a cup of coffee from the carafe in the center of the tray.

"One's definitely monochrome, silvers," Maggie answered, hopping up onto one of the folding chairs, seated now across from Digby. The vulpesin had poochy bags under his eyes, having slept poorly throughout the night. Mem poured a second cup and brought it over to him, for which he gave a silent nod of thanks. "The other's varied."

"I see. Maggie, can we have a moment?" Mem asked politely.

The kobold girl nodded, hopped down off of the chair as easily as she'd hopped up, and Mem spotted a tinker's travel toolkit peeking out of her dress's wide front pocket.

Mem leaned down close to Digby's ear and whispered, "You were whispering in your sleep last night."

Digby stiffened, she felt his shoulder become hard as a rock.

"I didn't catch a lot, but you said Vanessa's name. Several times."

"The others," he mumbled back.

"No, they didn't hear, I don't think. Sirock slept like the dead, and Biff only got up once all night, I think to go take a piss. He wasn't gone long."

Digby nodded, and Mem waved Maggie back over. The kobold girl resumed her seat with a grimace, reached into the padding under her lower back, and drew out a bullet for Digby's firearm.

"Ah, a bullet," Maggie said, turning it this way and that. "Who's got the firearm?"

"That'd be me," Digby said muzzily, reaching down to his light travel bag beside his chair and pulling out the shoulder rig, removing the gun from its holster. "Recently acquired it at a machine shop."

Maggie was up and around the cold fire pit in an instant, her wrist clenched firmly in Digby's grip, her fingertips on the butt of the gun. "You're fast," he commented, letting her go slowly.

"You're faster," Maggie said, rubbing her wrist.

"It's just reflex." He offered her the gun. "Sorry."

Maggie popped open the chamber and spilled the bullets out into her pocket, then took an eyepiece from within and scrutinized the machine.

"What're you looking for?"

"Imperfections, ways to adjust it," she said. "I'm a bit of a tinkerer." After a minute's examination, she gave him a perplexed look. "Did you say you bought this at a machine shop?"

"Yes, why?"

"Because whoever sold it to you sure as hells didn't make it," she answered, pulling out a slender tool and rubbing along inside one of the ammo chambers with it. "This is ancient, pre-First Age."

Digby leaned forward in his seat, now eyeballing the weapon with a fresh appreciation.

"How would that end up in a small machine shop in an unknown town," Mem asked.

Maggie switched to another tool, and seemed to be making some kind of adjustment to the sight on the end of the barrel. "Easy, really. The Unified Scientific Front has been dumping off ancient tech in shops like that for years, trying to make it blend in with current stuff," said Maggie. "Nobody really knows why. But that's not what you folks are looking into, now is it?"

"No, but it's definitely a matter to bring up to somebody later on," Digby said. "Biff? Bring that notebook of yours over here," the rogue called, and the burly barbarian half-jogged over with pen and book in hand. "Note: look into Scientific Front dumping ancient tech with new stuff. Why?"

Biff dutifully scribbled away in his notebook, then looked at Digby with pen ready.

"That's all. Grab me some of that bacon, yeah?"

Biff came back with a few strips, which the vulpesin nipped at evenly. "The varied nest, you said it's about a day south of here?"

"If you left now, you'd come across it about an hour before nightfall. Here you go," Maggie said, handing the gun back. "Don't try to fire any incendiary rounds from that thing. The chambers are wide enough, but an incendiary's cap will fuse to the chamber, and you'd have to have an F-4 pry clamp to get it off of there. That, or someone with an adamantite letter opener to get between the cap and the chamber flat. And as for those varied rendermen, best to be careful: there's more than a few trade caravans that've come too close and gotten ambushed. Those things will attack pretty much anything that isn't one of their own, and they seem to enjoy it from what I've heard."

"I'll keep that in mind." He holstered the gun and put on the shoulder rig. He folded up his chair and carried it to the back of the wagon, sliding it inside. "Weather's cleared up, we should get moving now. We need to check out the nest as soon as we can, because it might not be the right one."

Mem, Sirock and Biff got their gear stowed, and Digby sat on the bench with the mage woman beside him. They got rolling, and the horses, quite refreshed after a good night's rest in environs they seemed more suited to, jogged along briskly.

When they'd been rolling for about a half an hour, Biff leaned toward the front. "Hey Mem? You said these things would probably like, worship this shield, right? Treat it like it's sacred?"

"That's right," she replied, reaching down between her feet for her light bag and pulling out her journal. She flipped through several pages of notes, then tapped a paragraph lightly. "Yes, right here, some notes I got from a veteran who used to hunt rendermen almost exclusively. He says that while most of them are savage, wild things, some packs develop signs of civilization, including constructing sophisticated compounds in their lairs."

"Fair to say such a compound would look different even from the outside?" Digby asked.

"It would, I imagine," said Memnock. "We may be able to avoid having to fight any wild ones if we make rolling passes by the lair entrances."

"Unless they're mythril," Sirock put in from the back, his copy of *Pronouncements* open in his lap. "Those ones are faster than wildfire, and they could catch us up quick."

"They're also highly vulnerable to magic," Mem replied. "I can always use a gust spell to push them away if they pursue."

"Good game plan," said Digby with a smile. "Simple, clean, plenty of room to improvise if it should come to that."

The majority of the morning rolled by without incident, the company having to wend southwest a little before picking up another broad roadway to travel directly south on. Several greenskin patrols could be seen sweeping their assigned territories on foot as they passed near towns and villages, but none of them attempted any contact with the company. Live and let live seemed to be the status quo for the region.

The company stopped for a meal break just before high noon, and as Biff fetched water from a nearby pond, he looked up and spotted a trio of ogres in heavy armor with uniform vests approaching from the other side. Their long, drooping ears looked scarred and malformed, and their movements were those of older men, from what the barbarian could tell. "Greetings, traveler," one of the ogres said in a voice so thick, it sounded like his was talking through a mouthful of raw syrup.

"Hey there," Biff replied, hoisting up the water pail and heading back toward the wagon, the ogres trailing close behind.

"We have had word from colleagues to the north your group would be passing through," the ogre rumbled as Biff handed the buckets to Mem. She poured a little in the pot over the cooking pit, and Sirock, standing over by the wagon, could be seen by Biff reaching slowly for the handle of his axe. "They say you are with the Freelance Adventurers Guild?"

"That's right," said Digby, rising from the grass and offering his hand. "Digby Narick."

The ogre just stared at him, then put his hand back toward one of the slightly shorter patrolmen, who handed him a scroll tube.

"What's this?"

"I understand you're already on a job, and this isn't time-sensitive, so just take it back to your bosses when you're done here in our nation." The lead ogre put the tube in Digby's still-open palm. The broad man crossed his arms over his massive chest, nearly as wide from side to side as the company's wagon, and gave Digby a queer look. "You a werewolf? Cuyotai?"

"Neither." Digby knelt and slipped the tube into his light bag before standing up again. "I'm a vulpesin, fox-man."

"And what is it your people are known for, wherever they're from," asked the ogre in a tone that conveyed a hint of mockery.

"Mostly?" Digby rubbed his chin and grinned impishly. "Rabies, I'd say," he said, and all three ogres shuffled back a couple of steps reflexively. The biggest one's expression went lightning-quick from dismay to hostility as Digby guffawed aloud at them.

"Very funny, little man," the ogre rumbled, wheeling about and barking at his men in their native tongue as they strode away.

Memnock clamped a firm, friendly hand on Digby's shoulder and leaned on him from behind.

"Any chance you could *not* annoy the locals, fox," she rasped.

***

Sirock read through another passage, then tucked away his *Pronouncements* and opened his trunk, plucking out a rashum study guide and checking the table of contents. Flipping to the short chapter on rendermen, he started reading through the material. There was nothing new here, and after only a couple of pages, he suspected there wouldn't be. He clapped the book shut and watched the countryside pass behind them out the back of the wagon, trying to enjoy the rich aroma of the still-damp soil of the farmlands and fields. A stamprous ranch with several of the beasts staring vacantly beyond their wooden barriers slipped by slowly, and the dwarf considered the creatures momentarily.

Orcs and ogres, and some hobgoblins, were much too big and ungainly to ride horses, so the lizard-like creatures made great mounts. Their diets weren't much different than that of a horse, though they often ate more animal protein and meat than their equine counterparts. As beasts of burden went, though, stamprouses had a reputation for being even dumber than oxen.

Just before he lost sight of the creatures on the ranch, Sirock saw one of them provide an example of this by ramming its head, seemingly without reason, into one of the thick support posts in the fencing.

He let out a sigh, thinking back on his previous encounters with rendermen. He'd only been in battle with a few of them, and regardless of which type they were, the creatures always fought like berserkers, using wild, sloppy attacks. Counterstriking worked best against them, and magic was good to have on hand. But these particular rendermen, if Mem's notes held accurate, would not be the simple-minded flailers he'd faced before. With advancements of behavior, their combat methodology might also be more evolved. *A nest is usually twelve to twenty in size, and they usually move and act in trios. Best odds, it's three-to-one against us, worst, nearly seven-to-one.* He let his eyes rove over his companions, and smiled to himself. *Either way, I don't mind those odds.*

Soon, he would be reminded that too much confidence can be just as destructive as too little.

Chapter Thirteen

Digby slid the farviewer shut and slapped the frame of the wagon's cover rapidly. "Go, go, go! They spotted us," he shouted to Sirock, who had the reins in hand.

The dwarf priest snapped them sharply, and the horses bolted forward with twin whines, pushed on by both the reins and the sight of the metallic, humanoid figures sprinting toward them. Perhaps two hundred yards away, in the side of a hill, nearly half a dozen of the silver rashum shuffled around outside of a cavern entrance. Three of the creatures, however, were presently charging the wagon, having spotted them in the distance.

Memnock once again stood at the back of the wagon, shoring up her mana reserves and preparing to unleash a spell that would, she hoped, slow down the creatures. They were still too distant to make out their shapes, though she could already tell that their arms had been morphed into tapered blades, prepared to attack as soon as they had their prey in range. The trio stayed clustered close together, and as she had hoped, they remained within only a lunge or two of one another.

After about thirty more seconds, Mem thrust out her left hand with a grunt, index and middle finger raised upward, her right hand clenched in a claw by her right hip. As the rendermen let out primal howls of pursuit, her spell took hold, and a wall of solid rock thrust up from the ground right in front of the creatures. She heard the distant but definite crash of all three monsters into the wall, and with a twist of her right hand, she compelled the wall to crash down on top of them.

Less than a minute later, when she confirmed there was no more pursuit, Sirock pulled back on the reins modestly to slow the horses back down to a quick trot. A couple of minutes later, another twitch got them rolling at a normal pace.

"That was definitely the wild silvers Maggie talked about," Biff said, flexing his fingers. He'd been in the back with Mem, hands clenched tight to the rope belt around her waist to support her on the wagon's rear gate. "Did she say how far apart the lairs are?"

"No, just that we'd come across them both before nightfall," Digby answered over his shoulder, pulling out the farviewer once again as they rocked along the uneven roadway. "How in the hells did those things spot us so far out?"

"Silvers and golds have the best eyesight according to all the known data we have on them," Memnock said, taking out her notebook from her light travel bag once again and perusing her notes. "Coppers are the smallest and weakest, but they also have a warning shriek that can travel for miles in every direction, so in varied nests they tend to serve as outward sentries and guards. We should definitely be on the lookout for them."

"Which ones are the foot soldiers in a varied nest?" Digby asked, still looking for sign of the next nest.

"Irons. They're slow, strong, and generally rely on strictly physical attacks. They aren't known for having any specialized techniques or magic at their disposal. Our biggest worry in a varied nest is if the alpha is mythril or adamantite, because those ones always have some kind of magic at hand and they won't hesitate to use it, even if it costs them the lives of their kin," Mem read from her notes. "More often than not, though, the alpha is a gold, and while they have some limited magic and intelligence, they aren't rated a discernable threat to any skilled group."

The company bounced along for another twenty minutes before Digby reached over and put a hand on Sirock's wrist.

The dwarf brought the horses to a halt and Digby leaned forward with his farviewer before pulling it away from his eye. "Two coppers, out there about a mile and a half. Looks like another cave entrance in a hill," he said, offering the tool to Sirock.

The dwarf looked, confirmed the rogue's observations with a grunt, then passed it back to him.

"It doesn't look like the sort of complex exterior we'd be expecting from our bunch. I vote we swing out and stay well out of sight, keep searching the area."

Biff thought about what Charlie had told him, and nodded his agreement with Digby.

Memnock said, "Okay, we move on, then. But where do we go from here?"

"We should maintain a southward trend, makes it easier to backtrack if we need to," Sirock offered, guiding the horses with the reins once more, angling off of the road into the tall grassland plains. When they finally angled back to the road half an hour later, the sun moving ever-closer toward the horizon, Digby once again grabbed his wrist, but this time quite suddenly and firmly.

"Oy, what's wrong," the battle priest exclaimed in surprise.

"Shhh! Look," Digby rasped, handing the farviewer to the dwarf and pointing to the east.

At first, all Sirock could see were the derelict remains of what looked like an old industrial park of some sort, a kind of business-focused area that might have been in development for Ja-Wen's protectorates before the Greenskin Nation was established, abandoned over the threat of inciting a war. It didn't look like anything they should bother with.

Until he spotted movement, similar to what they'd seen from the silver rendermen along one of the broad concrete roadways along the development's western exterior.

Sirock handed the farviewer to Memnock and switched places with her, and she watched a pair of the creatures making what looked like a methodical patrol, engaged in what she assumed was conversation among their kind. She also spotted what passed for decor with these creatures, as she found herself staring in disgust at corpses of various sentients rammed onto broken girders and positioned in less than polite postures with one another at various points around the exterior of the area. She handed the farviewer to the vulpesin rogue and whispered, "Well, I believe we've found our nest. Now the question is, which of those factories or office buildings is the shield going to be in?"

"If they're smart enough to set up routine patrols and establish a dwelling in pre-existing structures, they're likely expecting intruders to use a quiet, stealthy approach," Digby said, loading some of the adamantite rounds into his firearm and checking his long knives. "And let's not forget they also managed to set up and execute an ambush on the caravan that was transporting the shield in the first place."

"Were they directly targeting that one just for the shield," Biff asked.

"No, they weren't," Digby replied. "You have to remember that these things will attack anything that isn't their kin. Rendermen don't just hunt and kill intruders on their turf; they're the sort that go out of their way to find anything with a pulse and destroy it. I recommend we blitz them, use an overkill smash entry and watch for where their backup comes from. That structure will likely be where the shield is."

"No planning?" Biff asked, perplexed. "Just go in and start smashing things?" A huge, dopey smile crossed his face. "I like this."

"Sirock, take the wagon around there." Digby pointed to a dilapidated structure off the west side of the road, what looked like an old way station.

The dwarf did so, hobbling the horses to hitching posts to allow them some limited movement.

"All right, Mem, what's the loudest, nastiest spell you can throw at the first ones on short notice and at medium range?" Digby asked.

Mem, flustered now that the moment was upon them, stood with her hands shaking at her sides, mouth flapping noiselessly as she mentally cycled through her rather extensive list of combat-ready spells.

"Stormrage," she finally muttered.

"Okay, you and Biff will take point and lead off with that, I'll be back and to your left opening fire after your first targets are struck. Biff?"

The young barbarian, jaw set, monstrous blade in hand, snapped his eyes onto Digby's like a machine, primed and ready to perform its designed function.

The sensation gave the rogue pause for a moment, but he quickly recovered. "You do not charge ahead of her, understand? Not until she's got her first targets down. Then you can pull ahead. Sirock?"

"And one, blessed Reyko gave no command to, for he was long known as one of her best warriors, and needed no guidance," he quoted.

Digby snickered, shaking his head at his friend's insight and preemptive verbal strike.

"Do you all have your charged stones," Memnock asked.

Biff patted a pouch on his hip, as did Digby and Sirock.

"I want to watch a few more minutes, see if there's more patrol on the paths. The two we saw are silvers, possibly rejected or willingly splintered from the pure silver nest we first saw. It makes sense to have them patrol the perimeter; they likely performed that duty for their home nest. But they probably won't be the only ones."

Digby tossed her the farviewer, and after finding a good spot to watch the exterior pathways with cover behind a kind of maintenance shack a dozen yards from rusting, broken fencing that surrounded the entire park, she took another look at the area. Along with the pair of silvers, she also spotted a trio of iron rendermen milling about in front of a structure that was either a factory or warehouse of some sort, never straying more than a few yards from its partially open doorway. The irons, much like the silvers, had taken on a generally orcish appearance in frame and composition, to better match the native sentients of their domain. She waited until the silvers had moved once again out of range, then crept back to the others.

"I think I've spotted their primary structure, and you're right, there's no good way to try and sneak in during broad daylight," she said to Digby. She began pooling environmental mana from the area around and into herself, her fingers flickering with streaks and swirls of crimson and yellow light. "The silvers make a full circuit every two-hundred counts."

"All right." Digby thumbed back the hammer on his firearm. "At the next one-hundred count, we go," he said, relying on Mem keeping track.

The wait wasn't actually long, though it felt like forever as his adrenaline began surging through his system, honing his focus down to a narrow edge. When Memnock snapped her fingers, he rasped, "Now!"

The company burst forth then, Mem and Biff leading the way to a wide gap in the fencing, remaining side-by-side as planned. When they were perhaps fifty feet away from the iron rendermen guarding the primary structure, Memnock unleashed a scream invoking the power of the Stormrage spell, planting her feet in a wide stance and thrusting both arms forth, a coruscating cone of flames sheathed in crackling lightning streaking at the rendermen. The three creatures flinched back, but the spell caught them in its fury, tearing into them and the shutter-like doors fronting the structure, rending everything in its path. The reek of scorched metal and blood flashed back over her and Biff.

As her spell raged forth, Digby took careful aim at the patrolling silvers, who were both wheeling back toward the sound of the assault. He gently squeezed the trigger, and one of the silvers stumbled back, blood flying from the gunshot wound to its chest. *Still not quite right,* Digby thought as he adjusted his aim for the second creature, which was sprinting toward him now, its blade-arms held out at its sides for streamlined running. *I was aiming for its head.* He took a deep breath, carefully aimed once more, and squeezed the trigger.

He managed to hit it in the shoulder, but the beast barely slowed down. "Oh, shit," Digby muttered as he started to adjust again, but his trepidation was cut short when Sirock leaped into the renderman's path and swung low and hard with his axe, cutting the creature's legs off at the knees.

It let out a horrific shriek as it flopped to the ground, blade-arms pitched forward to try to catch itself. Because of its forward momentum, it ended up plunging its arms into the street, piercing right through the carefully laid bricks making up the roadways.

Sirock wasted no opportunities, and whirled around, burying his axe in the back of the screaming creature's head.

"Come on, let's get inside," Digby said, but Sirock pitched forward then with a grunt, and the first silver stood behind him, barely standing as blood pumped out of the bullet wound in its chest. "Godsdammnit," the vulpesin snarled as he fired two more rounds into the renderman's forehead at point-blank range.

The beast dropped back, stiff as could be, the vibration of its impact on the ground tangible.

A brief look at the dwarf showed a narrow gash through the backing of his armor. Blood splashed down across his backside and legs.

Biff had already charged into the blasted-open entrance of the building, which appeared, now that they were entering, to be a large warehousing facility. Digby spotted him about ten yards in, swinging his huge blade savagely against the arm-blades of a towering iron renderman, two more of the creatures dead on either side of the barbarian. Memnock was crouched down with an arc of blue translucent shielding magic a few yards in and to his right as a pair of copper rendermen pummeled at it with hammer-shaped fists. Digby, the stench of the magical explosion still playing hell with his perception, holstered the gun and drew out his long knives.

When he darted around her shield and stabbed the first of the coppers, it didn't even seem to have noticed his presence beside it. The tempered steel blades stabbed through its neck and the side of its head almost effortlessly, and it fell at his feet. As the second copper wheeled to face this new threat, Memnock launched a spike of magical ice through its midsection, flinging it away shrieking like a banshee through the air to crash into a towering shelving unit, which tumbled over with a cacophonous crash.

A sweep of the eyes showed Digby that Biff was now in trouble, backing away as he defended himself from five iron rendermen, bleeding freely from wounds in his sides and his legs. The creatures seemed to have figured out that they weren't going to make much of an impression swinging high on the barbarian, and they'd opened up a handful of wounds on his less-protected lower limbs. Sirock joined his side, and together, they began pushing the footsoldiers back, though not before one landed a lucky stab through the dwarf's left biceps. Digby watched, stunned, as the battle priest hacked off the offending blade-arm at the shoulder, yanked the appendage free, and rammed it right through the assailant's head with a primal snarl.

Had Memnock not been paying attention for other assailants, the rogue vulpesin might have been maimed or killed moments later. "Digby," she shouted as she planted herself in front of him, a fresh curvature of defensive power arced out between herself and a neon-green skull of magical force streaking at the vulpesin.

When the spell struck, her shielding was blown apart, absorbing most of the energy, but not all. Enough force spilled over to blast her and Digby both back out almost to the warehouse's ruined front.

Digby was up in a crouch swiftly, though he quickly ascertained that Memnock had taken the worst of it; the left side of her face had swollen instantly, as if a troll had punched her in the eye. *Without that shielding, she or I would be dead,* he thought, spotting a shimmering, slender form about sixty feet away in the building, glittering gold exterior stalking toward the company methodically.

"You dare to desecrate these hallowed grounds," an alien voice called out, wet and snarling, as if an animal had learned the secrets of pushing sound out of a mouth never designed for such use. "Surrender now, and your suffering shall be made small, a quick death for all of you! I'll even promise to cut off the woman's head before my flock can violate her flesh."

Digby helped Memnock up into a sitting position, and Sirock and Biff made their way over toward them, the barbarian's steps stunted and stuttering from his various lacerations. The gold renderman's spell had blasted a clear path through all of the shelving between it and them, and Digby saw two more silvers flanking it, one on either side. The gold was clearly the speaker, and the pack's alpha; visible mana swirled around its legs, another spell assault being prepared.

"Give us a moment," Digby called out through the wreckage between them, making to help Mem to her feet and slipping his hand into one of her pouches, pinching one of the stones she'd locked a healing spell on and swiftly withdrawing his hand. The magic flooded her immediately, restoring her face to normal in the blink of an eye. "We're a bit battered, here," he added. "Stones, fellows," he rasped to the dwarf and barbarian, both of whom, blissfully, demonstrated that they knew what he was getting at.

The smoke-darkened interior of the structure, and haze of battle obscured the air between them and the rendermen; this would allow them to regroup immediately without being witnessed. "We have no quarrel with you. We are on a mission to recover an artifact, a shield we have been led to believe is in your possession. That's all we want."

"I know," intoned the gold renderman, wending its hands in arcane gestures in the air, glowing glyphs shimmering before it. "Just like those others who came before you. And like them, I offer you one last chance at mercy. Take it, or share their fate as playthings for our young and excitable. They do so enjoy having things to stab throughout the day, and your kind hold an awful lot of blood."

Digby shook his head slightly; *what others,* he thought. *I thought we were the only ones who'd taken this contract.* That question would have to wait until they got back to Breck, *if* they got back. For the moment, they had to focus on either getting away or pressing forward with a new attack.

The decision was taken out of their hands, however, as a bestial roar rumbled through the warehouse. A broad blur of purplish-blue fur and muscle streaked past the company on their right, and a moment later, Digby, Sirock, Memnock and Biff watched as a chimera barreled headlong into the trio of rendermen, smashing into them broadside by turning itself sideways at the last moment. The gold alpha's spell lanced out just before it struck, a triangular beam of white power that flew off-target, blowing out a gigantic section of the wall to their side and evaporating everything in its path. The warehouse groaned and trembled from the sudden damage to its structural support, but otherwise remained standing.

Before he could try to stop him, Digby watched Biff launch himself forth, shouting, "Charlie! Be careful!"

The chimera flung a silver away effortlessly as magical flames wrapped around the other one from the goat head on its shoulders. The gold renderman swung a wild kick at the beast, but a massive foreleg came up to block the attack.

Sirock broke off next, then Memnock, with Digby bringing up the rear as they followed after the young barbarian.

The chimera loosed a howl of agony as it blocked the kick, half a dozen gold spikes jutting through its defending leg.

The alpha followed up with a swift thrust of its palm, an unseen magical force propelling the chimera away, blood spraying from Charlie's ruined leg.

Biff arrived in range to bring down a vicious overhead chop with his broadsword the next moment, but the alpha moved swiftly, swinging its left arm, morphed into a shield of its own, up and across to deflect the blow. Now only a few feet away, Digby saw that the alpha had taken on a more hobgoblin-like appearance overall, which might explain its combat prowess.

Sirock moved in to flank the alpha, and between Biff and the dwarf attacking, the creature started backing away, both arms now ending in shield shapes to ward off their assaults.

Stepping over broken shelving units, Digby spotted, perhaps fifteen yards away, a kind of raised dais in the center of a wide, open floor space. Standing on the center of the dais, surrounded by dozens of trinkets and scraps of cloth torn into arcane patterns, was a multi-hued kite shield, shimmering like a rainbow in the last daylight coming down through a skylight in the warehouse ceiling overhead.

The vulpesin rogue, accepting his limitations in combat, knew what to do: sticking to what he was good at, he swiftly snuck around the fray and made a bee-line for the shield.

As the rogue separated from his company, Memnock used a modified ice spell on the alpha, four ice lances forming over the creature's head and driving down into it. The lances didn't pierce its gold exterior, as such was not her aim. The moment the tips landed, one on each shoulder and one on each elbow joint, the ice lances liquified, spread over the renderman, then reformed, locking its arms in place by encasing them in ice.

"What devilry is this," the alpha snarled.

Unable to move its shield-hands into position to defend itself, the alpha grunted as Biff's broadsword bit several inches into its left hip, and Sirock's axe smashed wetly into its rib area on the right. They'd both cut through the alpha's gold flesh exterior, and when they yanked their weapons free, the alpha stumbled backward. "You, will, die, here," it croaked, conjuring more mana into its chest.

What spell it might have used on the warriors, they never learned. The chimera pounced from behind the alpha, pressing it flat into the floor. All three heads lunged down, and among the alpha's horrified screams and thrashings, the scrape of something hard on metal could be heard. After a few seconds, the screams turned wet and weakened, and with a wrench, the alpha's severed head was flung away from its limp body.

Digby stutter-stepped up next to the chimera, the kite shield strapped over his left forearm, and let out a weak laugh. "Well, I suppose we owe you some thanks," he said, patting the beast's shoulder with his free hand.

The goat head turned toward him and raised one thick eyebrow curiously.

"Charlie, was it?"

The lion head let out a 'harumph', and the chimera got off of the alpha then, limping away from the company, out of the building, and out of sight.

Sirock swiftly trundled through more of the wreckage around them, and came back, the alpha's head held in his hands. He led the quartet wordlessly back out of the warehouse with the head held out before him, a move that Digby realized was quite sharp as they got outside. Nearly a dozen assorted rendermen of several breeds had assembled in a semi-circle a dozen yards from the blown-out entrance, and at the sight of Sirock and their alpha's decapitated head, they appeared to visibly deflate, shuffling away from the company.

Still without a word exchanged between them, the company returned to the wagon, unhobbled the horses, and stowed their gear in the back. Sirock hurled the alpha's head away with a grunt, clambered up into the driver's bench, and patted Memnock's leg as she took up the seat beside him.

After securing the multi-hued shield behind Mem's main trunk, Digby stretched out as flat as he could in the little space he had, hands folded together on his chest. Biff, worn out and still feeling battered despite the healing effects of the stone he'd used, sat to one side, hunched forward with his chin on his palms.

"We're gonna have to talk about it at some point, aren't we," the barbarian asked.

"Yyyyup," Digby replied, staring straight up at the cloth cover overhead.

"Even if I don't really get how it works?"

"Yyyyup."

"Are you gonna tell the Headmaster?"

"Nope."

"We can keep it just between the four of us?"

"Yyyyup."

Biff was silent for a moment, and Digby asked, "Sound good to you?"

"Yyyyup."

Chapter Fourteen

They had all been relatively subdued on the trip back, and were now only a couple of days away from Breck. The young barbarian had been the worst of them, saying not a single word since Sirock had used the reins to lead the horses and wagon away from the industrial park the rendermen had been living in. Not even Memnock had been able to coax any dialogue out of him, and he'd spent several afternoons riding along in the back with his head in her lap, letting her run her fingers gently through his hair.

The roadside inn drew close enough now that they could see several people milling around out on the front deck. "Glory be," Digby said, urging the horses on a little swifter with a twitch of the reins. A valet stableman waited for them all to take out their light travel bags, then guided their wagon toward the guest stables after giving each of them a ticket to retrieve the wagon the following morning.

After checking in with the clerk, the quartet split up, each going into their rented rooms without a word spoken between them.

Memnock made use of her bath almost immediately, stripping out of her worn, grungy travel clothes and soaking herself in a tub of water hot enough to stay steaming for a good twenty minutes, scrubbing herself clean finally when she'd felt her entire body go loose. She got dressed in long, loose white pajama pants, a plain white long-sleeved shirt, and a lightweight white nightgown. She then pulled on a sturdy pair of house shoes and sat in a cozy chair situated by the window in her room, which looked out on the grasslands in back of the inn and a nearby woods. She had made certain to get one of the rooms facing the woods before, even though they were generally smaller than the rooms at the front half of the inn facing the road.

Around midnight, she turned off the lights in her room, then crept out into the hallway to the door of each of her companions.

Memnock didn't usually indulge in such subterfuge, but she poked a single finger under each of their doorframes, and one by one, flooded their rooms with sleeping magic.

Once she was certain there would be no surprises from them, she headed down to the first floor of the inn, slipped softly through the kitchens, and exited out the back employee door, walking toward the woods. From one of the deep pockets of her bathrobe, she withdrew a small bottle of olive-green fluid, pulling out the stopper and dribbling it very slowly as she walked in a broad circle.

She stepped into the circle proper then, putting the stopper in the bottle and replacing it with a pair of smoothed, cube-shaped chunks of ruby. She took one in each hand, strode to the center of the ring she'd created with the fluid, and set them as far apart as her full arm-span. Then, she stepped out of the circle, facing the woods once more, and drew mana from her surroundings instead of from within her own personal reserves, shaping the energies to ride through the ring and the ruby cubes.

The stones glowed brightly like candles, while the ring throbbed with a dull green light.

Its purplish-blue fur rippling with its low, slinking movement, the chimera stepped out from between the trees, into the center of the circle, and sat on its haunches like an enormous canine.

It turned its three heads this way and that, considering the ring, then aimed all three sets of eyes at Memnock. "This magic is rather ancient," the chimera said with its lion mouth, its words sounding as if spoken in the common tongue. "Or rather, it is a modern adaptation of an ancient magic, yes?"

"Yes," said Memnock in response. "Biff calls you Charlie, is that right?" she asked, hands on her hips.

The chimera nodded its central lion head.

"I am Memnock. I won't take up too much of your time. I suspect you are impatient to finally be away."

"Whatever makes you think that?" the beast asked, one foreleg twitching slightly, the puncture wounds from the alpha renderman's morphed spikes still scabbing over.

"You've remained farther away each day on our return trip, and have spent less and less time near us. Simple observations," she replied. "Do you know what first drew you to him? To Biff? Is it something you recognize?"

The chimera let out a sigh, the expression on all three animal faces turning exhausted and, if her eyes told true, a little saddened, regretful.

"To tell you the truth, I have no idea," it said gently. "Initially, I was going to attack your company, had my hearts set on it."

Intriguing, have to make a note of the plural there, Mem thought.

"But the moment I laid eyes on him, sitting at the back of that wagon, I felt this overpowering urge to be his friend, to help him. It was like a magic I've never seen or heard of before, except it wasn't magic, not precisely. Well, not magic that he was actively or even passively using. It's difficult to describe, because I'm not sure how it works."

Memnock slowly paced the outside perimeter of the oily green ring, keeping mana flowing through it with a twitch of mental effort and folding her arms over her ample chest. "And it didn't feel like the beastmasters' Call of the Wild power being invoked?"

"No, nothing at all like that," Charlie replied. "That can be resisted by my kind with a modest effort. This was something far more subtle than that, subtle and unarguable. It felt like something had taken hold of my mind, and convinced me in an instant that the world would just make more sense if I became his friend, helped him. And so, I tried."

Memnock halted when she'd come around three-quarters of the circle, facing the beast on its right flank. "Did you waver before our encounter with the rendermen nest?"

"A little, once, yes," the chimera admitted. "I'd stayed away for a couple of days after you cleared the marshlands, mainly because I had to avoid a rather sizable horde of undead things and their necromancer mistress. With greater time and distance, I felt that urge to help start to falter, to wane, but it didn't go away entirely, so I returned as soon as I could."

Memnock completed her circuit around the chimera, and chewed at a thumb nail.

"You're worried about him, yes?"

"For him, more like, but yes, I'm worried," Memnock said. "You're starting to pull away from him, and I need to know if that's a sign of some sort, if he was hurt in that battle worse than he's let us know."

The chimera let out a rumbling little chuckle and grinned kindly at her.

"Miss Memnock, human, do not worry over that," he said. "Biff is not injured in that way or that badly. It's just that, well, I can feel whatever force it was that convinced me to follow and help him now telling me it's time to let him go, and to move back to my old life and old terrain, which is due north of here. After tonight, I will likely not see him, or you, ever again. Now, will you answer a question of mine?"

Mem nodded silently and dropped a hand to indicate he should feel free.

"Where did you learn of this ancient spell?"

"From an old tome of philosophies and theories written down by Thesilis Arbory, a mystic. There aren't many mystics left in the realms, and their libraries have all been either lost to the ages, or hidden away by means only their own order know of undoing. But every mystic kept a set of journals where they wrote their musings and experimentations down. I have one from my mentor, which she felt I might benefit from."

"A wise woman, indeed," said Charlie thoughtfully. "Very well. And now, I must ask of you a favor, before I go." Charlie's wings flapped out to either side.

"What would that be, Charlie?"

"Watch over him, Memnock," the chimera said gravely. "I know not what he is, but there are those in this world who, if they figured it out, would surely put him to ill use. He does not deserve that." Without awaiting a reply, the chimera's wings beat rapidly, and it flew off over the treetops, heading north out of her line of sight.

"I think I can manage that," she said, using one foot to break the circle in the grass and retrieving the ruby cubes. "I think the three of us can."

***

Biff eased down into his chair at the large, polished commons room table with his tray, his eyes still half-lidded with sleep. Since returning to the guildhall two days earlier, he hadn't slept well, his whole body sore, his mind playing over the course of his first job from beginning to end. Already possessed of a terrible short-term memory, this forced recollection proved an almost painful experience, and he wasn't entirely sure if there weren't parts he was fabricating out of pure cloth for the sake of filling in the quiet gaps.

Yet as Memnock sat down across from him, the pain in his head receded, and all of his worries melted away. Freshly washed and wearing a plain but more form-hugging yellow dress under her white cloak, she fairly radiated health and good cheer, which lifted his spirits. She smiled warmly at him and said, "Good morning, Biff."

"Mmm," he replied, sipping his coffee. He grimaced at its bitterness, reminded quickly why he always laced his with plenty of cream and sugar.

"Sirock not come through yet?"

"Uh-uh." Biff's eyes roved over the morning crowd of his fellow guildmates in the commons hall. "Didn't see him at all yesterday. Do you know where he was?"

"Sirock always disappears for a full day after we get back from a job," Mem replied, spearing some of her eggs and practically inhaling them. "Does a full-day cleansing ritual, part of his faith. Plus, I imagine he wanted to have Nancy fix his armor properly, so he would have taken some time to catalogue all the damage." As she took a sip of her own coffee, a stout, thickly-scarred hand slammed down flat on the table, fat fingers splayed wide, startling both Mem and Biff into looking at their new arrival.

Sirock had not only cleaned up in terms of bathing, but he'd also gone to the trouble to re-braid his beard, something he'd not done in almost half a year. The fury fixed on his face, burning out from his eyes, spoke of trouble.

"He's scarpered," the dwarven battle priest snarled through clenched teeth.

"What," Biff asked, unfamiliar with this word.

"Digby, the little thief," Sirock snapped. "I just asked Vikas about our commission, and he said he gave the money to the fox, says Digby told 'im he'd handle dividing it out among us. That, apparently, was the day we got back," he yelled, slamming his hand down on the table again for emphasis, his jaw clenched.

"Sirock, calm down," Mem said, seeing the concern in every face around them, the men and women who were their colleagues reaching for weapons or drawing up mana to subdue their guildmate if need be. "I'm sure there's a reasonable explanation for this," she continued, though she felt like she'd just been kicked in the stomach. *How could he do this to us*, she thought furiously. *Why would he? Aren't we his friends?* She reached out for Sirock's arm, and as her fingers touched the soft cotton of his commoner's green tunic, he visibly softened, letting out a deep sigh, shoulders drooping.

"Where does Digby usually go when he isn't staying here off-the-clock?"

"One of the whorehouses, oft as not," the preacher replied.

"So, we'll all eat, have our coffee, and then start looking for him," Mem said, directing Sirock to a chair. "I'll fetch you a tray, okay?" She rubbed his shoulders for a moment, kissed the top of his head as he sat down with a 'harumph', and shuffled away toward the serving line.

"Like she's my bleeding mother sometimes," the dwarf muttered.

"She does have that kind of air around her sometimes, doesn't she?" Biff asked with a grin. "I like it."

Mem came back a minute later with a tray laden with sausage patties, bacon strips, and three large hash browns for the dwarf, which he thanked her for before tucking in. She set a cup of coffee by his left hand, and the three of them enjoyed a much mellower breakfast together.

Until, that was, Digby sat down at the table's remaining available seat. "Well, I'm glad you're all here," the rogue vulpesin said with a sweep of his hands to indicate his friends. "I've got some big n—," he managed before a fist sent him into the darkness of La La Land.

***

When he came to, it was because of a near-freezing sensation against the point where his lower jaw connected to his skull, and Digby's eyes fluttered open to find his head in Memnock's lap, her hand against the soft point of impact sheathed in magical ice. He took that for a good sign: she'd only use a healing spell if something had been broken outright. With a groan he sat up, and saw that the quartet had moved to the guild's stables, the smell of horse dung and moist hay pungent, overpowering. Biff stood leaning back against a support strut a few yards away, one arm barring Sirock beside him.

"Oi, good to see you too, Sir," Digby quipped thickly, getting up on his feet and brushing off his trousers.

Memnock shuffled over to Biff's other side, and the three of them stood like interrogators across from the vulpesin.

"What's this, then?"

"You disappeared, Digby," Memnock said evenly, folding her arms over her chest. "And with the entire payment for the contract, too, didn't even tell us you'd turned the shield and paperwork both over to Vikas. Given that you are, well, a man of subtle skills—"

"Thief," Sirock grunted. "Bloody orcs have it spot-on there."

"We have ample reason to suspect the worst," Mem continued as if the battle priest had not interjected.

Digby chuckled, and pressed a hand to his forehead. Why not find the humor in this? After all, they had not given him any chance to explain his quick and furtive actions upon their return, and they were now back among the other guild members, most of whom did not hold him in precisely high regard. For two whole days, his closest companions would have been exposed to every snarky comment made about the sneaky little fox in their guild's midst.

"What's so funny, Digs?"

"The fact that I'm about to make all three of you feel very, very foolish for not trusting me." Digby reached into a pocket in his loose brown trousers and pulled out a set of keys. "If you want that explanation, I'd ask you to follow me." He headed toward the open barn doors out of the stables. Back outside, with the sun beaming down on them, the other three now walked almost right on his heels,

Wouldn't want me to try and make a run for it, would they?

Digby said, "Do you remember how that alpha said that others had come before us for the shield, back in that warehouse? Said it plain as day, though you might not have caught it, you were all still recovering from having actually engaged in the fighting, not my forte, direct combat you understand? Not among my 'subtle skills' as you put it, Mem," he quipped, pleased to see as he looked over his shoulder that she at least had the good sense to blush, to show some embarrassment. "But when someone says something that seems to go against everything I know to be true, I take notice. So, when we got back, I went and had a few words with Vikas.

"Turns out, while we were on stand-by, he sent another team out to try and complete the job," Digby said, turning onto Gambler Street, swerving to avoid a gaggle of children kicking a round, red ball along the way to one another. "Now, when he told me that little nugget of information, I asked him if that team happened to be the Tafferton twins and their wives, since we haven't seen or heard from them in nearly half a year. He tells me yes, indeed it was they, and yes, they're likely dead and buried. Well, who here can tell me what happens when a guild member attempts a contract and is killed in the line of duty?"

"Hazard pay," Sirock said.

Digby raised a thumb's up with a snap of his fingers.

"Precisely! Hazard pay! And it hadn't been noted on the contract when we shipped out! So I ask Vikas if we're going to get that, and he informs me that no, sorry, that money's not in the current slated budget, it'd have to wait for the next go-around. I'll take payment now, then, for all of us, I says, and he agrees with a great big smile, and hands over a small coffer with the payment all arranged in bags."

"Are you taking us to wherever you stashed the money, then," Biff asked, looking around the neighborhood Digby had led them to. It was one of the more middle-class areas of town, one he'd not yet visited.

"Yes and no, lad." Digby pulled three of the keys off of the ring in his hand. "You see, I got to thinking, as I was leaving his office, that we seem a good fit, the four of us, yeah? And it's always so crowded in the guildhall, and we've all got our secrets, right? Things we'd prefer not to have spread around among our colleagues, yeah?" He came to a stop at the base of a set of steps leading up onto a porch at the front of a fair-sized residential home, turned around, and faced them. "Right. Hands out, yeah? They all match, so Biff, if yours works, they'll all work," he said as he deposited a key into the barbarian's hand. "Go on, try the door." He pointed over his shoulder up at the front door.

Biff didn't need another invitation; he was blissfully devoid of long-lasting wariness.

"And although Biff there is new to our little fold, I think he's one of the best, truest companions any of us could hope to find in a misfit guild like the Freelancers."

"It works," Biff called out, pushing the door open. He came ambling back down the steps with the key keld out, but Digby curled the big man's fingers shut around the key. "Who lives here," Biff asked.

"We do." Digby dropped the other keys into Sirock and Memnock's waiting palms.

The two of them couldn't even clench their fingers shut as they stared at him, unable to process what he was saying.

"Purchased in full, with a private stablehouse to undergo construction starting next week, and still plenty left over for us to start furnishing the place. All I got us each thus far was a bed, so that'll have to do for now." Digby nimbly skipped up the steps ahead of his dumbfounded colleagues. "Well? Come along," he said, and they followed him inside, Sirock walking on legs so stiff he looked like a cartoon robot.

The front door opened directly on a kind of family room, which presently had a single old couch and two simple armchairs. An old-fashioned money coffer sat in the middle of the floorspace, the lid open. "Is that—" Memnock started to ask.

"Yes, it's the remainder. It's about fifteen-hundred gold. I know, I know, should be more with the hazard pay, but I decided not to hassle Vikas for that extra money in exchange for one thing."

"What's that," Sirock asked, using one foot to nudge the coffer lid shut.

"The wagon and horses from the job," Digby said with a smile. "They're ours just as soon as the stablehouse is up. No other members are to use them from here on out." Digby reached into his tunic and pulled out a couple of papers, offering them to Memnock. "Their names, by the way, are Thunder and Lightning. Bred and raised together, brothers of a sort. Those are their lineage proofs and title holdings."

"They're in my name," Memnock said with a snicker, shaking her head. "Why?"

"You were the one taking care of them most of the time," said Digby. "It stands to reason they'd be considered yours first."

Memnock flung herself at him in an impulse hug, dropping them both to the floor with grunts and laughter.

"So, does this mean I'm forgiven, lads," Digby asked as he looked over the shoulder burrowed into his neck up at the dwarven battle priest and the young barbarian.

Sirock gave Biff a raised eyebrow.

The younger man nodded, and together, they jumped on Memnock's back, laughing like children.

-Fin

Afterword

Thus concludes the first tale from Tamalaria's Fourth Age. Oddities abound with a new cast and a world setting placed over a thousand years before *Freedom or the Fire*, the tale of Byron of Sidius and his unlikely rat-tag crew, yet they all bring with them their own challenges and charms.

I'd like to briefly relate a little about the origin of these characters, as this is something of a point of pride for me. I've been involved in tabletop role playing games since I was twelve years old, and have a deep love and respect for the classic that started it all, *Dungeons and Dragons*. A couple of years ago, I was invited by a friend on Facebook to join a DnD-themed discussion group on the site, where I mostly interacted by way of providing comments on pictures posted by fellow members asking 'Write this creature's background', or 'What happened here?', simple prompts that often led to the kind of passages one might expect from tried-and-true swords and sorcery sorts.

But at one point, I found myself making light of some of the tropes of old, and even ended up using this previously unknown character, Biff the Barbarian, as a sort of comedic foil to lighten the mood and bring some levity to some of the posts and debates raging back and forth through the group's wall. A lot of folks responded positively to these quips and short passages, and over the course of perhaps half a year, I had developed these constant companions for him; Digby, Sirock, and Memnock, all trying to keep the big dope from getting himself or them killed, or at least maimed.

Finally, someone asked me, 'So, what's these guys' story? What's this Tamalaria place?'

And now, we have an answer.

-March 28, 2017

Books by Joshua Calkins-Treworgy

Forward Shamble
Motor City Shambler
Strange Camp Fellows